The Rainbow Track

The Multidimensional Travellers, Book 2

Arwen Jayne

Copyright © 2023 Arwen Jayne

Disclaimer

While reference has been made to some real locations all other names, characters and places are fictional; the product of my overly imaginative mind. Any resemblance to actual persons, living or dead, businesses or places is purely coincidental. This is especially the case with the Gun Barrel Highway which I have only travelled in my imagination and via the web. Elements of the story were loosely based on outback travels I've undertaken elsewhere in Australia.

The same goes with any technology, science or metaphysics mentioned in this story. While I've always had a thirst for knowledge I can't honestly say that school, or having someone tell me what to do, were ever a good fit. I was often too busy daydreaming in class to learn. Most of what I now know I've taught myself, late in life, or it's come from direct experience, the people I know, from dreams or the vivid recesses of my mind.

Acknowledgements

Thanks to all my fans, friends and family who support my work with their ongoing help and encouragement. To Jen for her valuable feedback on the first draft and finalising the front cover. To Erin and Al for letting me base a character on their dog Clyde.

Cover Photo Credit

Photo by Robyn and Noel Drummond, used with permission

Author Note

I've been lucky enough to spend extended periods of time in Australia's outback. In writing this book I drew on that rich fabric of life on the outback roads. The last three years have been good to me. While Covid raged around the planet I've lived a quiet existence but yet a rich one. Technology has meant I could keep in touch with friends, learn Irish and research online. That research returned me to shamanism, ancestral healing and astral travel, allowing me to delve deeper. Like my other books my soul explorations guided my writing. It's always a great deal of fun wrapping it all up in a story.

1

Reilly lay unconscious on the cold dark bitumen. Congealing blood plastered the side of his head. Other bodies lay on the ground, almost uniform in their jeans, bike boots and patch jackets. Surviving gang members disappeared into the shadows as the cop car's siren echoed down the street. An ambulance followed not too far behind, its familiar flashing lights and blaring siren enticing pedestrians who'd come to gawk at the carnage.

The lead detective slammed the door on his vehicle, marching towards Reilly's comatose form. "Check this one. Looks like he's still breathing."

The paramedic shook his head, not convinced of the man's survival, "Pulse is weak. I doubt he'll make it. I'll set up a drip and get some blood into him but..."

A reporter, either fearless or uncaring, shoved a microphone under the detective's nose. "Can you tell us what happened here Detective Flaherty?"

"Back off Massey! I just got here didn't I? Get back behind the cordon or I'll have you hauled off for obstruction."

"The public has a right to know."

"Yeah, yeah. That's what you guys always say. Damned cliche. I think the public already knows they've got a gang warfare problem. Now git."

Grudgingly the reporter retreated.

Flaherty bent down to talk to the medic attending to Reilly. "I need him to live. I need someone to hang all this on."

The paramedic rolled his eyes, "You want me to save him so you can hang him."

Flaherty smirked, "Not literally. But someone has to answer for this. He'll do."

The medic ignored the cop, prompted by a missing pulse that had him suddenly commencing CPR, "I'm losing him. Mick," he yelled to his colleague, "need that damn defibrillator over here. Now!"

I was a helpless onlooker, panicking for Reilly but I couldn't get to him. I was desperate to push through the police cordon and be by his side but some invisible barrier was blocking me. Fearing for his life I sent all my love and the healing energy that I knew I could muster and sent it to him through my outstretched hand, my one and only good hand since I'd lost the other in a bomb blast when I'd still been working as a war correspondent.

Reilly gasped as his heart came back to life. His eyes fluttered open and stared straight into the cop's gleeful face.

"Got you now, you bastard," Flaherty crowed. "The rest of them?"

The medic turned to her partner. "Status on the others Mick?"

"Dead as dodos. Head shot on that one. Knife to the gut over there. He bled out. There's a good patch of blood over by the entrance to the alley. A trail of blood leads that way."

"Hmm," was all Flaherty said, then spoke into his comms. "Where the hell's forensics? What's taking so long? I've got blood drying here."

I watched the scene play out, horror clenching my belly. There was nothing I could do.

"It's a bleed'n dream Ry. For fuck's sake wake up." Reilly shook me. Something of his swearing registered in my confused brain.

Jim took my hand and kissed it. Their combined effort pulled me from the dream. My eyes sprang open and stared into his, mesmerising slate grey eyes that verged on blue. "It's not real. I was only dreaming. Ugh. I hate it when they're so real."

'It was real," Reilly muttered. "Once upon a time. I warned ya that if we kept no mental barriers between us we'd get each other's memories of the past."

I relaxed, my shoulders uncrunching, "Damn. You nearly died."

"I did die. No-one could ever explain how I came back to life before they even got the defibrillator set up. Though now it seems I had some human angel watching out for me."

"Me?"

"How else do you explain it?"

"I honestly don't know," and I didn't.

Jim coughed to get our attention. "I'm as intrigued as both of you and just as happy for Reilly's life. But we have a meeting to go to."

"You two head up," Reilly decided. "Tell them I'll be there in a few moments. They're lowerin' our load to the deck. I just want to go and check on somethin'."

Knowing Reilly as I did whatever checking he had in mind would be thorough. I got a sense that something about the cargo we were going to be transporting was bothering him. Or he was just being suspicious. But I had other things on my mind. Like how the hell could someone in the present heal someone in the past? What if I had never met Reilly? Never shared his memory just now? Would that mean he would have died back then? Was I predestined to be here now, in this relationship with these two wonderful men, albeit one at times a little gnarly? I wasn't complaining but my head was swimming under the weight of questions, tossing in a stormy sea.

Jim gave me a tug. "Let it go Ry. Come on or we'll be late."

Captain Wilcher's meeting area, just off to the side of his shipboard office, hardly counted as a conference room but it was secure. Apparently we needed a soundproofed area for this little get together. We'd already signed non-disclosure agreements so why the continuing secrecy?

What little we knew about the proposed operation was what they'd already related to Riley. The outback had been unexpectedly blessed with ample rain over the last few months. Enough that a number of unsealed roads, somewhat euphemistically called highways, were even now flooded and badly eroded. Under the cover of transporting goods, bypassing the affected areas, we were to test some sort of prototype engine.

Wilcher frowned as we entered, "Where's O'Reilly?"

"He's coming but I wouldn't wait. Something's worrying him and he's gone to check on it."

"He has to do that now?"

I shrugged. "It's not my place to question the Third Officer, sir, at least not when it comes to his work."

Wilcher smirked at that, "I'm glad you qualified that statement. Okay Jackson, Northey, take a seat. Let me introduce you to everyone. Deman of course you know."

I nodded to my old time friend and sometimes otherworldly ally. "Dem." The charismatic shipping magnate was in his element at the business table.

Another man, equally confident and alert, extended his hand across the table, "Dan Sutton, Sutton Innovative Technologies."

We shook his hand and he introduced the others who'd come with him. One of the women, who if I looked past her no fuss office attire and if my aura reading wasn't packing it in, seemed to be surrounded by an electric blue field that literally prickled my senses. Dan introduced her as Terri, his wife, assistant and part owner of his company. Strange mix of roles if you asked me. The other man with Dan was of darker complexion and wore even darker glasses that seemed out-of-place in the meeting room. And I couldn't read him. Security? My eyes widened a little when Dan introduced him as his wife's other husband, Thallon. Not his husband but her husband. But who was I to quibble when I was mixed up, intimately, with two guys who were best friends but exact opposites of each other? Maybe this lot would have a few hints on making such things work.

The last in the group was a young woman who looked out of place in this high powered gathering. Her eyes sparkled with impish amusement. She wore patched jeans and a bright yellow tank top that left her shoulder tattoo of a kitten playing with a ball of wall, fully visible to all the world. I could feel the energy coming off of her and much of it was mental. She was clearly an irrepressible ball of energy, lots of clear yellow and orange colouring the auric field that surrounded her, overlaid with a deep blue. And I had a vague sense that she carried another soul within her. Was she pregnant? But the bump hardly showed.

"Hi, I'm Tess," she grinned.

"You must be the engineer," I guessed. But at such an age? Didn't it take nearly a decade to get that level of engineering skill? Yet she seemed hardly more than her early twenties.

Tess grinned at me, almost as if she'd heard me, "Mr Northey's one too I hear."

Jim groaned at the title "Drop the Mr please. Just Northey, or Jim when we're not on the ship. Electrical engineering's my thing. I make no claims to any knowledge outside of that field."

Dan looked at his notes as if checking, "Except perhaps for the background in cybersecurity and hacking for the authorities in your country of birth. Even some officially sanctioned safe cracking."

Jim winced, "Those files are supposed to be too high level for anyone outside of the highest levels of international government to access. I got out of that field."

Well now, that I hadn't known.

Reilly strode purposefully into the room, distracting everyone from his best friend, "And my background before sidesteppin' my career was in mechanics. Reilly O'Reilly, pleasure to meet yas." He shook hands all round. "Sorry for bein' late but somethin' worried me about the cargo we're proposin' to transport. I couldn't get a better look until they got it down to deck level, just now. The container's been tampered with."

Wilcher's eyes narrowed, "The seals have been broken?"

"They have. Very carefully so the trespass is hardly visible unless you look closely. But the locks are secure which makes me think that whoever messed with it had a key to relock them. I wouldn't have bothered to inspect it yet but … call it a gut feelin'."

"Because of the suspected smuggling operation you heard whispers of on the ship's last voyage," Dem, the ship's owner, assumed. "I'd hoped we'd caught those who might have been involved in that."

"Apparently not," Reilly observed.

Dan cupped his chin and thought, "Isn't it just a load of Persian carpets for that salesman in Alice Springs, the one having the closing down sale?"

But there was a lot you could roll up inside a carpet, I thought to myself.

"Exactly," Reilly absently responded to my unspoken words.

Fortunately the Captain knew of our telepathy. "Outloud, please. Though I suspect I'm the only mere mortal here."

"No-one would ever think of you as 'mere', sir." I placated. "I was just thinking that there could be stuff hidden among those carpets. There is a way to find out, sir."

"One of your out of the body odysseys," Wilcher assumed, having seen me do the trick before when we'd been battling pirates on our last trip. Apparently he thought nothing of speaking about such things in front of these people. But then he knew that Dem was a multidimensional traveller like me and if the auras I were reading of the rest of them, or not as in Thallon's case, were anything to go buy I doubted they were, in any way, ordinary.

"It would only take me a moment. But I'll need to be close to Reilly while I do this." I needed an explanation for me sitting on the Third Officer's lap in the middle of such a meeting.

The Captain sighed, still not quite resigned to the relationship I had with one of his most senior officers and his ship's eletro-technical officer. For the most part we kept our unconventional relationship low key but the Captain knew. "Do what you have to Jackson but be quick about it."

Dem nodded at me but I heard his voice in my head, *I've got your back if you need.*

Thanks.

Our silent exchange earned a glare from Reilly. *Get your ass over here Ry, we haven't got all day.*

Jim telepathically chuckled.

I settled on Reilly's lap and fought with myself not to overtly snuggle in his arms. Instead I just leaned back onto his reassuringly hard chest. Both my men worked out, as did I. I could feel Reilly's every chest muscle but I couldn't let it distract me. I focused on my inner space and slipped into it. Into that otherworld that was increasingly becoming my second home.

I was somewhat unsurprised to find Dem beside me. Though in this world he looked more like an Anglo-Saxon warrior in his tunic and leggings, with his etheric sword unsheathed and ready by his side. "Reilly's not going to like you being here."

"Perhaps not, but he'd want you safe. He's in charge of security after all."

"And who's keeping you safe?"

"Rachael's Mum. She has a long reach."

"Lydia," I said. It made sense. I didn't know all there was to know about Lydia Greenfell, orphanage administrator and wielder of magicks but she was my mentor. If Dem said she was watching over him I knew she was with me too.

I am, I heard her reassuring confirmation in my head. Though she was undoubtedly somewhere hundreds of miles away.

"So where to?" Dem asked. "You're the one who knows your way around the ship."

Shit, I'd forgotten to ask Reilly for directions to the container.

Here, I got an instant picture, straight from Reilly's mind.

I forgot you could hear me here!

Anywhere darlin' and Deman's right, your safety overrides my feral desire to rip his throat out for bein' there. Now hurry up. The Captain's gettin' restless.

I projected myself to the container and Dem followed. Even in the etheric I could just make out the barely visible break in the container's seals.

"See here," Dem pointed. "An etheric taint of the person who broke the seals."

"Like a fingerprint."

"Of a kind. Look at the colours."

"Hmm, dark green, almost the colour of an avocado skin and mustard yellow. Not a pretty colour scheme exactly but memorable."

The green suggests elements of deceit and greed in the person's character, Lydia telepathed to both of us.

"And that other yucky colour, the one that looks like baby poop gone wrong?"

Ugh, did you have to say that? I suspect this individual is inherently lazy, prefering to take rather than to work too hard. It may also suggest a certain amount of illness. Even, dare I say, in the liver or gallbladder area.

"Great profiling Lydia." Though it didn't tell me what the individual looked like, only their aura.

"The question is, have you seen any of the crew whose aura matches this?" Dem wondered.

"To be honest, I don't go around staring at people too hard. Tends to give them the creeps."

There are ways to do it casually out of the corner of your eyes, Lydia commented. *Just don't touch it. You don't want any of that energy attaching itself to you. Think of it like a virus.*

Gah! I was so over viruses. Particularly after being unable to disembark for the last week because of some nasty virus that was doing the rounds of the city and the Captain didn't want his crew infected. Viruses tended to spread rather well in the confined space of a ship. But that was another matter. I glared at the gungy coloured etheric taint, wishing it wasn't there. "So how do we get in?"

"Nothing's solid in this dimension," Deman reminded me.

"Just walk through the walls of the container, through the carpets?"

"Why not? We don't need air in this dimension."

He had a point.

I walked up to the container, scrunching up my eyes against any impact with the wall and just kept on walking. I opened one eye, then the other. Okay, weird. I was in a sea of carpet but it didn't feel like it was there. "Anything?" I wondered.

Dem waved me over, the outline of his aura clearly visible through the carpets. "Over here. Methamphetamine I think. Bags and bags of it. Rolled up inside the carpets."

"Shit." An isolated community like Alice Springs didn't need that hitting their streets. "We'd best head back and report this." But I was momentarily mesmerised by a pulsing dark green light inching its way towards Deman. It had a vague resemblance to a giant worm, only this one made of murky, pulsating light.

Deman held his sword at the ready but was backing out of its way.

Get out of there now!, Lydia yelled into both our heads.

The fear and concern in her voice told us all we needed to know. We didn't have to be told twice.

I merged back into my physical body. Relieved when I looked across the table and found Dem in one piece, though a bit pale of face. "You alright, what was that thing?"

"One of the nasties that inhabits the etheric. Lydia calls them penge. Damn things are always hunting me in there."

"Why?"

Wilcher growled. "You can discuss your trip later, what did you find?"

"Drugs." It sounded like the easy and obvious answer that it was but we all knew it was about to complicate our venture. Big time.

The Captain swore then went to yell out to his chief officer who was manning the bridge. "Pertwie, get me Border Force on the line."

Dan groaned and buried his head in his hands. Terri gave him a reassuring pat on the back.

"Couldn't we just dispose of the drugs and pretend it never happened," Thallon wondered out loud, seemingly oblivious to the implications.

Dem shook his head forlornly, "We need to bust the smuggling operation that's been plaguing my shipping line. This will complicate and possibly delay things but there's no need for them to know about what we're really doing."

"Save that explanation until the Captain comes back in," I suggested. " I want to know about the penge."

Jim laughed, "Watch out, she's got her journalist hat on."

Terri puzzled over that. "But no-one in the mainstream media's going to pick up a story about the creatures that inhabit the etheric realm."

Ah, yes, but she didn't know. "I have a blog, with a growing following. I've been blogging about my otherworldly experiences. So, Deman, tell us. Why's a giant glowing worm made up of murky green light hunting you?"

"A what?" Dan stared at me in horror.

Tess leaned forward, enthusiastic to know more. "Do tell."

Deman grumbled, none too keen to go into it, "Lydia, ah, a metaphysical consultant who works with us, thinks it's because I've yet to transcend the need that led me onto the path of acquiring wealth. It's not the being wealthy that's bad," he explained, "but the fact that I, possibly, go after it out of some deeply ingrained survival need to thrive. She thinks it's driven me to act a time or two less than magnanimously with my competitors."

"You mean you've eaten them like a ravenous shark," I suggested. "Not," I added quickly, "that you've acted any differently than any other business magnate out there." Hell, if you couldn't tell a friend the truth, who could?

His eyes narrowed on me, "You're exactly right but that's the problem. The bug senses what I am. You might say it resonates at my frequency. It homes in on that frequency. It wants to feed off my similar energy. If it did I could become very ill, even mentally, while all the while it would be feeding my desire for success and wealth. Hell, I could become a megalomaniac. Try for political power. That sort of thing."

"Ew!" I made a face. None of us needed a twisted, off-the-rails, version of Dem becoming *el presidente* of some unsuspecting country, least of all ours. "So what does Lydia suggest?"

Deman made a face back, "Therapy." He said it like a rude word. "Something about me needing to recognise my self bias, its causes and making peace with that side of myself. Like where exactly am I going to find a therapist that I can talk openly to about energy sucking bugs?"

Thallon rubbed his chin as if in thought, a very human gesture yet something made me think he wasn't human. "I might know someone."

"Leigha," Terri enthusiastically agreed. "Though there's no knowing where, um, she might be. She works remotely with her husband's team but I believe if you leave a message on her answering machine she may get back to you, especially if you say you know us."

Thallon closed his eyes for a moment, blinked and then picked up the pen in front of him and wrote down a number. He passed it along to Dem. "Worth a go."

"Hmm," Deman didn't sound convinced but I couldn't see how he could keep going into the etheric dimension if those things were after him.

Wilcher returned, "Border Force are on their way. What did I miss?"

"Nothing Captain, we were waiting for your return."

"Well you'd better hurry up. We've only got about twenty minutes before the Border Force inspector gets here."

And what was the bet the inspector's name would be John Smith.

"Tess, would you do the honours?" Dan asked.

Tess bounced up like a spring that had been waiting for release and went over to the electronic board, bringing up a screen.

"We started out looking for an ex military three seater with a twin cab capable of moving your twenty foot container across variable terrain. What we actually settled on was a commercially available Mercedes Benz Zetros. 6 by 6. Crew cab. It seats up to four people in a very comfortable cab. The one we acquired had a mobile home built on the back of it which should suit all your accommodation needs, though we've had to crib some space for the conventional fuel you'll be carrying. Attached to the back is a twenty foot container trailer with off road suspension and floatation tyres that should handle any sand you meet along the way.

From the outside the Merc looks like what it started life as but under the hood. Well that's a different matter. It now runs hybrid technology. From the cab you'll be able to switch from its normal engine to the prototype. Because of the secrecy surrounding what we've developed we've got a security code for lifting the hood of the truck. It will also recognize your hand prints or voice commands."

"Ya haven't said much about the prototype yet," Reilly pushed.

Tess paused, thinking, "Do you know about the maglev train system?"

"Where the train hovers over a magnetically charged rail and the rapid switchin' of polarity propels the train along? Kind've of. What has that to do with dirt roads in the outback?" Reilly frowned, wondering.

"Well, instead of artificially constructed rails you'll be riding the electromagnetic currents that run around the earth."

"Ley lines," I'd assumed.

Tess pursed her lips, "Not specifically. Ley lines are powerful conduits but only one major one runs from just north of Broom, up in the far North West of Western Australia, through Uluru in Central Australia, down to Bairnsdale down in Victoria. Firstly there's no need for you to track so far North and secondly it's the more common fields of current we want to use for testing. The technology is of no use to us if we're restricted to travelling along the main ley lines. Not to mention that many of the world's major sacred sites are built along ley lines and since most of them are major tourist attractions their custodians wouldn't like our trucks whizzing past, so we've had to look at alternatives."

Damn, there went my stopover in Broome. "So from here to Alice Springs, via where?"

"Meekathera. We don't want you firing up the alternate engine near civilization so you'll only use it for short stages." She changed screens to a map, "Here, here and here."

Well no-one would see us, for sure. There was hardly anything out there but a few abandoned gold fields, desert and forty five or more degrees celsius temperatures. Certainly no roads to speak of. Well maybe the somewhat euphemistically named Gun Barrel Highway from Wiluna to Yulara but it was hardly a road. More like a dead straight clear patch of dust engraved into the ground

"Electromagnetic currents only run in one direction," Jim pointed out. "How do we go back in the other direction?"

Tess looked smug. It's all to do with attraction and repulsion. You use one of those one way and the other on the return."

Jim sat back in his chair, "Genius. And you came up with all of this?"

"Hell no, I just built it. It was Terri's idea."

"Just a concept really," Terri shrugged her shoulders. "I'm no engineer. Tess and her mates worked out the details. But it still needs proof of concept. That's why you're here. Jim and Reilly, you have the collective skills to fix problems on the way or at the very least diagnose and describe the problem to us. Ry, we want you to document the tests. Let us know what you observe. Anything on this plane or the astral. We don't want any unforeseen side effects."

Neither did I. "I can do that for you."

Pertwie poked his head in the door, "The inspector is here."

"Send him in, Pertwie, thanks," Wilcher acknowledged.

"Actually, it's her, Mahala dePlankas."

So not Smith, I mused.

Tess quickly switched the screen off and returned to her seat.

Inspector dePlankas was an imposing woman. Tall and rangy. Dark eyes, assessing, scanned the room, us and took everything in. She offered Wilcher her hand. "Thanks for the call Captain. As Mr Merkwood there knows we've been trying to get to the bottom of the smuggling operation plaguing his line for some time. You've inspected the cargo?"

"The seals have been broken. Not in an obvious way but on closer inspection it was clear," Reilly answered.

"You're the ship's security officer?" dePlankas asked though it seemed she already knew who she was talking to.

"Third Officer O'Reilly," Reilly acknowledged.

"I'd be interested to know what aroused your suspicions O'Reilly?"

"It's supposedly a load of Persian carpets headed for a closing down sale in Alice Springs. The vendor's been pressuring us to get the delivery to him on time even though he knows that multiple roads south of the Alice are cut off at the moment due to flooding and washouts. What does it matter if he closes down at the end of the month or next? Yet he's prepared to spend a lot extra to get the delivery on time. Just didn't sit right with me."

"Hmm, why the urgency, indeed, when everyone else in the country right now is having the same logistics issues with getting their supplies? No offence Mr Sutton," she nodded to Dan.

"None taken."

"So you opened the container to inspect it?"

"No, we didn't want to arouse suspicions that we knew something was afoot. The Captain thought it best to discuss the matter with Border Force first."

"We appreciate that, but I was led to understand that you know what's hidden inside the load."

The Captain groaned and rubbed his forehead as if it pained him.

I relieved him of having to divulge the truth. They could shoot the messenger instead. It wasn't like I had a long standing maritime reputation at stake. "I'm psychic, Inspector dePlankas. Not a seer or fortune teller as such but I can see what is, if that makes sense. I used my abilities to ascertain the nature of the cargo."

DePlankas didn't look as doubtful as I thought she might. Instead she seemed interested. "Describe the contents."

"Well wrapped, probably waterproof bags, about this size," I showed her with my hands.

"And it's methamphetamine, you think?"

"It's just a hunch," I fudged. I didn't know exactly how Deman had managed to tell but I wasn't dropping more than one of us in it.

Thanks, Deman murmered in my head.

"And is there anyone on board this ship who can attest to your psychic abilities Jackson," dePlankas wondered.

"I can," Reilley was quick to answer.

"Me too," from Jim.

"Damn it," swore the Captain, "Me too."

"And me," Deman acknowledged with a nod from across the table.

The others kept quiet but Tess winked at me.

Inspector dePlankas seemed to think about that for a moment, pacing the room, then seemed to come to a decision. "Okay then. Let's say Jackson is right. Mr Sutton, do you mind us putting surveillance on your truck."

Dan didn't look happy. Terri whispered in his ear. He nodded. "On condition that it does not include GPS tracking of the truck's location. You can put spy cams on the container but not in the cab or the living quarters of the crew."

The inspector looked suitably intrigued. "Definitely we will respect your crew's privacy but why no locator? It would be useful."

"Dan, tell her just enough and get her to sign a non-disclosure," Deman suggested.

"If this is about commercial in confidence I'm quite happy to sign anything you want to throw my way," dePlankas offered.

"It's a little more high level than that," Dan explained. "We're testing technology and couldn't have you discussing it with your bosses. We don't know who we can trust in your department."

"I see," the Inspector stared down her nose at Dan. "Honestly, if the technology was of national importance I may indeed feel the need to relay my findings. I understand the position you're in but you must also see mine."

"The technology is irrelevant to catching your smugglers," Dan asserted.

"Are you sure of that? The smuggling might be just an add on to their real interest."

"There are parties we wouldn't want finding out about the technology," Deman agreed with Dan. "You'd understand that some technology is in the world's best interest and shouldn't be locked up, hidden away or privatised by the unscrupulous."

"What can you tell me?" the Inspector asked.

Everyone looked at each other for answers, unsure.

"If I may," I had an idea. "Let me read her."

DePlankas stared at me, wary, "There is much in my head I don't need you knowing about Jackson."

I shook my head. "Not mind reading. Just let me assess your aura." She didn't need to know that I'd be deferring to my mentor for an assessment.

She gave her okay and I rose to stand in front of her.

"What do you see?" the Captain asked, mildly curious.

"The colours are clear. Red, but it's a healthy red. Some blue. And there's an overlay of purple."

I concur, Lydia whispered in my mind. *She's essentially a career woman with an astute mind but that purple also suggests some psychic ability. I have no concerns about her, Ry.*

"You're communicating with another," the Inspector surprised everyone except me and Lydia with the comment.

I smiled and nodded. "I am, and that is all I'll say. I have others I need to protect, Inspector dePlankas. There's no need for you to try to recruit any of us, because of our abilities. We all have our own lives and I ask you to respect that. As you ask me to respect the boundaries of your mind."

DePlankas acknowledged my comment with a nod, "A fair trade indeed. You're a canny one Ms Jackson. Very well, you have my word. No recruiting the psychics among you." Her eyes tracked the room, letting us all know that she knew more than we'd like. "Do I pass muster?"

"Yes."

Dan sighed, "Tess if you could bring up the screen again and do a quick recap."

2

So here we were, out of the city, in a private plane hanger next to a landing strip. "Who owns this place?"

"Some friend of Deman's," Reilly muttered. "Just one more international millionaire with a stake in Western Australia's mining industry. The thing is we're well out of the public eye. Let's not ask too many questions."

"I like asking questions," I growled.

Jim tapped my head, "Put the journalist away for now Ry. We're just the delivery guys in this top secret enterprise."

"Hmm," delivery guys who were expected to fix or at least analyse any problems along the way. And me? I'd do what any good ship's deck officer cadet would normally do. Document, take readings, check the weather forecasts, double check our course headings and manage communications. And amongst all that take photos of the breathtakingly stark and arid scenery. There had to be a story or two out here if I kept my eyes and ears open. Something I could report on without breaching our non-disclosure agreements.

A nondescript white government vehicle with Commonwealth of Australia number plates pulled up outside the hanger: DePlankas, and she had a friend with her.

The 'friend' woofed, excited, wanting to be off the leash. A giant of a dog with a coat that glistened various shades of brown. Distinct whiskers drooped down the sides of his muzzle. Eyelashes the envy of many framed eyes of the clearest orange-brown.

"He won't hurt," Inspector DePlankas assured, "Unless you object to cuddles and sloppy licks. Okay if I let him off?"

"Sure," though I immediately doubted my sanity as the biggest dog I'd ever seen came bounding towards me.

"Clyde!" DePlankas yelled.

The dog braked, almost comically, his front paw digging into the ground. He looked at me, mournful and hopeful.

I weakened and walked up to him. "Nice Clyde, good Clyde. He's huge," I commented.

"Hence his name, short for Clydesdale."

"A Cú Faoil," Reilly noted in a tone of reverence as he went to stroke Clyde's shaggy coat. "He's magnificent. Ya keep him in excellent condition, inspector."

"Did you say koo-fweel?" I wondered. I hadn't even known Reilly could speak any actual Irish.

"I did. A hound of wolf or wolfhound if you prefer. He's a little big for a sniffer dog isn't he, inspector?"

"There are times his size comes in handy. He's not much use as a guard dog as he's too friendly but he'll easily catch a fleeing crim, if needed. It's in his nature to bring down large quarry like wolves. We've had to train him when not to go for the kill. Like a lion they aim for the throat and finish their prey a good shake. Clyde's trained not to do that to humans though he will go hunting for his own food if he thinks he's hungry. We keep him well fed and on a leash if he's outside. Clyde, heel." Clyde attentively walked beside her as they went to inspect the container that was now loaded on the back of the trailer.

Jim came to stand beside me as we waited to see if the dog would confirm what Deman and I believed we had found.

Clyde suddenly stopped in his tracks, sat and gave two short woofs.

DePlankas smiled, patting her friend, "Excellent Clyde." The Inspector turned back to us. "I'll take that as confirmation."

"But we're not opening up the load?" Reilly sought confirmation.

DePlankas shook her head. "No, the less it looks like we've found the real cargo the better. Now, tracking. Can we negotiate?"

"Sutton Innovative Technologies will have our location at all times. They'll keep you advised," Reilly gave the Inspector a steely eye.

DePlankas stood her ground. "That doesn't help if they offload the cargo."

"And tagging our vehicle wouldn't have helped with that," Reilly pointed out.

Jim was enjoying the tug of war as much as me but intervened, "I have an idea. I think I can steer a fine fibre optics cable into the load. Sort of like key-hole surgery except I won't be cutting anything away. I could plant some microscopic radio-frequency identification devices inside a couple of those bags of drugs. I'd make the tiniest of holes in the packaging. No-one except us would ever know."

"What do you need?"

While Inspector dePlankas went off to organise that Clyde, who she'd left behind, and I checked our supplies for the trip. Although I wasn't too sure that Clyde wasn't checking for tasty dog treats. There was a hopeful gleam in his eye.

My phone vibrated in my jeans pocket and I pulled it out to see if I wanted to take the call. Scammers, telemarketers, pollsters, and politicians had all taught me healthy caution when it came to answering the phone. I smiled when I saw the name, "Bosun, how are you? How's Horatio?" Though arachnophobic to the core I had some kind of connection with Bosun's pet tarantula, dare I say even a soft spot.

"I'm well. Keeping busy. Unfortunately maintenance doesn't stop just because the ship's in port. About Horatio, that's why I'm ringing. He's not in his home."

Shit. "Hell, the Captain finds out he'll flip." Wildlife onboard the Merkwood II, whether pets or not, had to be contained while we were in port. It was a nightmare of a quarantine issue. Normally pets weren't allowed but the Captain made a grudging exception for the Bosun's pet who, in a way, had become an unofficial mascot for the boat. Having escaped Bosun's cabin on numerous occasions Horatio now had a home up on the ship's bridge, hidden out of sight in a purpose built enclosure under the communications console. I'd explained to Horatio through some kind of non-verbal communication I had with the spider that he needed to stay put until we were back at sea. Knowing Horatio's curious nature I was guessing he'd gotten bored.

"You're telling me. I was hoping you might have had some sense of where he's at."

"Honestly, I've been a bit distracted," which might have been part of Horatio's problem. I'd kind of been neglecting him. "When was the last you saw him?"

"Last night when I went up to feed him a cricket. I'm at my wits end."

"Look, I know the Captain's limiting shore leave to try and keep that virus away from the crew but you can still get deliveries. Go online and find a plastic spider about the size of Horatio and put it in the cage. And remove one leg just in case some observant person counts them." Yeah, Horatio had gotten his name not just because he was a seafaring spider but because, like me, he was missing one limb.

"Ry, you're brilliant. I'll get right on that."

"Good luck." After saying our farewells I hung up, though now I worried. There wasn't anything I could do at the moment so I sent a mental note to Aranya, the uber-protector of all arachnids and somehow my protector too. *I entrust him in your care.*

She didn't often communicate with me but I felt the warmth of her smile. Did large majestic scary and beautiful spider beings smile? Maybe not in her face but there was a shared sense.

I put the distraction to the back of my mind and went back to checking supplies with Clyde giving me the occasional head bump, reminding me to pat him again. He seemed to have an insatiable need for pats. Was this the world's cuddliest dog?

Inside the mobile home part of our rig was everything you might need in a mini-home. A compact yet fully equipped kitchen. A tiny bathroom including a shower bay. And a bed that just might fit the three of us but it was going to be cosy. I hoped I wouldn't roll out of bed during the middle of the night. Though usually I slept in the middle. Don't ask.

The table, a fold out attached to the wall, could just about seat four, intimately. There were power and USB slots in the wall near the table and the bed that gave me some hope of having the internet. I trusted Jim to have arranged some satellite broadband as there wouldn't be much of anything else where we were going.

Clyde circled the mat at the foot of the bed, pawing at as if to check it for softness before he lay down. Truthfully I expected it was just a comfy place for him to watch me from. I might go to a kitchen cupboard and pull out some yummy biscuits. In his dreams. "I'm sorry Clyde, we haven't stocked any dog treats."

A curt woof seemed to ask, why not?,

I felt more than heard Reilly come in the door. He surveyed our accommodations. "Well it's compact."

"It's that. But we'll have the great outdoors if we get claustrophobic."

Reilly rolled his eyes, "Yeah, dust, flies and heat. Might be alright at dawn and dusk." He eyed the airconditioner that was fitted into the ceiling. "Does that thing work?"

"I have no idea," I reached up with my good arm and flipped the switch. Nothing. "Hmm."

Reilly frowned, "Well we're not going anywhere without it. I'll put it on Jim's to-do list. Speaking of which, Jim and the inspector are heading back into town, to her headquarters, for some bits so they can tag the drugs. Mahala's keen for our furry friend here to accompany us."

"She's probably got a tracker in him."

"Most likely but she also thinks he might be an asset if we meet up with any undesirables on the trip."

"He's a wolf hound," I pointed out. "He might look intimidating but he's more likely to smooch strangers to death than to be an actual guard dog."

"Apparently he can act," Reilly grinned, "Clyde, guard." He pointed to me.

Clyde instantly sprang up, positioning himself in front of me. Lips went back revealing vicious teeth, drool dripped from his beard and the growl, well I imagined the Hound of the Baskervilles would be proud of the show.

"Clyde, at ease." Reilly commanded.

Clyde's growl instantly turned to a grin and he settled himself back on the mat before licking the drool from his smile.

"Impressive."

Clyde's tail thumped the ground at my obvious praise.

"Okay he stays, but what are we going to feed him, other than a stray thief or two?"

"I'll head in with Jim and Mahala. Her headquarters must keep supplies for the dog. Are you alright for a bit? We're going to need the space in the car."

"You go, I'll plug my laptop in and work on my blog. I might even go for a walk and take the camera with me. See what there is to see on the property."

"Take Clyde with ya if you do. And stay in sight of the hanger. We can never be too sure who might be watchin' us."

"No-one knows we're out here or what we're doing," I assured him.

"Let's hope not. We'll be back in an hour or two. If ya need anythin' ring. We can always get the property owner to send one of his employees out."

"What do we know about this owner?"

Reilly shrugged his shoulders, "A friend of Deman's. A Mr Homes. We're invited for tea tonight."

I frowned, "For dinner?"

"He called it tea but I understood it as dinner," Reilly quipped.

"I'll dig out my best frock and pearls," I joked.

Reilly hmphed, "Our maritime navy uniform will do for the occasion and that's all he's going to get." He wrapped me in his arms and gave me a deep kiss. "Pearls wouldn't suit you anyway. Fire opal maybe."

"I'll make a note to seek one out. See you when you get back."

He paused at the door, "By the way, I'm not gnarly."

Shit, yeah I had had that thought earlier in the day. "Only in the most awe inspiring way. I like your gnarl remember. I like everything about you." I walked over to him at the door. We grinned at each other like silly kids then sprung at each other. From desperate kisses Reilly went straight for my neck, like a vampire looking for a vein. I moaned and yielded. Clyde broke the moment by giving an uncertain woof.

"At ease Clyde. And ya thought he wouldn't make a guard dog."

"I wasn't thinking of him protecting my virtue."

Reilly laughed at that. "I'd better go or the Inspector might start wonderin' what we're up to in here."

But we knew Jim was distracting her, since he could read both our minds. "I'm guessing I've got one damned big hickey on my neck now so I'll save your reputation by staying put. Have fun shopping for dog food."

Clyde got up and woofed excitedly.

Reilly eyed him speculatively, "He understands way too much that one. We'll be back as soon as we can," he stole one more kiss and left.

I spent the next hour updating my blog. With the main heat of the day finally abating I decided it was time for a walk.

As if sensing my mental shift Clyde was instantly up and attentive.

I looked around for a rope of something I could use as a lead but there was none. "You going to behave Clyde? No chasing down hapless wildlife. Okay?" As if I'd get any agreement on that front but I guess if we were both going to get a walk I'd just have to hope.

I grabbed a bottle of water and my camera then locked the rig and the access door to the hanger, pocketing the key. Clyde and I wandered off, mindful of Reilly's request to stay in sight of the hanger. Made sense anyway as most of the landscape looked the same out here. It would be easy to get lost in the sand and the scrub.

I spied an ancient, weatherworn outcrop of sedimentary rock that looked like it had erupted out of the ground long ago. The red dirt monoliths looked like smooth edged statues straight out of some *avant garde* artist's workshop. There had to be some photos there so we headed in that direction. Clyde galloped there and then back as if to say hurry up. His sheer energy was almost exhausting to watch.

When we reached the first of the monoliths I wiped the sweat from my brow. I took a drink from my bottle and then cupped my hand and used it to offer a welcome drink to Clyde. A single slurp later and it was gone but he looked at me with a grin and wagged his tail. "You can have more before we head back."

I took a moment to savour the feel of the place, leaning back against the great monolith. I took another moment to laugh at the antics of my mind that thought of tales of heroines falling through ancient rocks into other lands. The stuff of books and movies. Yeah, well. Yet there was something here. A deep connection with place, the here and now. In just this one perfect moment in time. I waved away the last of the day's bush flies from settling on my face as they searched for their own drink from my skin's moisture. I should have grabbed a fly net from the rig but it hadn't been uppermost in my mind. Having just spent time at sea, as trainee crew on the Merkwood II, I'd forgotten about such things.

I did my best to ignore the flies. As long as one didn't crawl up my nose. "Clyde, stay!" I assumed he'd understand that. It was a fairly basic command. I watched him lay down and settle at my feet then I closed my eyes and linked to what I felt.

Reilly would be cross if I slipped over into the other dimension without him to guard me but with Clyde at my feet I felt I'd compromised. I drew a deep breath into my body, visualising it travelling all the way down to the earth beneath my feet. I was grounded and connected to this dimension. Though I kept my spirit anchored in this world I allowed myself to become hyper aware of the tiny particles that made up my inner vision. I looked through them into another world.

As I relaxed into the vision I spied a man walking towards me. He looked out of time, clad in little more than a loin cloth. He was tall and lanky, almost wiry. His dark complexion contrasted against the grey of his wispy beard. He spoke in a language I didn't know but yet I understood. How paradoxical was that? But then I had telepathic links to some people so perhaps I shouldn't be so surprised.

"Hello," seemed the safest, almost universal greeting.

"Welcome to my country," he acknowledged me with a nod.

His country? I suddenly felt like an interloper, trespassing where I shouldn't be. Maybe this outcrop of rocks was sacred to the local people who'd once lived here.

"Be at ease," he assured, in his own language. "You're welcome here. I only come to greet you and to bless your journey."

"You know what we're about?" I guessed.

"I do. We are greatly interested in your world at the moment as it is reaching a critical juncture. Long ago your dimension split from ours. Choices were made and are still being made, that have ongoing ramifications on all the dimensions, all the universes. Another choice point is coming. We see you, Ry, as a bridge between our respective existences. Though why ours is referred to as a dream while yours is termed reality is a source of much amusement to us."

"But, I'm not of your people." He looked like he belonged in the dream time that the first nations spoke about.

"Which term would you prefer; rubbish, hogwash, nonsense…? In the time before, your ancestors were all one tribe. Haven't your own scientists proven that by tracing the bloodlines of everyone now on your version of the planet back to the few survivors of the last great split? And, if you want to be particularly picky, I'd look to your great great great grandmother, the daughter of a settler, who fell in love with a cattle drover. He was a man steeped In the traditions of your country, trained in the ancient wisdoms."

Hmm, it seemed I'd be checking my DNA and having a long delve into the family archives.

"Or you could just ask them to tell you in a dream. While they have reincarnated many times since part of them remains immortal, beyond time and space. All your ancestors watch over you. Forgive them any mistakes they made because of the times they lived through and send them love from within your present reality. That will create the connection you need."

The vision of my visitor began to fragment. There was still much I wanted to ask him. "What is it you want me to do?"

"Be true to yourself. Trust yourself. The rest will unfold," and frustratingly he disappeared.

I opened my eyes to my current surroundings. My phone was ringing urgently. "I'm fine Reilly."

"You were off-line," he growled.

By off-line he meant he'd lost our telepathic connection while I'd been in the trance.

I understood his worry and anger. "I wasn't in the other world. I just happened to have a vision."

Reilly hmphed but sounded appeased, slightly. "We'll be back soon. Get yourself back to the hanger."

"When I'm good and ready." I wasn't about to yield easily to his authority, outside of work. He needed to be reminded I was my own person.

He was worried, came Jim's mental chide.

Which no doubt meant that Jim had been worried too. I sighed. "Oh, very well. I'm heading back now." I hung up the phone.

When I got back to the hanger Mahala was heading off with Jim to the container, cable hung over her shoulder and she carried what looked like a fishing tackle box of bits. Jim was fervently studying an instruction sheet.

"Don't forget to fix the air conditioner Jim," Reilly yelled after him.

Jim didn't bother to turn around. I heard his, *you don't have to yell*, reply in my head as well.

Reilly grunted and turned his attention to unloading the dog food from the car. There was a surprising amount.

"Where are you going to put all that?"

"In the storage space under the bed."

We had storage space under the bed? This was news to me.

All was revealed as he released a catch under the bed and the whole thing, mattress, bedding and all, tilted up to reveal a considerable space, already partially taken up with tools and assorted camping paraphernalia. "I guess Clyde's not going to go hungry. Don't suppose you came back with a lead for him?"

Reilly pointed to a bag of bits including dog treats, a couple of balls, a well worn and partially chewed soft toy and a lead.

Since Reilly had the job of packing well in hand I grabbed my phone and went to sit in the front cab, out of the way. "Hey, Mum, how's it going?"

"Really well. Just came back from the hairdressers," she fluffed her hair on the video call. "What do you think?"

"Snazzy Mum. You always have a way of looking great."

"Sweet talker. Are you staying safe? You're not near that virus outbreak in the city are you?"

"No Mum," I guess no matter how many times I'd reassure her on that one she'd still worry. "The three of us are taking a truckload of goods from the ship up to Alice Springs, via the Gun Barrel Highway."

"Well at least you're sticking to a highway. I'd worry if you were going on some outback dirt track."

And wasn't it good that Mum wasn't telepathic. I could only hope she never felt the impulse to look up the Gun Barrel Highway on the internet.

"You know the guys wouldn't risk my safety."

"I know darling. But I'm talking to my one and only daughter who's made her name by tracking to some of the most dangerous places on the planet."

And even though I didn't do that anymore, not since losing my left arm, somehow trouble still found me. Pirates, assassins, smugglers …hmm. Don't go there. "We're taking a guard dog with us on the trip. Must be the biggest wolfhound I've ever seen. His name's Clyde, short for Clydesdale."

On cue Clyde pushed his way into the cab and gave a friendly woof in greeting, as if he'd heard the other voice on the speaker and come to investigate.

"Well hello there Clyde, aren't you a beauty. Don't suppose you can send him home to me when you've finished your trip?"

"Sorry mum, he's not ours. He's on loan. He likes the wide open spaces and he's very much a working dog." I suspected our Clyde needed a job to do or he'd get bored.

"Oh well, now let's get down to business. You didn't ring me just to introduce your new friend."

"Er, no. Question. All my ancestors were descended from English farmers - right?"

Silence, "Well, mostly. There is one wild story that one lady on my side of the family was a bit of a rogue, a black sheep. I couldn't get any information out of my gran when I was researching the family tree. It was like a wall suddenly went down and I could get nothing more out of her. She fobbed me off by saying that no-one in that time knew the first names of their parents."

"Definitely fudging."

"I think so."

"But you did your DNA. Anything interesting? What haven't you told me about mum?"

"Well this is a turn around. You've had no interest before now."

"That's not an answer Mum." A bit of telepathy would have been useful here but even if I had that sort of connection with Mum I wouldn't want to pry. My mentor Lydia had strongly pushed respect for boundaries on me. "What was the wild story you'd heard whispered?"

Mum cleared her throat. "That this lady did a Lady Chatterly. She had it off with a visiting stockman. The trace of DNA I found suggested he must have been at least in part indigenous."

"Wow. I'm guessing in your Gran's time that wasn't something to be spoken about."

"Poor woman, I can't imagine how hard it must have been for her. Unmarried. A child out of wedlock."

"There's no evidence she ever married?"

"Nothing in the records I could find. Hell, I only have a surname to go on. Kelly. Her parents' property was somewhere North West of Perth. In Wajarri country, I think. Don't take any of this as gospel. A good genealogist doesn't believe anything until she sees the paper trail."

And yet a shiver went down my spine, something resonated with what she'd said. "You're a great genealogist mum and I'm sorry I didn't show enough of an interest until now."

She waved a hand in dismissal, "I'm delighted you're interested now. But I'm curious. What brought this on?"

"I had a vision." I couldn't tell her about the true purpose of our trip but this much I could tell. So, since Mum was open to such things, I shared what I could. In turn, excited by what I'd told her, she gave me an overview of all my inbuilt heritage.

When I finished the call Reilly was at my back. He put a hand on my shoulder, seeking connection. "All good?" I knew without a doubt he'd heard the conversation, if not by ear then at least through our shared mind link. He probably felt my mental turmoil and surprise.

"Yeah. I'm still left pondering a mystery but I know more than I did before. Mum, at least, is 82% from Britain and Ireland, 12% French-German. 4% Nordic, probably Finnish and 2% Indigenous Australian. Go figure."

"Irish eh? I wonder if we're distantly related?" Reilly mused.

I laughed, trust Reilly to home in on that, "Show that interest to my mother and she'll have you spitting saliva into a DNA test quicker than you can blink."

"I'll bear that in mind. Jim's finished both his jobs. Mahala's left and wished us bon voyage."

"Was I on the phone that long?"

It was Reilly's turn to chuckle. "Come on. We need to clean up and make ourselves presentable for dinner."

Ooh, that was a nice thought. A shower.

Reilly waggled his finger. "And do ya 'av any idea how long our limited water supply would last if the three of us took our usual showers? It'll be a wash from a sink full of water."

"Damn."

3

I'd almost been expecting some kind of chauffeur driven limousine would pick us up. The property owner was a friend of Deman's after all. But then I was a friend of Deman's too, having done most of our schooling together.

Instead a king cab ute pulled up and we all got in. Except for Clyde who got to ride in the back which, if the grin on his face was anything to go by, he enjoyed immensely. Jeff, who turned out to be the owner's son, pulled up in front of the big house. Reilly frowned as Jeff went around to help me down to the ground. "She's not a bleedin' invalid."

"Hush Reilly, he's just being a country gentleman, aren't you Jeff?"

Jim, taking his cue, walked over and offered me his arm before Jeff could, "When in Rome."

Reilly growled. "She hasn't even done her karate practice today."

"Neither have you," I reminded him.

Jeff looked between the three of us and shook his head. "You three are like an old married, er…triple."

I shook my head, "Don't say the M word Jeff. It tends to freak us out." Not that we'd ever be allowed to marry each other in this country. Maybe being a dual citizen I could marry one under Seychelles law and the other under Australian law? You couldn't class it as bigamy if it involved two guys could you? It would be something like bi-androgyny? Was that even a word? If it didn't exist in law then they couldn't stop us? Could they?

"Ry," Reilly covered his face with his hands, as if in pain.

Hmm, I focused on the architecture of the house instead. Not a colonial build, well not entirely. They'd kept the 1800s ornate white painted iron lace work on the wide front verandah but the rest of the building looked like it had been modernised and expanded.

Jeff opened the front door for us and welcomed us into a wide entrance hall that ran the fall length of the house. Halfway down the hall a wooden ballastraded stairway led to an upper floor.

We were greeted, not by some stiff shirted butler, but by his sister Essie, "Mum's still busy making the hors d'oeuvres and dad's got god knows what on the go. But trust me, whatever it is will be delicious. Can I show you around the house, or get you a drink to have out on the verandah?"

Simultaneously I said house and the guys said drink.

Jeff laughed and ushered Jim and Reilly out leaving me with Essie, "It's a grand place you've got here."

"It is now. It probably started out plain enough when it was built back in the 1890s. This would have been the main house with several families living nearby in simple two room workers' cottages. These days the property doesn't need so many hands as we have equipment, vehicles, even a helicopter to help round up the cattle. But we still have a few hands, though these days we house them better than then."

"Do you have any photos of the place as it was?" I asked, curious.

"Ah, if it's history you're after, follow me." Essie led me to a large room that looked like it had been turned into a mini museum. Black and white and sepia toned photos found place on the walls among shelves of all kinds of mysterious objects, such as you might find on an old farm. Old fashioned shears for shearing sheep, a genuine butter churn, Tilley lamps, petrified wood … even what looked like to be a few dinosaur bones.

"Wow, you've got quite a collection here."

"They're no longer really ours. We're more like custodians since my parents gifted the contents to the State. The government museum has catalogued what we have and occasionally borrows bits for displays or to take and show schools. This is more like an offsite storage facility but it helps to keep the pieces where they were found."

"That's very generous. I wish more people looked after the past that way." So much of Australia's early colonial heritage had already been lost but perhaps that was a rant for another day. My attention was drawn to a group of photos, children seated in front of their extended families. No-one smiling as no-one did for the camera in those days. "Do you happen to know any of the history of the early families? It's just that I only found out today that I had ancestors in this vicinity."

"Ooh, hard," she rubbed her chin. "You got a name?"

"Only a surname, Kelly. That's all my Mum could get out of my grandmother. Going by DNA and what records we do have, the woman would probably have been alive sometime around the mid 1800s."

"That is early. This part of WA only started to be developed after some explorers went through around 1851. Some of the area was opened up to farming but it wasn't until gold was found in the 1880s that people really moved in." I could see her mind thinking as she strode purposefully to a drawer of old documents. "There's an index here somewhere. Ah here it is. Kelly, Kelly… James Rossiter Kelly and his English wife Melba had a land grant… ooh… not far from here." Essie put on white conservator's gloves before handling a precious map.

"Let me see," I'd gotten a lot better at reading maps since I'd been training as a cadet Deck Officer. "Is it okay if I take a photo of this?'

"As long as you don't use a flash. The light can damage the old documents, they fade quicker."

I took my photos. I already had a rough idea the place would be on our way. I only had to persuade Jim and Reilly it was worth the slight detour.

Jeff poked his head in the door, "Come on you two. Nothing can be that interesting when Dad's dishing up his masterpiece."

"Philistine," Essie countered, rolling her eyes before we followed him out the door. "Ask him about artificial intelligence and its use in modern day farm management and he'll talk for hours but history…"

Jeff laughed, "Essie's an arts major. Archeology, historical preservation and a bit of palaeontology thrown in for good measure. Damned waste of time if you ask me." But he didn't say it unkindly. More a jibe between siblings.

"Isn't it a bedrock of modern management theory that the best indicator of the future is the past," or something like that, I jibed back. I think the original statement had more to do with people's behaviour.

Essie slapped me affectionately on the back, "Well said."

Dinner, tea, whatever you wanted to call it, passed amiably. Jeff pinned Jim's ears about his ideas on the uses of remote sensing and robots in farming. Reilly talked tractors and trucks with Max Homes, the masterful chef of our fine meal. Essie helped Amelia, her Mum, clear the table to make way for the deserts. My help met with a certain amount of hospitable resistance, being one armed, but I was not one to give in easily. And it gave me more time to pick Essie's brain on the history of the area. I was truly grateful for what she shared. I had a picture building in my head now, what life must have been like for my ancestors. It gave me some of the connection I was looking for.

Before we said our farewells for the night and gave thanks for a meal well shared, Essie took me to one side and pushed a card into my hand. "If you find anything more about your ancestor let me know. I've written a few contacts for you on the back as well. Ed, that's all I know him as, has a breadth of stories about his people, some might have been cattle drovers. And this guy, Stef Maxwell, has his own private historical collection. If you say I sent you he might let you see it. I think he's on your route. Not that I've been told too much about what you're up to but it seems much more than a simple delivery of goods to Alice Springs. Dad's been shutting the door whenever he speaks to his old friend Deman about it."

"Sorry about that. I can't tell you either but I really appreciate your help. I know it's not why we're here but somehow I feel this trip is about much more for me. A reconnection with some deep level of the past. Not just within the last two hundred years but way further back. This is just the start."

Essie looked at me curiously, "How do you intend to connect further back?"

This was a secret I could share. "I, I don't know what you'll think of this, I can journey out of my body and as of today it appears I can have visions as well. The man I saw in my vision told me I could contact my ancestors. I haven't a clue how but I intend to try."

Her eyes widened in surprise and delight. "You have got to talk to Ed. Tell him what you just told me. I'd be very surprised if he didn't agree to help you contact them."

"I'll do that then."

"And tell me the outcome."

"Well, we'll be back this way on our return."

She looked pained. "You're not going to keep me waiting that long are you. Keep me posted."

I had an idea. "I have a blog. I share my explorations and some of what I experience in the otherworld on it. I keep it up to date." I gave her the web address. "But I'll give you a call on anything I can't put in the blog."

"Deal," we shook on it.

4

Jeff dropped us back off at the hanger. To tell the truth, I was ready to stop the frantic rush of the day. The pace had been full on since we'd left the ship in the morning, picked up the rig, come out here and everything that had followed on from there. I watched Reilly secure the hanger door. "I hope that's not the only way in and out."

He pointed to the far end of the hanger, where various bits were stacked. Drums of who knew what, a ride-on mower and a spare wind sock, among other things. "There's a fire exit down there. It only opens from the inside."

Clyde barged ahead of us, following Jim into our mobile home. "Well I guess that answers where Clyde's going to sleep for the night."

Reilly frowned. "I was thinking he could patrol the hanger bay."

"Are you going to tell him or shall I?" I grinned, knowing I'd bet on the dog winning that argument.

Jim looked up from putting food in the dog's bowl, as we came inside, "You got a bit more on your ancestor."

"I did," which reminded me that I needed to text the details to Mum.

"Hmm," was all Reilly said but I could read his mind.

And I was getting used to deciphering his tones, "I know, we didn't intend this trip to be an episode of 'Looking for your ancestors.'"

"It's important to you so we'll fit it in," Reilly decided.

Nice of him to agree but then he was kind've nominally boss of this little enterprise. "I'll contact Deman when I have a moment and brief him. If it's an issue we'll leave my investigations until the way back."

"Oh no you don't," Jim surprised as with a groan, "or it'll be spinning in your head all the way to Alice Springs."

It pained Reilly to agree but,"Jim's right. That busy brain of yours will go into overdrive. Text your Mum, Ry. Then let's get to bed. We've got an early start in the mornin'."

Clyde burped then licked his chops before settling himself down at the end of the bed.

"Really?" Reilly asked the dog.

Clyde stared him down with his searing golden eyes and a 'try moving me' grin. Dog 1, Human 0.

Reilly swore something in the Gaelic tongue which I was just coming to realise he spoke more than a little bit of. I'd wrongly thought that Irish was only spoken in remote far West pockets of the Republic of Ireland but apparently it was still spoken by some in Northern Ireland as well. He neatly folded his clothes and placed them on the chair near our tiny fold out table and then clambered into bed, after bestowing one last glare on Clyde. Then he snuggled up against my back and pulled the bedclothes up around him.

Jim, facing me, waggled a brow. I waggled mine back. It was a kind of morse code. We moved into a deep, satisfying kiss.

Reilly growled. "I thought everyone was tired. I was restrainin' myself."

"Well don't. I pushed my backside invitingly into his crotch as I leaned more into Jim, trailing my tongue down his divinely sculptured neck. Jim moaned but if his mind was too blissed out to think his cock still had enough presence of mind to find its happy place, deep inside my vagina.

I heard a condom being released from its wrapper and then shrink wrap being ripped with a vengeance as Reilly fought to open a fresh bottle of lube. Those sounds alone sent a shiver of anticipation down my spine. It took all my focus to keep my attention on licking Jim as I waited for Reilly to take me.

And then there he was and I was full. Oh so full. I yielded to both of them in complete and utter trust as they flowed into their now well practised dance. One in, one out. Liquid heat built inside my cunt. My heart beat louder in my chest. Breaths came shallower and faster.

"Not yet," Reilly swore. "Ya've got to both hold on 'til I say."

Both Jim and I groaned as we struggled to maintain that fine edge without falling over it.

"Faster," Reilly ordered, "Go deeper Jim."

"I can't ..." I wailed. "I can't hold on."

Reilly scruffed me by the hair and turned my face to his. His emerald green eyes piercing mine with his command. "You will hold." As he thrust into my core. We both felt Jim's struggle, edging on frustration. "Now!" Reilly yelled.

I screamed. Jim yelled out, "Yes!" The bed seemed to be rocky ground for a moment.

Then two curious eyes looked over the end of the bed, as if to say WTF, what the hell are you lot up to? Then Clyde let out a woof and resettled. Reilly rolled his eyes at the dog's antics. "At least he didn't try to rescue ya."

"I'm not sure how I go having an audience."

Jim chuckled. "I don't think any of us were aware of him until just then. Now go to sleep." He pulled on his trusty sleep mask and rolled over. He'd taken to wearing one when it became apparent that I often got up at least once in the middle of the night and rather than have me fumble around in the dark Reilly had ordered me to, quote, 'switch the damn light on', end quote.

I sank into the deep dreamless sleep that comes when you finally give over to the body's needs. A few hours later the dreams started. This time, at least, I had a sense that I was dreaming.

Jim was determinedly packing a brand new backpack with anything that would fit. His Mum was sitting on the bed, watching him, tears streaming down her face. "Where will you go?"

"You won't tell him?" It was a plea as much as a request.

"I wouldn't do that to you." She dried her tears as she thought about how they might keep in touch. "I've got a private post box in the city. I use it for things I don't want your Dad to know about." She wrote the address down. "Write to me there."

Jim hated that his mother had to live a life where she felt she needed to hide stuff from the man she'd married. "I'll write as soon as I get wherever I'm going. Honestly, I'm not set on a particular place yet but I'm thinking further West." Seattle held appeal but could he afford it?

As if sensing his mind his mum took an envelope from her pocket and handed it to him. It contained a stack of notes.

Jim gasped when he saw the amount. "Mum, I can't."

"You can and you will." Her spine straightened now. "He gives me an allowance to do the weekly shopping. Anything I haven't spent I've stashed away. Look Jim, it's too late for me to start over. He's never allowed me to work. I have no skills. I've got no way out. You're young. You can rough it for a bit. Let me at least have this in my heart. That you escaped." Fresh tears threatened.

Jim knew he had to then, "Okay. I'll do this for both of us. And when I eventually earn enough to get a place of my own you'll come."

"I will."

Though Jim had his doubts that she'd ever make the break. Over the years his father had weakened his mum's faith in herself.

"What will you do?" She eyed him curiously now.

Not what his Dad wanted, that was sure. The man had made a booking to send him to a 'program' to straighten out his somewhat nebulous sexuality and then had plans of having him join the family business. "I've always fancied getting into electronics."

His Mum nodded encouragingly, "You've the mind for it."

"With what you've given me I should have enough to pay the entrance fees to get into a university if I can find one that will accept me."

"You'll need your school certificates…"

They both jumped at the sound of a car door slamming out the front of the house.

"Go," his Mum urged. "I'll send you anything you need." She nodded to the adjacent window.

"Good thinking." He kissed her on the forehead and fled.

"Where the hell's my dinner, woman?" came the yell from the front of the house.

Jane's shoulders sagged. She took one happy look at the window through which her son had just left and then steeled herself for the nightly confrontation.

I was woken from my 'dream', by Clyde's low growl. He was up and at the mobile home's door. Nose pointing in the direction of concern.

"Somethin's out there," Reilly decided, quickly throwing on some clothes and shoes but before he could charge out the door I grabbed hold of his shirt. Clyde was just as eager to go and get whatever it was but we had no way of knowing if whoever it was was one or many or whether they were armed.

"Aren't you forgetting something?" Reilly was always quick to take charge but sometimes, in his hurry to respond to situations, he forgot the strengths of those around him.

Reilly looked at me and froze. It was that moment of comprehension. I'd given him time to think. "Ya're right. How quickly can you shed yer body?"

"As quickly as you can cuddle me." He'd been charged by those in the know to protect me during such adventures.

Jim, who was awake now too, nodded his approval. "Jeff gave me the codes to patch into the hanger's security cameras. I'll go and check the monitors in the cab while Ry goes on her scouting mission. Clyde, you can come with me." Clyde wrinkled his eyebrows expressively but followed as asked. Clearly he thought he had better uses, such as hunting intruders.

I nestled into Reilly's strong arms and let go, wishing I had Horatio, the spider I reluctantly called friend, with me to put the frighteners into whoever was out there. I was surprised then when I felt his etheric presence. I turned to stare into his multifaceted eyes. "Well you are a good friend aren't you." I guess it didn't matter he was somewhere, AWOL, on the Merkwood II. I was conflicted between the need to find out where he was and the need to go and investigate our possible intruder. Though it could be just a possum Clyde was worrying about.

Stay on task, Reilly firmly ordered in my mind.

Right. "Let's go Horatio." I projected my consciousness outside the rig, outside the hanger and together the spider and I roamed. No one could see us unless they were in this realm so there was no need for stealth.

I saw him. A pale man with almost platinum blond hair or maybe grey hair that had gone white but he didn't look that old. The dark green and mustard yellow aura that surrounded him was undoubtedly familiar. The man grumbled to himself, frustrated, trying to pry open the fire exit with a pinch bar. "How about you go spook him Horatio, while I go see if I can find his transport."

The man's ute, what some might call a truck, was an old model Toyota flat tray. The vehicle had been famed in its time as indestructible which made them common enough in the outback. Though these days the Isuzu Dmax 4x4 was becoming the much sought after vehicle of choice. As to electric vehicles no-one was quite sure yet how they would work out here, when sometimes the nearest charging place might be several hundred kilometres away. Only time would tell. Personally I thought there was a better future in hydrogen power or turning the surface of a car into one big solar panel. Some futurists even talked about making the roads themselves the charging stations though that would hardly work on a dirt road outback. Possibly when the scientists studied the data from our current proposed trip they might come up with other alternatives. But enough of cars. What I needed was a number plate,a make and a model. *Can you write this down, Reilly?* I gave him the info, just in time, as the now screaming man came barrelling towards the vehicle, dived into the driver seat and drove away like the hounds of hell were after him. I guess I wasn't the only one with arachnophobia. "Well done Horatio."

Horatio's etheric presence came near me. I felt his longing, as ever, for experience and adventure, then he faded back to his body. He'd been out of his body without someone to watch over his physical body, wherever that was, but I knew the uber being of all spiders, Aranya, kept a special look out for him. I sent her my thanks before returning to my own body.

"Got a good picture of him," Jim announced as he and Clyde returned from the cab of the big rig.

Reilly had written down the details I'd gotten, "Send this and your picture to Mahala. Let's see if he's a known quantity."

"I don't think he'll be back tonight," not the way he fled the scene.

"Remind me to thank Horatio for the scare routine," even Reilly had been impressed by the results. Though he hadn't seen Horatio in his giant, menacing etheric form I think he had a sense of it.

"Let me just give Clyde a dog treat by way of reward. Then perhaps we can get some more sleep."

I liked that idea.

Our sleep ended with two phones ringing furiously. Reilly dived for his and I went for mine.

"Mum! We're three hours behind you."

"Oops. Sorry dear. But if that's the case it's 6am where you are, don't you have work to do?"

Hmm, "You're right. What's up?"

"Well those names you sent me last night. My curiosity got to me and kept me up late looking into them. I found the bloke easy enough. And," she paused for effect, "his marriage to one Melba Davies. Not English, Welsh."

Welsh? It appeared I had another thread to my mixed up heritage. "What about the daughter?" The mysterious ancestor who'd done a runner.

"Well I'm not sure yet. Still a few leads to check. It's looking like she might have gone East to Sydney. I've found a plausible marriage and a christening for a child born not long after that. The name of the groom on the marriage document and the christening record is simply given as Jimmy. He signed his surname with an X. Makes me think he may have been indigenous as they often didn't have surnames back then."

She was evading my question. I knew she wasn't sure of the facts yet I had to know "Just give me what you've got Mum. I won't hold you to it. Who do you think was James Rossiter Kelly and Melba Davies daughter and who was her child?"

"Melba Kelly, but when she married she took the surname Drover. Since it was Jimmy's occupation it kind of makes sense. Their child was one Rosie Melba Drover. An interesting lady. Ended up running her own business in Melbourne, a small local newspaper. Imagine the obstacles she must have had to contend with back then. Though who she married and how she connects with our existing family tree I have no idea. I'll keep looking."

My ancestor, a journalist. My heart sang with the connection. Reilly tapped me on the shoulder. "Thanks for all that Mum. Got to get moving. Let me know if you find anything else."

"And you. Take care of my girl."

I'd try. "Love you Mum," I hung up. "Okay Reilly. I feel the vibes coming off you. What was your call about?"

"That was Mahala. They ran the photo Jim got and the details of the car you saw. The car's stolen. No surprise there. But the photo. The hair colour's all wrong but they're pretty sure it's one Frederick James Leary."

"And that means something to you?" I felt his unease.

Reilly raked his unruly flaming red hair with his fingers as if trying to brush away the past, "He was the enforcer for the bike gang who kidnapped my best friend at the time. He came to me and told me that if I didn't do what they wanted he'd be swimming with the fishes, on the bottom of the Farset River, by morning.

"A tiger kidnapping," Jim surmised.

I hadn't heard of such a thing. "A what?"

Reilly seemed genuinely surprised I hadn't heard the term. "It's an Irish invention that's since been exported around the world. Say you want to blow something up. You don't want to do it yourself because you don't want to go to jail for it so you kidnap someone who's important to someone else. Instead of the ransom being money they want a crime done."

"And let me guess, if you go to the police you never see the kidnapped person again. Only in this case it wasn't a bomb they wanted you to plant."

"I was to deliver a package to the rival gang. I assumed it was some kind of contraband. The meeting had been set up beforehand. I was just the errand boy. But when I got there it turned out I was being used as the bait to get them there. It was an ambush."

Yeah, well I'd seen how that had gone down. "And the police didn't believe you."

Reilly scowled. I felt him thinking me naive. "If I'd said anything, and I mean 'anything', I wouldn't have survived 48 hours in jail. As it was I only had to bide my time and get early parole for good behaviour. And, thankfully it kept me out of my father's way. A roof over my head, food and no parental beatings … though I won't say there weren't other beatings. Thankfully word got out fairly quickly that I could stand my own in a fight and was quite capable of exacting my revenge when none of the guards were looking. I wasn't looking for a power base, like some try to build in jail. I just wanted to be left alone to see out my time."

"Bugger naivety. Reality doesn't change what should've been."

"Pisses me off too," Jim muttered, which was surprising. Our Jim was easy going and not known for negative outbursts.

"So Fred Scumbag sent you to the place I saw in my dream."

Reilly's eyes sparkled with mirth at my name for the man. It was the result I'd been hoping for.

The real question was why Fred had turned up now. "Do you think it's a coincidence he's following us? He could just be a hired thug with an agenda related to the drug shipment."

"Reilly frowned, "I don't believe in coincidences."

"Why would he come after you now?" Jim wondered. "Surely he can't hold a grudge after all this time."

"Ha!" Reilly seemed to find that amusing. "And what of the MacDonalds and Campbells up in Scotland? That grudge has been going on hundreds of years. And do you think the Ukrainians are going to easily forgive what's been done to their country? No, Fred hated my old man for some reason. Why I don't know but since no one in their right mind would come after my father Fred may be looking for someone else to vent his grudge on."

"Then he's making a big mistake," Jim decided for all of us. But Fred Scumbag didn't know the man Reilly had become, we did. He had a backbone of steel, the mind of a strategist and a fiery temper that always seemed to be, at the very least, on a slow burn. And we loved him.

Clyde watched us intently with hungry eyes, clearly waiting for us to think of other things, like food. "You'll get fat. I pointed out to him." The dog did his best to look innocent. I could almost swear he understood me. But then again, if I could commune with a spider dogs shouldn't be any harder.

"The dog's right," Jim decided for me. "We need to fuel up for the day. Ry, you do the drinks. Reilly, toast, you can't mess that up."

Reilly growled. "And our masterchef is doing what?"

"Gluten free strawberry danishes. Well, actually they were a gift from Adeela, she and Cook made up a batch for us. I'll heat us up a few."

My mouth watered. "Yum but ....."

"It's what the people in Denmark have for breakfast" Jim countered, knowing where my mind was going. "I don't see too many fat Danes running around, do you?"

"I haven't met many, I couldn't say."

Reilly shouldered me, "Hasn't anyone ever taught you not to question a good thing. I don't think we need the toast though."

He wasn't getting out of kitchen chores that easily. "You can feed Clyde then," I smirked.

Clyde woofed in agreement.

"I thought we weren't supposed to be feeding the dog more than once a day."

I laughed. "Good luck explaining that to him," I went to put the kettle on.

5

We headed out into the red dust under a startlingly blue sky. The light here had a quality all its own. It painted the landscape in the most saturated palette of colours you could imagine. All except for green which was decidedly muted in its tones. A few spindly sage green shrubs dotted the landscape. Interspersed with straggly pale grey saltbush that provided the main food for the local animals. But in between the usual plants was a carpet of desert blooms, cheerful yellow and white daisies and red Sturt Desert pea, that had thrust from the ground at breakneck speed after the recent rains. They still held onto the last of their blooms, frantically trying to set seed before the last of the moisture in the ground was sucked out by the unrelenting sun and the scorching midday heat that often went well over forty degrees celsius.

I pulled down the sun visor, only to scream.

Reilly braked to a stop, managing not to jackknife the rig. Jim swore as he barely stopped his computer tablet flying off his lap. Clyde looked up and whimpered, shaking uncontrollably like he had a sudden case of the chills. Perhaps the dog was as arachnophobic as me. I took a deep breath and held my hand out to the cause of the chaos. "Horatio, you're not supposed to be here." Though it did explain why he wasn't in his enclosure back on the ship. "We went over this. You're an illegal migrant." It was bad enough for humans who tried to get into the country, often to end up languishing in off-shore prisons for years while they hoped that one-day, maybe, someone in authority would review their case and let them in. For critters like Horatio it was worse. A death sentence if caught.

Horatio stared at me guiltily but he seemed to be calming down from the mutual fright of his discovery.

"What the hell are we goin' to feed him?" was Reilly's immediate, practical concern.

"Locusts, if we're unlucky," Jim offered up that not particularly encouraging news.

"The recent rains, you think that will bring them on?"

"Already has. There was an outbreak reported this morning out in the wheat belt."

"Oh great," Reilly swore. "Just what we need. If we hit a mass of them they'll block up the rig's radiator and god knows what else. Let alone remove any hope of seein' through the windscreen."

Jim didn't seem as worried. "I've downloaded an app that tracks the main swarm. With luck we can avoid them."

"There's not many roading choices once we get to Wiluna," I pointed out. It's the Gun Barrel Highway or nothing."

Jim studied the data he had to hand, "Unless there's an unfavourable wind that drives them our way they should stick around the farming areas. There's not much food for them the further out we get. Should still be the odd one or two though."

"And those we feed Horatio. What about now?" Our Brazilian Black Tarantula possibly hadn't eaten for a couple of days.

Jim frowned, considering that. "I'll rig up a bug catcher. There's got to be a jar I can use in the pantry."

Reilly grumbled to himself. "First genealogy side trips, now a hitchhiker. Well I guess there's no turnin' back now so find somewhere for Horatio to call home for now and let's get back on track."

"Wait a minute. He needs somewhere better than the sun visor to hide out in. It'll get too hot up there."

"What about the glove compartment? It's dark and cosy," Reilly suggested.

"You don't think he'll get too hot in there?"

"He's Brazilian," Reilly pointed out.

"The dash will get scorchingly hot under that sun, as the day warms up," I countered, worrying for the creature I reluctantly called friend.

"Give me a moment,"Jim disappeared off into our mobile home and returned with a roll of aluminium foil, a cotton tea towel and a cardboard box. He passed Reilly the box while I got out of the way, nursing the spider. Between them they emptied out the glove box, scrunched up foil and used that to create insulating batts then lined the interior with the cloth. Reilly found a drill from somewhere and drilled holes into the glove compartment door.

"This isn't our rig," I reminded him.

"Do you want a cool spider or not?" Reilly growled.

Jim sat back and studied their handiwork, satisfied. "That should do him for the bit. Next major stop I'll rig up a thermostat and duct some air into there if necessary. Should keep him the same temperature as us."

"Unless we stop for a while," I worried. The airconditioning in the cab only worked while the vehicle was worried.

Reilly groaned but was clearly thinking ahead. "The town of Cue's up ahead. It should have a big enough IGA store that we can buy some kind of container we can quickly adapt for carrying him about." He emphasised the 'quickly'.

With our spider securely housed, we were underway again. I went back to enjoying the scenery. Initially what all looked like unending scrub and dust started to take on more detail. I saw differences in the trees as we got further out. The desert blooms started to peter out but were replaced by a garden of another kind. Lone majestic granite boulders that appeared to have been placed in the landscape by chance. Anthills rose from the ground. A flock of desert pigeons, scouring the ground for seed. For a while a pair of emus raced alongside, as if keeping pace with us, until they veered off to run along an old fenceline. I thought I saw a fox but it scurried into the salt bush before I could be sure. "It's beautiful out here."

"It's nice to visit but I don't think I'd want to live out here," Reilly decided. "You'd be up against the heat, the flies, the petrol guzzling distances, lack of infrastructure and not to mention the lack of green grass and rolling hills."

I eyed Reilly speculatively. "You miss Ireland?"

"In a lot of ways no but the landscape. It's what I grew up with. It's what seems normal."

"Yet you prefer to live out on the world's oceans."

Reilly shrugged his shoulders, "There's a freedom out there. It's the kind of freedom that some who have been without freedom crave."

Some like him. "Were you in prison long?" It was a topic of conversation Jim and I had avoided with him but after my dream the other night I was curious.

"They could never prove I'd actually been the one who did the killings. But the detective ya saw in yer dream, he was determined someone was going to be accountable. Especially as the gang leaders had gone to ground."

"Including Fred Scumbag."

That got a laugh out of Reilly. "Includin' him."

Jim looked up from his computer tablet. "My map's showing me that we're close to an old homestead belonging to the Kelly family. There's a gravestone marker might be worth checking out."

I scruffed him by the back of his sandy coloured hair and kissed him hard on the lips. "You're a wonder Jim. You've been beavering away quietly there and we didn't even notice. All I was getting from your mind were glimpses of map references and boundaries."

"I got into the government's land registry and cross referenced it with satellite photos of the area. Slow down Reilly or we'll miss it. Should be right about now."

"Hmm," was all Reilly said as he brought us to a stop. He kept the engine running to keep the cab cool for Horatio and for us when we got back in.

At first glance there was nothing out there but a few piles of rusty timber, masonry and timber, all that remained of a few buildings. It was a sad sight. Even rocks tended to break down out here, the scorching sun combined with the occasional night time frost splitting them easily. It was a miracle that there was something more than dust.

I got out and was immediately accosted by the hordes of annoying little black flies that were starting to move as the day warmed up. Reilly reached behind his seat and handed us each a fly net. Thankfully one of us had thought ahead. I hated to think what we looked like but it did keep the flies from crawling all over our eyes and up our noses. They craved moisture.

"Over there," Jim pointed.

I squinted into the sun and saw what he was looking at. A lonely piece of rock with a plaque. I wandered over to it.

"Just their names and their birth and death years," I noted. I jotted the details down and took a photo. Mum would want the evidence.

"See what you can feel," Jim suggested.

"They're just bones," Reilly pointed out the obvious.

Even so, "Jim might be onto something. I've got to give it a try." I sat on the ground, after giving a cursory glance for ants or other bities. The sensation of the flies crawling on my arms was hard but I focused and managed to retreat my consciousness within. Then I sent it down into the earth, along with my request, what do my ancestors want me to know?

I instantly felt the regret and guilt of having driven away their daughter. It wasn't a sensation I could say was coming from them rather than my own preconceived notions but it felt true. I connected with a sense of them having battled the environment to farm the land. They were hardy people. Hard working and stoic. But they'd never really gotten over losing contact with their daughter. They'd seen out their time on the land until first James and then Melba had passed away. Though there was something about her final years. I felt that the local tribe had kept an eye out for her, dropping her off the occasional wallaby for food or bringing her things from nearby towns. And when her time had finally come they'd called the region's minister to perform the rites. A simple unmarked grave. Which left me wondering who had erected the plaque. Had their daughter come back to visit them, only to find them gone.

I was winging it. I was new to such ancestral connections but I thought it important to reassure them. To tell them their line had continued and that I was one of their descendants, even if we hadn't yet made the link. I knew. And I felt their smile of joy. Crying softly I came back to myself. To Reilly's firm arms around me; to Jim stroking my hair.

"So they were yours."

"I believe so." I wiped a tear from my cheek. "I may never officially know, unless Mum can find the paper trail that will link the Drover family to her tree but, yes, I know they were mine."

"You feel okay to go on?" Reilly asked but I was aware of his worry that the day wouldn't wait for us.

"I can mull it over in the cab. Sorry, I'm not being of much use to you yet on this trip. Wasn't I supposed to be the navigator or something?"

Jim affectionately squeezed my shoulder. "I've got that in hand for now. You can pitch in once we start testing their new fangled technology. For now, mull."

I arched an eyebrow, that had almost sounded like an order from Jim, "Let's get out of these flies." I took one more look at where my ancestors had lived their lives then followed Jim and Reilly back to the rig.

6

Cue was a welcome surprise of a town. Once the thriving hub of the Murchison Gold fields, with a population of around 10,000, the sign at the town limits claimed a current population of only around 120. Its historic buildings included a police station, a gentleman's club if you please, a masonic lodge, mines offices, a grand shire office and various pubs and shops.

"We haven't got a lot of time," Reilly warned, "not if we're to make our designated campsite before dark. Take your pictures for your blog but be quick about it. I'll stay with the truck."

"How about I go and get us some ice creams?" Jim offered, knowing he was on a winner.

"Best wait until Ry's nearly back or they'll be puddles of goo."

"I won't be long," I promised. I grabbed my fly veil and my camera and hopped out, leaving Reilly to go and top up our fuel at the local petrol station which also boasted a truck bay for parking such a big rig. Not that there were a vast amount of vehicles parked in the streets. Towns like these survived on supplying the local property owners with groceries, equipment and repairs. Other than that they hoped the odd passing tourist might stop on their way to Meekatharra. A hopeful cafe boasted its wares on the chalkboards strategically placed on the footpaths but most who stopped in the town would grab a take away at the petrol station while they filled up their vehicle and used the restrooms. With the disease outbreak back in the capital there were only a couple of 'grey nomads' to be seen, that ever roaming population of retirees in caravans and mobile homes. I grabbed my photos and returned just as Reilly had finished paying for our fuel and Jim was returning with our ice creams.

"You want the chocolate mocha, the blueberry surprise or the dairy free orange almond?" Jim asked, knowing full well our preferences.

Hell, there went the calories for the day. I took the orange almond. It tasted even better than flourless orange cake with all its syrupy goodness.

Reilly swore and took the chocolate mocha. "I shouldn't be eating this but thanks, Jim."

Jim laughed, enjoying the mental moment of Reilly savouring the chocolate. "Now, as it turns out I'm rather partial to blueberries."

My moral dilemma resolved, bar a minor twinge of guilt at Reilly having to take one for the team, my mind shifted back to the day's agenda.

"So, onward ho?"

Reilly rubbed his chin, not looking entirely pleased that further delays lay in our path, "I asked about your Ed as I was paying. He drew me a mud map of where to find the guy."

Jim frowned. "Mud map?"

"You know, 'turn left at the first paddock corner, take a left at the black stump then cross the dried up creek' kind of map."

Jim shook his head.

I felt for Jim. I knew he'd rather put his trust in a set of GPS coordinates. "By the way. He's not 'my' Ed."

"Well he's on the way. We either see him now or on the way back. Frankly I don't want your mind spinning. The sooner we get this ancestral stuff sorted the sooner we can focus on what we came here to do."

Made sense. I knew myself enough to know my mind would be working things over and wondering about the man James and Melba's daughter had run off with. "Okay."

We passed on through the almost abandoned town of Reedy, now little more than a crossroads, accessing nearby mines. We took a slight detour along Boyd St to see what was left of the town and then continued on our way, along the Great Northern Highway.

"What are we going to do when we camp tonight?" Fred Scumbag had tried to break into our hanger the night before. Tonight we'd be out in the open.

"I plan to set up an electronic perimeter," Jim explained. "It's unlikely he'll be back tonight after the scar Horatio gave him last night but if he does we'll know. How's Horatio doing anyway?"

I took a peek inside the glove box. "He's in the back corner but I sense his hunger." I sent Horatio reassurance that we hadn't forgotten about him.

"Next stop I'll get my makeshift bug catcher out." Jim promised.

"Worry about that later," Reilly took a left, at an ant hill.

"I'm not sure that's a road Reilly."

"It's got a solid base. It's dry. Won't get any better on the Gun Barrel Highway I assure you."

Hmm, that was reassuring… not.

The 'road' went parallel to a fence line and led us to the door of what could as much be called a 'building' as the ground we'd travelled on could be called a road. It looked like someone had found some straight-ish long dead trees and used them as upright posts for a structure that was little more than a loose collection of rusty tin.

An old yellow dog struggled to its feet and gave a cursory woof.

"Is that a dingo?" Jim wondered.

"It's technically illegal to keep a dingo as a pet. The law considers them a wild animal. I doubt his owner would want him outed."

A man who looked as old as the dog wandered out to greet us. "Don't mind old Yella. He's not a pet. He just lives here."

I smiled in greeting, "Got no problem with him." Hell, we were harbouring an equally illegal tarantula. "Looking for Ed? You be him?"

His eyes narrowed as he studied the three of us, no doubt silhouetted against the glaring sun, "Who wants to know?"

I imagined we looked a little formal in our work uniform of black pants and white shirts, though to avoid the traumas of buttoning one-handed mine was a polo shirt. "Name's Rylee Jackson. This is Jim Northey and Reilly O'Reilly. We're from a ship that recently docked in Freemantle. We're transporting goods through to Alice Springs but I have an agenda of my own. Essie Homes said you might be able to help me. I'm trying to make a connection with an ancestor who lived out this way, back in the 1800s."

"Ms Essie, eh?" His features softened, slightly. "And you ain't been into Perth?"

He'd obviously hear of the disease outbreak. I placed my one hand over my heart, "My word of honour."

He noticed then that the stump of my other arm hung loose at my side. "How'd you lose that?"

"Got blown up in a hell hole of a war torn country. I was interviewing a contact about women's rights in her country when her house had something large dropped on it."

Ed frowned again. "Reporter?"

"Was," I assured. "These days I'm a trainee Deck Cadet." I decided not to tell him about my blog as that might count as journalism, which I sensed he had an issue with. I went for distraction instead, nodding toward Reilly. "He's my boss."

"A Captain?" Ed's eyes widened, speculating.

"Third Officer, in charge of security, and trainees," he smirked in my direction then offered the man his hand. "She won't give you any trouble."

"And will you put your hand over your heart too?" Ed asked, curious.

"Not sure I have one. Unless it's her."

Jim rolled his eyes at Reilly's response. Of course the damn man had a heart. "I don't mean to interrupt but we've got a dog in the truck. Any chance we can let him out while you decide if you like us or not."

Ed chuckled. "Now you I like. Okay let him out. The old fella here won't bite."

Not like its owner, I assumed.

"You'd best come in out of the sun."

I'll just go and catch one or two live bugs for Horatio, Jim sent to my mind. The less questions on that front the better. "I'll join you in a minute or two. Nature calls." It was a good enough excuse.

"I'll join you," Reilly declared.

Great. Now they'd put the idea in my head I needed to go. "Don't suppose you have anywhere I could use. It's been a long trip so far this morning." And I didn't fancy squatting amid the flies and the heat. I could go back to our mobile home and use its mini bathroom but having gotten this far with Ed I didn't want to give him a chance to turn his back on us.

Ed grunted. "Porta loo out the back," he pointed. "I'll go and put a billy on the stove. How you have it?"

I guessed the brew would be figuratively strong enough for a teaspoon to stand up in but I'd stomach it for the sake of sociability. "Black thanks. Jim's the same. White and one for Reilly if you've got."

"Only condensed milk."

"Great." It would have to do. Reilly could growl at me later if he didn't like it.

The 'restroom' was a curtained off area in a lean-to at the back of the shed. Slightly less flies. I told my mind to ignore the spider's nest in the corner, stepping around it to wash my hands in the retro hand basin that due to the chipped enamel was clearly a salvage job. I didn't care about the aesthetics. It did the job and it was clean. Actually the whole shed, apart from its appearance of having been thrown together out of whatever parts were at hand, was remarkably tidy. The dirt floor, clearly recently swept. And except for the loo's resident spider the rafters seemed pretty cobweb free. Most of all it gave shade. Nearly all of its openings, sorry windows, opened to the shady side of the shack, drawing in the coolest air. If you looked past appearances it was a really well engineered structure, eco-friendly even. "Well set up place you have here Ed. Protects you from the worst of the elements I'm guessing."

Ed, somewhat suspiciously, took the praise. "Summers out here get over 40 degrees celsius all too often. Middle of the day you need the shade."

"Not much wind and rain out here to worry about," I thought.

"Oh, we get a few willy willies. Wouldn't like one of those hitting the shack. Get the odd dust storm though. Usually takes me a week or more to get the dust out afterward. As for rain, you don't want to be out here if we get a freak one. Believe it or not the shack's on a rise. Can become an island here, looking out on waterside real estate," he laughed. "Though most of it runs away quickly enough, down to the salt flats."

I tried to imagine the rise the shack was built on. I hadn't noticed. It could only be a couple of inches. I sipped my tea and my hair nearly stood up. Hell there was enough caffeine in there to keep me motoring along all day.

Oh hell, Reilly moaned in my head. *Only drink enough to be polite. We'll be in in a minute.*

"Why do you want to connect with your ancestors Missie? Trying to claim aboriginal heritage so you qualify for some benefit. Is that it?"

So he was a cynic but I guessed finding an aboriginal ancestor in your family tree was becoming as popular as finding a convict. "I'm paid well enough for what I do Ed. I might have been nearly blasted to oblivion but I've landed on my feet. I've got citizenship in this country and the Seychelles. And I've got two guys who love me." May as well be honest about it.

Ed choked though, "Two. Those two."

"Yes."

"So what do you hope to gain? Everything your kind do is about gain."

I decided taking offence at that wouldn't help my cause. "Two reasons. The first is easiest to explain. My mother is custodian of our family history and she's trying to get the complete picture, as least as complete as the records will allow. For me though it's…" How did I explain this? I suspected Ed demanded absolute honesty even if it might seem implausible. "I travel between dimensions. It's something I started to do after my accident. I've had a very good mentor," I added. "Lydia's encouraged me to work on healing my ancestors' karma, not only for their sake but that I might learn from their wisdom. To know what to shed of the past and what to keep going forward."

Ed leaned back in his chair and considered me. He squinted his eyes and I had a sense he was reading my aura. Quietly he got up and went to a jar in his kitchen, taking some substance from it.

Jim and Reilly came in just as quietly, sensing something was up. Reilly scanned the room, noted the white tea and took it to go and sit in a nearby chair.

Before taking his tea Jim looked over to me, checking on me I thought, *he's been testing you.*

We're strangers, even if Essie sent us here. Can't blame him.

"Shush," Ed growled, as if he'd heard our mental chatter. He wrapped a few of the leaves he'd taken from the jar in a clean tissue and passed them to me. "It would anger my own ancestors if I shared my tribe's rituals with you. If you are worthy you will discover what you need to know yourself. But these will help. You'll want these to produce smoke, not burnup in the flames. So when your campfire is dying down, put a flat rock in the centre of the fire and then place these leaves on it. You will need to inhale the fumes. I sense you have powerful guardians so your men can either choose to travel with you or watch over you. Be sure to only seek out those ancestors who best serve your highest need. We're all related, even to the rocks and trees, the elements and the animals. On the cosmic scale we are all one great tribe but many have lost their wisdom and pursue only their own self's agenda. Speak your intent clearly and give thanks when your journey is over."

Reilly, who I sensed in my mind was aggrieved we'd come all this way to no apparent purpose, cleared his throat. "We cannot join her on her search and leave her or our rig unguarded. Someone tried to break into our camp last night and we have reason to believe he may follow us."

Ed stared at Reilly before answering, "Your trip is not wasted, Grumpy. But she must find her answers her own way. If her ancestors are willing they will help her. I will speak with my own ancestors and see where I may assist. But as to your enemy of old. He will not bother you tonight if you camp on the North side of Lake Andeen. There's an old town site there with a cemetery. It is sanctified ground but you may park near it. Your enemy expects you to travel through, to push on to Meekatharra today. A change of plan will confuse him. Whether he assumes you've gone on ahead or backtracks is not yet decided. The future is not fixed."

7

So, with Reilly duly grumbling about not being further along our route, we took Ed's suggestion and camped at Lake Andeen. We checked in with Deman but he had no concerns about the delay. Our only requirement was that we returned to the port of Fremantle before the Merkwood II next sailed as, I thought smugly to myself, we were an essential part of the crew. Okay, maybe a trainee deck officer was not so essential but Jim and Reilly weren't going anywhere without me so that made me essential by default.

"Damn right," Jim nipped my ear in a way that had me sucking my breath in.

I'd learned to see past Jim's placid, polite good nature. He didn't have a dark side but it definitely had a few kinks in it.

Jim laughed at my thoughts, "We'll have to see about that later. I think, first, Reilly's got some idea of getting a small fire pot going."

"We brought a fire pot with us?" What hadn't we brought?

"Nah, but he's found a discarded one where someone must have camped and left it behind. There's not a lot of timber around here. You and I have been delegated to go and find some."

"Delegated, huh!" But it was a chance for a walk to stretch the legs. Clyde bounded after us joyfully, eager to 'help'.

We startled a couple of big red kangaroos that were still dozing in the shade of a few rocks, having not yet really woken up for the night. They bounded off, annoyed. Clyde wanted to give chase, not seeming to realise that he really shouldn't take one on. A roo that size, almost the size of a human but bulky with it, could easily disembowel a dog with their powerful claws. "No, Clyde." Thankfully Mahala or someone else on the Border Force had trained him well. He drooled but held his ground, staring longingly in the direction they'd gone.

Even being careful to check for nasty crawlies, Jim managed to find an armload and I filled the sling I often used for a one armed carry, then we wandered back to camp. Clyde followed but pausing once or twice to stare into the landscape, hoping to spy something else on the bound no doubt.

Reilly already had a small fire going by the time we returned with our offerings. "Great, we'll put a bit of that on but not too much. I don't want to attract attention to our camp."

"Are you thinking we'll put the leaves on that?" I wondered.

"Got a grid we'll put on top. We can rest a pan on that and add the leaves. They shouldn't burn that way, just give off their fumes. I think that was Ed's intention."

"Can we wait until these flies go."

"That won't be long. They won't stick around once the day starts to cool. Fancy a cuppa?" Jim asked.

"Sounds great. Though I'll give a pass on any snacks. Something tells me I should do this on an empty stomach for best effect."

"Wise," Reilly agreed, "I've no experience in such things but we can use a late dinner to ground and bring us back to the real world afterwards."

"We?"

"Well you're not doing this on your own. Me or Jim. Choose!"

"What if the person who goes with me meets up with their ancestors too? Which of you is most comfortable about that?"

"Great," Reilly muttered. "Both Jim's and mine are likely to be bigotted homophobes. Add into mine a criminal and alcoholic mindset."

"So a hell of a big opportunity to heal your ancestral karma." I mused.

Reilly frowned, "We can heal the dead?" He didn't sound convinced.

"They're only dead in our time-space reality." Well it was a guess but going on my experience in the otherworld it made sense.

Jim looked intrigued by the possibilities. "If he healed his ancestral karma, what would that do? What would be the consequences?"

Our electrical engineer, ever the scientist. "I have no idea but if we're connected to our ancestors then maybe we're part of a stream of energy and any karmic taints act as blocks to that energy, limiting our personal potential and the potential of the collective."

"Damn, that sounds important," Jim decided. "Reilly, you've got to do this."

"Why? I don't need my karma healed? What if it changed something fundamental in me." Reilly was digging in for a fight. "Come to think of it. Shouldn't we be thinking of the effects it might have on Ry?"

I walked right up to Reilly and looked him dead in the eyes, "Your identity is what you make it. The rest is genetics, experiences and the unbounded source of us all. This will just be one more experience among the many you've had through aeons of lives. But what if there is some extra strength, skill or knowledge that's been blocked from you because of the actions of your ancestors or even you in a past life. Wouldn't we be all the stronger for anything we could regain?" Not to mention it might be at least one less blot on the collective consciousness but I needed to sell this to Reilly in practical terms a strategist would appreciate.

"What about you Jim?" Reilly asked, clearly not wanting to deprive the man of the experience if he wanted it.

"Actually, I've done some of my own ancestral journeying."

"You have, why the hell didn't you say?" I was shocked. Hell, I could have already been picking his brain for knowledge if I'd known it was there.

"Because it was years ago in a South American jungle with a shaman who gave me a pretty nasty concoction to drink. Believe me, it wasn't an entirely pleasant experience and of no use to us here and now as it would be hard to duplicate in Australia, even if I knew all the ingredients."

"You did an ayahuasca ceremony," I was awed. "Tell all."

"Later. I'm thinking we're doing this tonight."

"Damn right," Reilly agreed, wanting the whole thing out of the way. "Okay, so I'll go in. You and Clyde hold the fort."

"I'd stand well back from the fumes the leaves give off then," I reminded Jim.

"Figured that. Look I'm not trained in protecting you when you do your astral walks, not like Reilly is. Would it be worth asking for some higher help?"

I was suddenly mindful of the ornate red and black peony tattoo that covered part of my shoulder and back. It had been placed there by the higher being who watched over Horatio and his like. "Hell! Shouldn't I make an offering to her before I ask? She's kind of above the mundane. I doubt my ancestral karma is high on her priority list."

"Aranya marked ya didn't she?" Reilly pointed out. "She wants ya as her representative so she'd want ya strong and capable. It meshes with her agenda."

"Sell it to her as a strategy." Well who was I to argue? I'd done much the same in my sales pitch to Reilly. "Okay. Still, something small by way of offering." I thought of Horatio's home in our truck's glove box. No doubt spiders in this environment would need protection from the hot sun too. I looked around and spied a few flat rocks. "Need help here. Let's arrange these into a shelter for the local lizards and spiders."

Reilly considered the rocks, "And snakes, if we make it too big."

"Small then." Not that I had anything against snakes but this close to a well used camp ground wouldn't be a good idea. I let the guys pick up on the image of what I had in mind. "Yeah like that." Not so it looked like a man made heap but rocks overlying rocks in such a way that it would provide plenty of homes for small critters.

They soon had it finished. "Step back and let me call her." I focused my mind in the centre of my tattoo and used that as my point of connection. "Aranya. I'm assuming you already know what I ask." Uber angelic being that she was. "Please accept this small offering for your kind as my token of goodwill."

A shiver rippled through my shoulder. She'd heard but was that a yes? I took it as one anyway. "We're a go."

Reilly rolled his eyes, knowing full well I hadn't had a definite response, "Fine, let's heap this fire up a bit. Jim, a couple of blankets to throw around us I think, in case we cool off when we're in the other place."

We set up our camp chairs away from the worst of the smoke. Hopefully the wind wouldn't change once we settled. Sometimes it seemed like fires had a mischievous will of their own and the smoke would follow you around.

Reilly and I cast our share of leaves into the pan, inhaling deeply then we went back to our chairs.

"Okay, just wondering how I go into a trance," Reilly asked.

"Connect with my mind, I'll guide you. Just keep your intent clear on healing ancestral karma"

"I don't even really understand what that is." But as the effect of the herbs took hold we went through into the otherworld together.

It was Reilly's first time in the astral realm. He'd been with me, in my mind, when I'd undertaken my journeys. Holding me close and surrounding me with protective stones given to him by our Seychelles friend and psychic police Lieutenant Sophie Camille. For this we'd shared the stones between us, placing them in our pockets.

Reilly looked around, interested, "I'd don't know what I was expecting but this isn't it."

"Always best to travel without expectations, in this world or in the 'real' one." As a journalist I'd travelled the world and quickly learned that expectations led to assumptions that were often dangerous or led to disappointment or frustration. Better to go empty of preconceptions and just be aware, see what was really there and stay damned alert. "Look, over there."

A tall, scruffy suntanned man with an orange beard and hair, much like Reilly's, was sitting on a rock, patiently waiting for us to notice him. "Well look at you," he eyed Reilly up and down. Who'd have thought, ey?"

"Who are you?" Reilly asked, clearly puzzled. I knew from his mind that he'd really come for me. He hadn't actually expected to have anyone interested in him.

"Don't tell me you don't even recognise your own father?" The man's eyes, as remarkably green as Reilly's, sparkled with mirth.

"You don't look anything like my dad."

"But I do look a lot like you. Don't I?"

I looked between them and had to agree, even down to the same unruly crop of hair, "He kind've does Reilly."

"My dad's mouldering in a grave in Belfast but when he was alive I can tell you he didn't have your height or build. And he certainly didn't have your smile. His face would have damned well cracked if he'd smiled."

"That would no doubt be whoever your mum married after her one night fling with me. A bonnie lass she was too. Serving ales at the Pig and Whistle. Charmed the socks right off of me."

This gave Reilly pause. "You're sayin' my mum got pregnant out of wedlock. Hell, that just wasn't done back then." Which would have been why she quickly realised her mistake and married the first willing male. "Why didn't you stick around?"

"I was only in port for the night. I was out fishing for cod when a storm blew up out in the Irish sea. Seemed the wisest thing to steer my fishing boat into port and get the hell out of it. I would have had to go through the storm to head for home on the Isle of Man so I headed over to Ireland instead. It's there I spied you mum." Then he winked at me. "See you've done well for yourself lad."

Clearly he didn't see I was missing an arm as my etheric form didn't lack one. I offered my good hand anyway since no one seemed in a hurry to do introductions. "Name's Rylee Jackson. Nice to meet you."

"Ah, I see it's your lady who has the manners. Fogal Quayle, at your service ma'am."

Gah, I hated that term. It made me sound like the madam of some brothel but I knew he was being polite. "Please just call me Ry. So, where abouts on the Isle of Man were you from?" I fell back on my journalist skills, questioning man as we'd be waiting forever for Reilly to do it. Reilly seemed to be too busy taking the man's measure and weighing the truth of what he'd said."

"I hail from the Port of Ramsey lassie. Still do."

Huh? "What do you mean still do?"

"This is only the part of me that wasn't birthed into your world. It's a bit too dense there for some parts of my soul. Why would I want all of me stuck in cycles of reincarnation down there?" He made it sound like breathing the pollution in Mumbai.

"So you're Fogal Quayle's higher self?" I assumed.

"That sounds a bit too hierarchical. I, like you, exist in all frequency or density bands, however you want to view it. Earth based Fogal's just my bit that's working out a few issues that can only be learned in that realm."

"But you know of his life."

"I know of all my lives, across all my incarnations, in all dimensions. Is it that you're thinking that time and space exists here?"

"No" And that was the truth, kind've, but it was only now that the clarity of it came to me. "But I'm still confused on one point. When I'm in this dimension and my body's back on Earth, am I my higher frequency self or a projection of my Earth based self?"

"What do you think?"

A question to my question, hmm. Was there a pattern here? "I don't feel that I'm anything more here than there."

"What is more? Do you have some set idea of what this higher self you talk about should be? An all powerful goody two shoes surrounded by trumpeting angels. Is that it?"

"Are you suggesting I have just as much power over my life on Earth?" Like, really!

"What the mind can conceive that realm can make real. Once you understand the rules and constraints you're working with. But with that comes great responsibility. Are you ready for that?"

"You're messing with her, Fogal. Poor girl's head's spinning."

I turned towards the new voice. She was bare footed and looked like the very land itself had given birth to her. Such was the grounded connection that radiated off of her. She wore little more than a loin cloth and seemed perfectly comfortable that way. White paint marked her breast and face with stripes and squiggles I had no way of interpreting. "Hello," I asked hesitantly.

"Welcome daughter of my heart. We sensed your coming and gathered together. Come join our circle and let's sing and dance together and share our stories."

"We?" But on the periphery of my vision I could already make out the group of women she meant, seating comfortably, waiting for me.

"Ry," Reilly warned. "Don't go away where I can't protect you."

The woman who had come to greet me tsked at him, "Look up young man."

We both did and gasped at what we saw, a web of starlight glittering with tiny spiders. The web stretched in all directions and around us. I knew in that moment that Aranya had heard my request and come to protect us. "We're safe Reilly, I'll just be over here."

"I can come over."

I looked at the gathered women, women who looked to be from many different races and nationalities. Intuitively I knew Reilly coming over to join in mightn't work. "I think this might be secret women's business, Reilly. I don't want to shut you out but I need to be respectful of my ancestors. Learn what you can from Fogal."

Reilly didn't look happy about it but nodded his head. "Just don't be long."

"Time has no meaning here, Reilly. We could spend an eternity here and still return to the moment we left on Earth."

Reilly rolled his eyes but settled down to yarn with Fogal. I followed the lady of the land.

I woke, enveloped in the warm blanket Jim had wrapped around me. The stars were out. I heard the thump of kangaroos moving around and the scurrying sounds of small rodents and marsupials. Everything, so alive, vivid, tangible.

Jim passed me a cup of hot chocolate, "Non dairy. I added a little of the yellow box honey you like. How was your trip?"

I normally didn't consume chocolate because the caffeine in it sometimes triggered a headache but right now the brew was welcome. "Mind blowing Jim. Much of it I'm not free to discuss so you'll have to pick snippets from my brain."

Jim shook his head, "I won't delve on purpose, only what your mind freely shares."

I looked over and saw that Reilly was still out to it which surprised me. I'd thought he'd be back before me. I let my mind connect with his and saw through his eyes that he was still protected by Aranya and still, even more surprisingly, enjoying his time with Fogal. "He's fine."

"So," Jim, still curious, set about interrogating me, "no details but can you tell me who you met and anything about what you did."

"They were from all lands, Jim. Women of power, grace and fortitude who'd lived many incarnations in many places and eras. Sometimes they'd been born as men when they needed a perspective that only a life as a man could give them but mostly they'd lived lives as women. Witches, priestesses, wise women, lovers, child rearers, cooks, wives and nuns. One or two of them had lives as warrior women and revolutionaries."

Jim chuckled, "Now why doesn't that surprise me? So, you talked."

"Some. But mostly we sang and danced. Their wisdom was in their songs and chants, and in the circuits we danced upon the ground. Even if I was permitted to tell you their secrets I don't think I could because it was a kind of non-verbal transmission of knowledge. Mostly from them to me but I shared my tales as well, even though I sensed they already knew my life. Jim," warmth filled my chest and tears threatened, "they were some of the most amazing people I've ever met."

"You're forgetting one," Jim beamed at me.

"Me?"

His kiss on my lips was neither insistent or needy, it was one of devotion.

"Bloody hell, I'm out to it a few minutes longer than you and you're at it." Reilly's sarcastic but friendly grumble drew Jim and me apart, reluctantly.

"What took you so long?" I countered, all the better to go on the offensive.

"Hmph. Turned out Fogal and I had, uh have, a lot in common." He looked at his watch and made a mental calculation. "Can you wait a minute, there's someone I need to call before she goes to the shops for the day?" It wasn't really a question. He pulled out his mobile phone and dialled. "Mum."

"Well hell, you suddenly remember I exist or somethin'." Jim and I listened in eagerly to the call Reilly had put on speaker phone.

"I'm sorry. For everything Mum."

There was silence, then clearly worry, "You well son?"

"Never better Mum. I have a couple of wonderful people in my life now. I have a job I love. I'm happy."

"Well bowl me over. Why the call then?" she asked suspiciously.

"No mum, I don't need your money. I don't need your help. I just wanted to say thanks to you for givin' me a life even though it meant you had to live with that bastard who thought he was my father."

"Thought?" there was a very long silence. "My god, you know."

"A Manx fisherman named Fogal Quayle."

"I didn't even know his name," his mum near whispered. "At the time I didn't care. It was a stormy night so the publican, Seamus, decided to ignore the regulations and kept the bar open for the night for those who'd have been drenched or blown away if they'd tried to go home. I'd helped myself to a couple of drinks while I was servin'. When I took, Fogal is it, when I took him up to a vacant room above the bar where he could sleep the night. Well ya don't need the details." she coughed to clear her throat. "So how'd ya track him down?" She was clearly over her shock now and curious.

"Uh?" her question flummoxed Reilly.

DNA I mouthed.

"Ah, I had one of those fangled DNA tests. Produced some genetic matches in the Isle of Man area. I haven't personally tracked him down yet but I believe he's still alive."

"If he's single I want to know," his mum demanded.

The two talked for a bit longer. Clearly there hadn't been an amicable discussion between them for some time and there was a lot of catching up to do.

Jim waggled his eyes at me and I smirked. We leaned in to continue our kiss.

"Bloody hell," came a nearby complaint. "Sorry Mum, yes I'll wash my mouth out when I get a chance. Got to go. Yes. I'll call soon. Love ya." He ended the call just as his Mum squawked at his closing comment. He eyed my mug of now cooling hot chocolate. "Any more where that came from?"

Jim made fresh cocoa and we drank it while the embers died down, there being something almost magical in the ebbing of the fire. Before we started to shiver we retreated to our mobile home. Clyde bounced up with a woof.

Reilly considered the dog, "Maybe we could hang up a sheet at the foot of the bed. It's a little disconcerting having an audience."

Jim smugly studied his fingers, knowing we'd find he'd already done just that.

Reilly clapped him on the shoulder as he spied his friend's handiwork. "Okay, I'm startin' to see benefits in this shared mind thing."

"Only just?" I teased. As I went to undo his belt. I knew what he wanted, satisfying his desire as I drew his cock into my mouth. Jim came from behind, licking, kissing and nibbling a path down my spine.

My mind went AWOL, going onto autopilot to bring Reilly to his orgasm while Jim found places on my skin I didn't even know were erogenous zones.

Reilly came, crying out in triumph then Jim took his chance to roll me over and enter me. My head hung over the end of the bed and suddenly Reilly rose above me only to lower his mouth to mine, to devour and claim.

Jim continued to thrust into me, knowing I wanted it that way. Then he leaned forward and took my left nipple between his firm lips and sucked, hard.

I came, writhing and bucking but Jim wasn't finished. Together we climbed that peak until he took us both over the precipice together.

I woke momentarily, warm, snuggled and wanted. Then I drifted back off to sleep where once again I found myself learning at the feet of my ancestors.

I woke to the sound of pelicans arriving at the lake on masse. The lake, normally a vast salt flat, had partially filled after recent rains and the birds had smelled it from possibly thousands of kilometres away. It was the only way to explain how they could know there was water there after so long.

I threw on enough clothes to keep out the early morning desert chill, along with my fly veil, just in case they rose for the day while I was out. Then I made a head motion at Clyde, inviting him to follow. We snuck out, quietly closing the van door, and left the boys to sleep.

The sun was just rising, in shades of tangerine and mauve. What seemed like a million or more pelicans were coming into land, like giant jumbo jets, all getting the okay from the control tower to arrive at once. It was mayhem yet no-one seemed to be crashing into each other. I couldn't hear myself over the cacophony of sound coming from the shore.

Clyde strained against the leash I'd put on him, "No!"

He looked up at me mournfully, pleading for me to not be so mean.

"They're trying to find nesting spots to have and raise their chicks." I said the words for my benefit but sent the dog mental pictures. Reluctantly he ceased straining against the leash.

Reilly, who must have woken shortly after me, came to stand behind me. He wrapped his strong arms around me and looked over my shoulder at the scene on the lake. "Can you imagine so many birds in one spot? They'll eat everything in there and shit the place up."

"You're such a romantic. And it's called fertiliser. That's why the lake grows so much algae and water weed, feeding the fish that hatch from the rains and need a short time to reproduce themselves."

"If any of them get past the pelicans."

I shrugged my shoulders, I didn't really understand the whole of it, "Must work. They've been doing this for millennia. Surviving years of drought, fish eggs waiting to hatch and frogs dug into the deep mud underneath the salt pans. Waiting for rains, maybe years down the track, that will start the cycle all over again."

"And what if it doesn't rain enough and it all dries up before they reproduce?"

"Nature's gamble. At times cruel and harsh. At other times miraculous. But you only ever see the offspring of the last big success."

"You really are good with the words Ry." He held me a moment longer then let me go. "We've got a lot of ground to make up today. A quick karate workout I think, before the heat of the day starts. Then breakfast and go. I want to get us well up the road before we camp tonight."

I knew taking the time for my ancestral odyssey had put pressure on our schedule. "Thanks for yesterday."

"Actually I think I should be thanking you. One thing. Once we head off, could you ring your Mum and see what she can find about Fogal?"

"How about I get her to go one better and have three DNA tests waiting for us at the post office when we get to Alice Springs. If they send them by fast courier they should get there in time."

"I don't want the cost to put your Mum out. If she sends through her details I'll reimburse her."

And I knew my Mum would hear nothing of the kind, "I'll ask. Come on Clyde." I let him off the leash having already sent him a picture of Jim waiting with a dog treat, which he was. "Go find Jim."

Clyde went racing back to camp, full of joy and exuberance.

"All that pent up energy," I admired the dog for it. "Do you think this morning's walk will stop him from getting bored the rest of the day?"

Reilly shook his head, "I doubt it."

8

Meekatharra came as a surprise. An old gold mining town to be sure but still very much alive. The football oval was even a shade of green. A creek, currently flowing, followed along one side of the main road, surrounded by leafy green parkland. There was an airport, a hospital, petrol stations, accommodation, a high school, police station and even a squash court. The central business district was modest but still had most of what you'd need, including a range of shops, a dentist, an accountant, vet, car repairs, a towing service and offices for a number of local mining companies and transport firms. "It's bigger than I thought it would be."

"Well, not big in population, only a bit over 700, but a lot of people pass through here on the way to mines, cattle stations or whatever ways they manage to eke out a living in this part of the world. It's a long way to anywhere else," Jim commented.

"So, we stopping?" I asked hopefully.

"Only for fuel," Reilly gave me the look that said what he thought. We didn't have time to dally around. "We can't be sure Leary isn't lying in wait for us. Hopefully he's well ahead by now, thinking he's chasing us but we can't be sure."

Even so, how much could Scumbag do in the daytime. "How about this? After you get fuel, park the rig near the police station. They should have security cameras around there. You can ring Mahala and see if they've found out anything more about him while Jim goes on one of his food scouting missions and I go and take a few photos for my blog."

"Fifteen minutes, no more," Reilly growled.

I kissed him on the cheek. "Thanks." I grabbed my camera, Jim helped me down. I took Clyde on the leash and made a beeline to the adjacent parkland so I could get a scenic foreground for a few shots of the town. I took a few photos of Clyde in the park for good measure. He was a natural, posing for the camera.

"Come on Ry," Jim whistled at me from the edge of the park, with an armload of goodies. "You know what he'll get like."

No, we didn't want to rile the Reilly. Though it was part of who he was and I loved him, rough edges and all, there was no need to make his day harder than it was. Or ours. He was my lover but he was also my boss. And he was right, we needed to get moving."

We hurried back. Jim passed his armload of nibbles to Reilly, stowed Clyde in the back and then gave me a heave up into the cab.

"Hmm," was all Reilly said. But he looked at his watch.

Oh well, eighteen minutes, hardly statistically noteworthy.

"Did you get some good shots at least?" he asked.

"That I did." I connected my camera to my tablet and pulled up the screen and showed him.

"Amazing, all I see is a few ordinary shops and a lot of dust and dirt but you saw that, enough to photograph it."

His comment pleased me immensely, "That's the art of it, seeing what isn't necessarily noticed."

"I love the photos of Clyde," Jim commented. "I'm thinking you'll have to give him his own page on your website."

"He belongs to Border Force," Reilly reminded us as he put the big rig into gear and headed down the road.

Damn, "You're right, I'd better clear it with Mahala before I make Clyde a star. By the way, did you catch up with her?"

"They've been backtracking over Leary's movements since he left Ireland. They haven't pinned down who he's working for yet but at the moment he appears to be in the country legitimately, on a travel visa, if you please."

"Legitimate except he stole a vehicle to get around in."

"I think the key word there is 'appears'. But they've got no evidence yet to hang on him. We're to keep an eye out for him but not to engage him unless he's a threat to us."

"So," Jim took his chance to interrupt. "Do you want to eat what I got now or wait til we get further up the road?"

"We'd best ask our navigator how far up the road it is to Wiluna?" Reilly was looking at me.

"Oh, well," I widened the view on the GPS and pressed a few buttons. "183 kilometres, about two hours if the road stays this good. Take the next right."

"What have you got in those bags Jim?" Reilly wondered.

"Locally baked sausage rolls and for Ry, a vegetarian pasty. The other bag's got muffins; raspberry, choc chip and a blueberry."

My mouth watering I knew we wouldn't be waiting for our treats, I got out of my seat, "We'll need drinks," and I went back to the kitchen.

Wiluna wasn't as big as Meekatharra but still managed to boast a well watered football oval and a swimming pool.

"Where's the turn off to the Gun Barrel Highway?" I studied the map and didn't see anything obvious.

Jim looked up the highway on his computer. "Look for a turn to the East to something called Carnegie Station.It's supposed to be the most remote station in Western Australia and at the point where three different deserts meet."

"Ah found it," it hadn't been where I was looking. "I guess they don't want to advertise it too much in case the odd unwary traveller gets conned by the name 'highway'." I sighed when I saw the distance ahead of us. "350 kilometres to Carnegie Station then another 500 kilometres to Warbuton. Crickey, it's a total of 1163 kilometres just to get to the West Australian border."

"Did you see the size of Carnegie station, nearly a million acres." Jim gaped at the data. "There's supposed to be a basic shop, some diesel, souvenirs, accommodation and hot showers."

"Hot showers!" my eyes lit with glee.

Reilly liked the idea too. "I agree a proper clean up before we head further east would be great, considering our limited water carrying capacity. We don't need their accommodation though, their campground will do us for the night."

Reilly knew I was getting numb in places that even well upholstered seats couldn't help after a while. "We've got to stop here, in Wiluna, briefly anyway. I need to head up to the shire offices and collect the permits Mahala's expedited for us. We can't go through the aboriginal lands on our route without them. Plus I'm bettin' Clyde could do with a run and Horatio probably needs a fresh bug by now."

Horatio! I'd nearly forgotten about him. I opened the glove box to check on him and he waved a hairy leg back at me. "He seems okay but yes, I think he could do with a break too."

"We should give him the run of the cab tonight," Jim suggested. "He's probably bored out of his brain by now, wondering why he came."

I communicated that idea to Horatio, with the caveat that he didn't come into our living quarters. "He likes that idea."

There were no official rest stops marked on the map so whenever we decided fatigue was at the point of claiming us we found a hard dirt patch of flat ground, just off the road and parked there for a cuppa and a snack. If Leary was behind us we'd be in trouble as there was no hiding out here. Hopefully he was ahead and I'd slowed us down enough with my short stops for photos to keep us well behind him. The recent rains had painted the desert a carpet of white, yellow and pink daisies that stretched as far as the eye could see. Given that it could be decades without appreciable rain out here it was a real treat. Apart from the flies that loved the cattle country anyway but had bred up to horrific proportions with the rains. We gave Clyde a run then bunkered inside our mobile home to enjoy our break, minus the flies.

Weary from hours on the road we finally arrived at the station. Reilly went to pay the camp fees. Jim took Clyde for a stroll and I wandered over to what looked like a small museum, dedicated to the guy who'd originally surveyed and built the road, Len Beadell. I took some photos for my blog followers then wandered back.

We parked our rig over to the designated campground. A patch of red dirt with a scattering of what locally passed for trees, though they were more like shrubs. They looked like they might condescend to grow a few new grey-green leaves, eventually.

"I showed Leary's photo at the office but they hadn't seen anyone by that description," Reilly informed us.

"Damn," that was a worry. There was no way of knowing if Scumbag was behind or ahead. Keeping a low profile he might have decided not to stop at the station. At least that was the hope. "I don't know about you but I'm heading to the shower," to my temporary idea of heaven.

Jim looked around, "The flies are ebbing. Fancy some barbecued eggplant Ry?"

"You bet."

Reilly grimaced. "Please tell me you're doing steaks as well."

"Hmm," Jim had been trying, with difficulty, to broaden Reilly's idea of food past meat and three veg. "How about minted lamb and rosemary sausages with sweet potato and carrot chips."

"Chips, sounds good," he grunted and went off to inspect the truck and our load.

"Sneak a little bit of that barbecue eggplant onto his plate," I whispered into Jim's ear. "It might surprise him. Oh, and the veggie chips do sound great." I gave him a thank you kiss then swung my towel over my shoulder and carried my wash bag and change of clothes in the direction of anticipated paradise.

By the time I returned from the shower the campground was starting to fill up with other travellers looking for somewhere to park for the night.

I stopped briefly on the way back to chat to an older couple who were next to their off-road rooftop camper. They were busy wrapping potatoes in foil to poke into the ashes of their fire but looked up as I approached and introduced myself.

"Praties," the woman explained, after introducing herself as Jenny and Jack.

"With bacon bits, mayonnaise and cheese," Jack added enthusiastically.

Heaven forbid. I smiled weakly, "Please don't tell my boss Reilly or he'll give up what we're having for dinner." I preferred to pretend Jim and Reilly were merely workmates when I was meeting strangers, at least until I knew how judgemental they were.

The woman grinned, "Would that be the one you were kissing before you went over to the showers?"

Caught, "Ah, no, that's Jim, he's a workmate and good friend." I emphasised the friend.

Jim must have picked up on my conversation mentally as he wandered over and put a possessive arm around me, "Dinner's nearly ready, Ry. You don't want to keep your 'boss' waiting. You know what he gets like." he winked at the lady and she laughed.

Okay, maybe people travelling this far out were of a different kind. I wished them both "Have a nice meal." As I left them to it I realised that neither of them had looked at me with pity because of my missing arm. Yeah, maybe the risks and hard work travelling this kind of terrain broadened people's minds.

"I think it's the breadth of the landscape and vastness of the sky," Jim decided as he walked beside me. "It's got to loosen up the mind. Give it more space."

My mind felt more spacious just thinking about it. But then I'd been to more than a few war torn dry flat countries that hadn't been conducive to that.

Reilly was busy dishing up our plates, "Did I hear mention of praties?"

Jim groaned. "Tomorrow night, okay."

Reilly seemed pleased with that. "That's fair. By the way, I fed Horatio and let him out to roam the cab for the night."

I snuck a bit of eggplant on Reilly's plate while he wasn't looking. He quickly spotted it and frowned, glaring at both of us.

"Praties," Jim reminded him.

"Hmm." But he cut off a small piece of it, chewed it and didn't spit it out. "Bearable."

After dinner Jim and Reilly went to shower while I put away the dishes we'd just washed up. I had some calls to make. But I reconsidered when I factored in the three hour difference between here and the eastern side of the country. Would Mum be in bed yet? I texted her instead, just to let her know where we were.

I didn't know what hours Border Force worked so I checked for any encrypted emails from Mahala before I went bothering her this late in the day.

Leary had been sighted in Thailand two months back, working as a bogeyman to intimidate indentured crew aboard an illegal fishing vessel. When the boat had been impounded he'd pleaded his case as a foreign national. They'd let him out but he'd never turned up to court. It was suspected he was still working for the mother company who had tentacles reaching not just into illegal fishing but also the human slave trade, people smuggling and drugs. He was small fish, as far as Mahala was concerned, but if he led to anyone further up the chain he'd be a good catch. Though, she emphasised, we weren't to take any unnecessary risks.

I did my best one handed typing to reply back to her. Simply that we'd received her message and all was well so far. Though I noticed Reilly had parked us bang smack in the middle of the campground with everyone else parked around us. We'd have to wait until some left in the morning, before we could leave, but it did mean we were effectively corralled. Anyone hoping to snoop around the rig would have to risk being heard or noticed by the inhabitants of the thin walled caravans, roof top campers and mobile homes around us.

My phone rang, it was Mum, "Got your message. I've got some news for Reilly."

I took notes. "Thanks a million Mum, now go to sleep."

"Don't you turn the tables on me, telling me what to do, sheesh." But she didn't sound too peeved.

"Love you Mum."

"Love you too. Now go and look after those guys of yours."

"They're out having a hot shower in the men's amenities block."

"Well I guess you're excused for not joining them then."

"Mum!"

She laughed and hung up, leaving me wondering if I was somehow living out one of my Mum's fantasies. If she only knew the half of it.

Reilly and Jim came in, Reilly still drying his wet hair. "Jenny and Jack have invited us over to sit around their fire pot. Seems Jack's pretty good on the guitar."

Reilly fetched a small tin whistle I didn't even know he had with him, let alone played and Jim went to find a disused beer carton to use for a makeshift drum, something called a lagerphone. I grabbed my camera, there had to be a good video or two in this.

9

We had a relatively late night of it, enjoying ourselves immensely. I certainly hadn't expected a trad session in the middle of the bush. Other campers had come over to listen and to sing along when there were songs they knew.

I went to sleep with music on my mind. Horatio crept into my dreams a time or two, letting me know he was on watch even if Clyde was off duty, sleeping at the foot of our bed again. Though I saw the dog's ears were ever alert, twitching at the slightest sound. And we had Jim's external cameras that recorded if they detected any movement close to the rig.

With my subconscious feeling safe it took me journeying into strange dream lands. If I'd expected to see more of Jim's and Reilly's memories I was wrong. The lady of the land who I'd met in the otherworld was waiting for me, on the other side of a large pool. We were inside some kind of room. The pool was an ornately embellished square. The water in it, abyssal black. "Come to me," the lady beckoned, "walk across to me."

Across the pool? Me, at best a one armed swimmer. I hated swimming over water I couldn't see the bottom of, couldn't touch my feet to the bottom.

"Not swim," she chided. "Walk."

Was this one of those 'test of faith' things? Hell, it was only a lucid dream. I stepped out onto the pool which turned out to be a black glass mirror, volcanic glass perhaps, with about two inches of water over it for effect. It was easy so I wondered at the purpose of the exercise. What was it meant to show me? Maybe my friend and mentor Lydia could tell me later. But the dream was shifting.

I was somewhere else, on holiday perhaps. I came across a large building full of people. An inn? Accommodation? Or a retreat of some kind?

A mute man greeted me with hand signals which for some reason I understood perfectly. He wrote my name down on the register.

"Just one night," I told him, not wanting to commit myself until I knew more.

The owner came over, "It's alright Mark, she doesn't trust us yet. My name's Pangur," she extended her hand.

"Ry. Um, wasn't Pangur some cat in an old Celtic poem?" I wondered.

"You've a good memory," the woman nodded. "The cat was the companion of an Irish monk and scribe who had fled his homeland because of the Vikings. He ended up seeking refuge in a German abbey where he wrote his poem as an aside in some material he was working on. Of course the poem was in ninth century Irish so no-one else knew it wasn't part of the text, just a note the scribe had made while he was working."

"A scribe," I mused. One with a slightly irreverent streak. I smiled at the thought of the poem and instantly liked the guy, even if I still wasn't sure of his cat's name sake.

"Come," she beckoned, "let me show you around."

We walked outside and in the way dreams sometimes shift I was suddenly in front of a tall strong man.

"Let him lift you up," Pangur urged.

Was this another 'test of faith'? I was sensing a theme here. In the waking world it wasn't my habit to trust without reason but I knew this for a dream so I obliged.

Had I closed my eyes as he lifted me up, easily with the palm of his hand supporting all my weight. It was either that or I was seeing with a different kind of sight. All around me was a great star studded cobweb. I was the web. Then the web morphed into star studded wings and flew. I knew not where. I simply became the experience. Suddenly I was back down to earth, feeling I needed to tell Jim and Reilly all about it. Then the morning phone ringing woke me. Jim reached over to the bedside table to get it and hand it to me. I knew who it would be, "Lydia."

"While the dream's still fresh in your head, give me your thoughts on its meaning. The meaning of a dream is as much about the subconscious of the dreamer as it is the dream."

And there I'd been hoping she'd just explain all. "Okay, I think the pool was square to represent the four directions. I need to demonstrate trust in order to cross the abyss. Trust again was a theme of the second part."

"Yes, trust. That you need to trust your allies who are willing to support you if you allow them. Importantly the abyss represents not only the boundless void, the ego that separates creation from the divine but also a clear and present danger that must be faced. The mirror aspect implies that what you experience of the danger will be a reflection of your inner self. The two inches on top represents an illusory quality. Your guide on the other says to walk on the pool, that is walk on water. To do this you must have faith in your ability to do the seeming impossible."

"So no tall order."

Lydia laughed but ignored my jibe. "The inn or retreat you came to in the second part represents a safe place where again you met a guide who asked you to trust. The strong man might be a metaphor for Reilly, though Jim does a fair amount of weight lifting, I'm not sure. Stars on the cobweb, hmm, maybe your wishes and desires which are enmeshed in the web or connections to people, places and things in your life. That the web transformed into wings in flight, perhaps the chance to morph yourself, free yourself, but only if you are willing to shed some of your ideological illusions."

"Ideological illusions?"

"What you believe about yourself and the world you appear to inhabit."

I loved the 'appeared to inhabit'. Lydia was always chipping away at my idea that the world was something 'real'. "And the guide being called Pangur?"

"Interesting that bit. An Irish flavour to the dream. A ninth century Irish monk's companion, perhaps unknown to him his spirit guide. Note that he was a scribe and you're a journalist. It's no wonder you would find a connection with a scribe and poet. If I remember in the poem the monk was focused on his lofty pursuit of old writings and their meaning while the cat was a down to earth character, carefree in his playfully chasing after mice. There's a time to be focused and a time to play. Other than that I couldn't say."

"And what did you dream about last night?" I wondered.

"Hmph," Lydia didn't sound happy, "More a nightmare. I was standing at the check-in counter of the airport and suddenly realised my ticket was in the suitcase they'd just processed. Not only that I was left without any money or idea and I couldn't remember the numbers of anyone to ring to get help."

"Cripes, are you worried about not having what you need to do something important?"

Lydia sighed, "Fear, yes. Probably it's because I'm worried whether I'm overstretching myself by building a music room for the orphanage. The bank doesn't seem to think the orphanage has enough collateral. Hell, I don't want to disappoint the kids. We have a couple at the moment who have a real interest. Would you believe they make instruments out of old tins and whatever guitar strings I've been able to buy them out of my own pocket."

"Have you spoken to Deman?" Clearly the richest man I knew. And the man who'd arranged for my extraction from a war torn country, at a moment's notice.

"He's my daughter's, well I'd say boyfriend but it's not quite that as they are both too independent. I don't want to use my association with him to impose on his good nature."

"And here's you telling me to trust those who support me. Back at you. Or I'll ring him and tell him your problem. He probably already knows but doesn't want to butt in."

"Damn it."

"Look, send him your business plan for the project and highlight the media opportunities for his company that his word in your bank manager's ear would bring. He's got excellent contacts. He might even be able to lean on someone for a government grant. It's not asking him for money, just his influence. At the very worst he'll underwrite the project. Aren't you the bookkeeper for your daughter's company?" Like should I have to tell her this?

"I guess I just needed the push."

"Anytime you need pushing, glad to help. And thanks for translating the dream. Now go back to sleep, it must be some ungodly hour there."

"You're a breath of fresh air, you know that don't you, Ry?" She hung up.

Jim took the phone back from me and replaced it on the side table, then leaned over me to kiss me.

"Long day ahead of us," was all Reilly said with a frown, meaning we didn't have time for a romp. Damn. Jim took his kiss anyway and then Reilly kissed me too, before rolling me over and spanking me on the bum. "If ya want another go at the hot showers ya'd better run and have at it while Jim does breakfast. I'll coax Horatio back into the glove compartment and give Clyde his mornin' walk."

Hot shower. "Yeah." I was about to grab my towel when I remembered my notes from talking to mum. "Contact details for your father. Middle of the night there now but later."

Reilly took the note, looked at it thoughtfully then pocketed it. "Your Mum's one resourceful woman."

"Yeah, wonder where she gets it from?"

It was Jim's turn to rouse me. "If you want that shower. Go!"

10

Having said goodbye to Jack and Jenny but hoping to meet up with them elsewhere on the trip we headed out into the desert for another long day on the road. Next stop the aboriginal community of Warburton, also called simply 'The Ranges' or Mirlirrtjarra to the local Ngaanyatjarra people. Reilly put the rig into gear and off we went.

"So we're not camping at Warbuton?" I asked for clarification.

"Can't, visitor's dogs aren't allowed out of the vehicle, inside the town limits." Jim explained. "But they do have a laundry we might use. I thought we'd put our dirty clothes through the wash while we have a late lunch come afternoon tea at the roadhouse. I've phoned ahead with our expected time of arrival."

Damn, that meant there wouldn't be much stopping for photos. "They do food at the roadhouse?"

"Normally they just do takeaways but they will put on a feed if asked."

"So we'll be out in the open tonight?" I wasn't liking the sound of that.

"And under the terms of our permit we're not allowed to camp more than thirty metres from the road. Speaking of permits, there's a bit in there about not taking photos of any of the local people unless they give you permission." Reilly gave me the look.

I rolled my eyes, "I wouldn't anyway. Even if it wasn't for all the privacy laws these days it's just not polite. Though that apparently doesn't stop the governments of the world using security cameras or facial recognition on us."

"You'd think differently if you were in an agency charged with finding crims", Jim seemed to be reflecting on something from his pre-merchant navy life. We knew he'd done some classified work but Jim hadn't offered up the details and we hadn't delved. Though I wasn't able to help it if I got fleeting glimpses of his memories in dreams and other times.

Time to change the subject. "Speaking of which Mahala emailed through some information on Leary. He works as muscle for various clandestine operations involved in smuggling, trafficking and the like. Tracking back through transactions they think there's an umbrella company called Plokamia but he might not know who he's actually working for."

"Plokamia," Jim spat out the name in disgust. "It's Greek for tentacles, and that's what they have. Tentacles reaching out, connecting them with most of the organised crime on the planet."

"You've come up against them, Jim?" Reilly asked, as curious as me.

Jim shook his head, "It's not something I'm at liberty to talk about. Let's just say they're bad. Really bad."

"I'm surprised then, that Mahala mentioned them, even in an encrypted email." Reilly mused.

"She'd know my past. She must have figured I'd recognise the name and take it as a warning."

"Okay, we're warned. How does that help us?" I wondered.

"It's always worth knowing what you're up against," Reilly said seriously. "We anticipate, we plan and we stay bloody alert."

We reached the road house, well in need of a break. Having dumped our washing in the coin operated washing machine we went to find our snack. Jim, as always, had ordered to everyone's liking. My stomach murmured in anticipation as I watched our plates come to the table. Not that we'd been doing it tough on this trip but the kitchen in our mobile home was limited. At the very least we had to be mindful of how much gas we used in cooking our food. That kind of limited us to what we could quickly boil, fry or grill.

"I only had sweet potato and pumpkin for your veggie chips," the cook, come waitress, apologised to me.

"No problem, They look delicious," as did the veggie burger and side salad.

Reilly's eyed with pleasure the steak and mushroom sauce she handed him.

Jim had gone for the risotto, which he accepted with thanks.

We ate in companionable silence. It might have seemed strange to anyone observing us but when all our thoughts were open to each other there was sometimes little need for chatting. We each knew that we were all focused on our food, savouring each morsel in almost a meditational calm.

I finished and was wiping my mouth with a napkin when the town cop rumbled in through the door, making a beeline to our table. He was a big man but I had a guess it was all muscle. He could have made two of me. I scanned his aura. Though purposeful in his approach he didn't seem angry so I didn't think we were in any trouble. "Hello officer," I greeted him casually. "Can I get you a seat?"

"No, thank you. I won't stay long. I just came by to check on where you're camping tonight. I received notification you would be coming through but few details about the why. Only that a criminal might be tracking you. I'd rather you didn't stay in town." It wasn't really a request.

Reilly had had a moment to take his measure. "That won't be a problem. We wanted to get further up the track anyway."

"But you're not going to tell me what you're about?" The officer was clearly fishing for more information than he had.

"As I'm sure you know, we're working with Border Force re the somewhat compromised cargo we're transporting to Alice Springs."

"Drugs," The cop assumed.

"You may be right," Reilly smiled, hinting at as much agreement as he could, "but I'm not at liberty to say."

"Figures. Okay, here's what I can do. I can be available on call," he handed Reilly a card. "Let's say you camp about twenty minutes out of town. Enough to be away from town but still within easy reach if I need to come out to you. There's a bit of an abandoned track here." He wrote down the coordinates. "You can camp there out of sight of the road but still be within the stipulations of your permit. I'll let the station at Warakurna know you're coming through tomorrow. Good luck."

"Thank you officer," and Jim meant it. "I don't suppose you can tell us if there have been any sightings of Frederick Leary?"

"Otherwise known as scumbag," I added.

The cop choked a laugh. "No. We haven't seen anyone matching the photo Border Force sent through. It may be that he's using a disguise."

"Or just trying to look ordinary and stay under the radar," was Jim's educated guess.

The cop nodded. "Makes sense. Since he's unlikely to look like one of the local mob my guess would be he'd try to pass himself off as a tourist. He'd have a distinctive accent though, wouldn't he?" He looked meaningfully at Reilly.

"What accent?" Reilly asked, grinning.

The cop rolled his eyes. "Well, here's hoping I don't hear from you. Have a good day." He left us to finish our meal.

As our waitress-cook came over to get our plates another woman came through the screen door. The waitress nodded to her respectfully, "Aunty." She found the older woman a chair and put it beside me. The woman, matronly and almost regal in her demeanour, sat down. "You may call me Aunty too." Without waiting for me to acknowledge that she continued on, as if on a mission. "Ed contacted me. He explained you're seeking your ancestors but he also had something else to say about you. He believes you travel the dimensions. Is he right?"

I was momentarily stymied by someone asking me about the very thing I talked to as few people as possible about. Jim and Reilly knew. Our boss, Captain Wilcher, unwillingly did. Deman and a couple of his close acquaintances. Even on my blog I kept my discussion of the metaphysical light, erring on the side of what the less sceptical might believe. But this woman was looking at me earnestly. Oh, what the hell? "Yes, I travel outside of my body. I have to admit though that I'm a novice. At times I'm not sure if I'm in a dream, the astral plane or somewhere else. The journeying I took with what Ed gave me," I was making an assumption here that he had told her, "it was somewhere different yet a protected space. I met many women from my ancestral lines. We sang and danced and we shared."

The woman nodded, seemingly pleased. "We had hoped you might experience that. As Ed explained to you there is much we are forbidden to share with you. There are always those wanting to study our traditions, make them their own and then make a dollar out of the book and lecture tour that follows."

"Cultural appropriation. I understand entirely. And me being a journalist," I wanted to be perfectly honest with her, "it just makes it worse, doesn't it?"

The woman laughed nervously, "Indeed."

"So I need to go within and discover things for myself," I intuited.

"It would be best. However I think I can tell you this much without disturbing my own ancestors. Look to the shamanic and animistic traditions of the world for ways to approach your journey."

"Using song and dance," as I'd experienced with my ancestors.

"Song and dance is a way of sharing knowledge. Not just with your ancestors but all that is. For instance, your tribal totem or your guardian spirits. You need to discover those. Watch how they move and act. Mimic that in your dance and music. No matter how crazy it may appear to onlookers. And try to go barefoot when you do it."

My eyes must have sparkled with mirth, "my guardian spirit is a spider. Not an easy one to dance."

"Of course you can. Watch how it hunts. How it weaves its web. How it hides and protects itself. Learn from him." She paused, seeming to realise she was travelling a fine line. "As you say, you must find your own truths." She rose to leave.

I stood out of respect, as she got up, "Thank you for coming to see me Aunty. Thank you for your time."

She grinned back at me, "I own no time girl." Then without looking back she left.

I wondered if the guys might tease me about attempting to dance like a spider but wisely they kept their thoughts to themselves.

We ended up spending an hour more waiting for our clothes to dry in the dryer out back and then continued on our way. Clyde, at the very least, would be needing a run by now.

We found our stop for the night but I had to wonder, "When are we going to use the new mag-drive?" I wondered.

"Mag-drive, I like that," Jim murmured approval.

"Tomorrow, at dawn," Reilly declared. "I intend a short test of fifty kilometres or less. If that goes well we'll stop for breakfast and then do an "as the crow flies" test that will take us to a spot on the road this side of Warakurna."

"Won't the cops there wonder how we got there so quickly?"

Reilly shrugged his shoulders, "We'll just say we were on edge and couldn't sleep so we made a pre-dawn start. We'll use up some time over breakfast to make it plausible."

The devilish look in his eyes gave me an idea how we'd be spending some of our breakfast break. "Okay, well then, I'd better take Clyde for a run."

"I'll do that," Jim offered. "You need to research shamanic dance rituals so we can give that a go after dinner."

"Do it yourself shamanism?" Even to myself I sounded doubtful.

Jim tapped me on the chest. "Gnosis. Remember what Aunty said, find your knowledge within. The Tibetans think the mind is located in the heart. And while we're at it some of the Buddhists of Tibet have a very old tradition that crosses the boundary between shamanism and Buddhism. Supposedly 18,000 years old. Research that as well as Tengrism, the ancient folk tradition of the Turkic and Mongolian peoples of Eurasia. Don't worry about the South American stuff for now. You haven't got access to the required psychedelics to go down that path, at the moment. Do look at African shamanism though, in particular that of the Yoruba, the Dogon, the Kalahari and the Zulu. That should give you enough to go on."

I winced at the thought of going near anything that smacked of voodoo but perhaps I was showing my own prejudices. "How do you know all this Jim?" I wondered, seeing yet another side of him.

He just smiled enigmatically, "I've dabbled. You know I've done ayahuasca under the guidance of a shaman."

"Then why don't you just tell me what I need to know?"

"Because, firstly I'm not an expert, and secondly because that's not the way it works. Each shaman must process his or her experience though their own soul. My interpretations would only work for me and the context I have lived in."

"But I'm not a shaman."

Jim gave me a disbelieving raised eyebrow look. "A shaman is defined as someone who moves between the visible and invisible worlds. Someone who uses metaphysics to heal, to anticipate the future and to control natural events. Now while I admit you've yet to show any signs of being a seer or being able to control the weather let's not be picky."

Hell, maybe I was.

"You're a natural," Jim continued. "But there's no need for it to define your identity. Most who become shamans go through some sort of transformative experience, like being struck by lightning."

"Or being blown up and surviving, minus one limb." Yeah, that had been about the point when I'd started doing weird things.

"Don't denigrate what you do by calling it weird." This from Reilly, clearly picking up on my thoughts.

"Okay, okay, I'll go research and see if I can plan out something basic we can do this evening." Though I didn't fancy going barefoot.

Jim tutted, "I'll sweep a patch of ground for you."

Reilly raked a hand through his hair. "And I'll go and make a drum for Jim, something better than the cardboard box he was using last night. Then I'm cooking."

Jim and I groaned together.

"Hmph," Reilly went off annoyed, muttering, "Ye of little faith."

So I spent a couple of hours online but most of what I found was either academic, historical or fluff and fancy. Though I managed to find one podcast series with some promising material, it would take me many hours to go through it all. I did listen to their episode on shamanic dance, even though I didn't have the benefit of having listened to all the previous episodes. I fast forwarded through their very first episode as I was running out of time.

The core of what he was saying was there was a seven stage process but first you had to at least be willing to see yourself as connected to everything. Plants, trees, landscape, other people and so on. When we came into this world we acquired a sense of separateness, seeing ourselves as isolated beings in a sea of existence. An existence seemingly filled with boundaries, hierarchy, and judgements about relative value. Such ideas were mental constructs, a miasma he called it. It was necessary to move past that illusion before entering on the shamanic path.

The first stage, if I was interpreting this right, was finding an empty space within. What he called becoming chalice or cauldron-like. Idly I wondered if that had anything to do with the Welsh mother goddess's cauldron and wisdom Merlin had found within it.

The second stage involved breathwork. Without having had time to go into the techniques more I had to go with my intuition that this involved breath awareness and in some way syncing it with the rhythm of the dance and the felt pulse of the earth.

The third stage seemed to me like a choice point. You either went down a ritualistic path which made the sacred dance akin to a pagan practice or religious ritual. Or, and this is what had stood out to me, you let your body and nature guide you. Both approaches had merit but the latter brought the dancer closer to the shamanic spirit path. But without someone to guide me I only had my body sense, my intuition and what I had shared with my ancestors to go on. For tonight it had to be enough.

"Dished up," Reilly yelled loud enough to break me out of my thoughts and get my attention.

I put down my laptop and put it into sleep mode, "Coming."

Jim was just washing hands after coming in from walking Clyde, who was happily snuggling down in his usual place, at the foot of our bed.

Reilly handed me a bowl of what looked suspiciously like Irish stew but without the meat. I tasted a bit. "Not bad," but I was suspicious. "You made this?"

Reilly, uncharacteristically, laughed, "It's a take away from the road house. I went back in and got some when we were waiting on the dryer."

Jim smiled, amused. "And there I thought you'd just gone to the men's room. You hid that one from us."

Reilly shook his head, "Not so much hid my thoughts. We've all agreed to not do that. But you didn't expect it of me so you weren't looking for the thoughts that would have given the surprise away. Anyway, Jim, you deserved a break."

Jim reached over and patted the Irish wolfhound on the head, "Clyde and I had fun, so thanks. But seriously, I enjoy cooking when I get a chance, so it's no chore. It's not something I get an opportunity to do onboard the ship so it's not drudgery for me. It's like being a kid playing in the sand."

Reilly looked at him puzzled so I interpreted. "He gets to play with all kinds of ingredients, cooking methods and presentation. It's an outlet for his creative streak." Though for me I preferred playing with words.

Jim nodded, "Exactly, much like Reilly likes puzzling out that new engine prototype we're testing tomorrow."

Reilly grunted. "Be better if I could get inside the mind of the girl who designed it."

"You want one of those brain downloads like in the sci-fi movies," I guessed. "Then perhaps you need to try and read the thoughts of those around you, not just Jim and me. Hone the skill. See where it takes you."

Reilly frowned. "What if I succeed and then I'm overwhelmed by all the mental noise."

I shrugged my shoulders, it was obvious wasn't it? "Then learn to block. Just because we agree to share our minds openly doesn't mean we can't exercise the blocking ability, just like we practise our karate. It's a defensive skill."

"Defence against?"

"The dark arts," Jim joked.

I rolled my eyes, "Against other people reading your mind."

"Shit. I didn't even think of that, only of blocking their stray thoughts. Could they intentionally put thoughts in my head?"

"That too."

"We're digressing," Jim intervened. "We can ask Lydia about this tomorrow. Tonight though, we need to concentrate on Ry's issues. You found out something in your research Ry."

Jim would have caught on to some of my thoughts but I knew Reilly had been busy engineering a makeshift drum for him. He'd been too focused on that to pick up on my mind. "I found that a planned, set ritual isn't the way to go. That would be using my brain's mind and for this I really need to use my body's intelligence. I need to connect with the animal, primal nature, part of myself. That's not to say there aren't a couple of techniques I can use to open myself to the process. How'd you go with the drum, Reilly?" I'd been dying to ask.

Reilly got up and came back with the result of his efforts, handing the rather heavy object to Jim. "It's all I oould do in the time," he commented apologetically.

"Amazing," Jim admired Reilly's inventive genius. "It's a wheel rim with some tarp stretched over it. What are these designs?"

Reilly shrugged his shoulders dismissively, "Something called to me to put them on. Just seemed right. The cross within the circle is the Celtic cross. I grew up seeing a few of them around. Probably where I got it from."

"It's the sun cross," I enlightened them both. "It actually predates Christianity. Possibly Norse in origin." Was it a symbol of Odin? I searched my mind trying to remember.

"Odin?" Reilly picked up on the thought but wasn't sure which god Odin was.

"The god of wisdom, I think. Comparative religion was only ever an idle curiosity for me," I admitted.

"Didn't Odin have two crow companions? Thought and memory were their names I think." Jim eyed the two rough crow silhouettes Reilly had drawn, one in each of the top quadrants of the cross.

"I have no idea." Reilly admitted.

"You just channelled it. Wow." I was impressed.

"I have no idea what you mean by that. Aren't channels to do with irrigation?" Reilly quipped.

"Don't be sarcastic, Reilly. You know damn well that channelling is bringing knowledge into this world from beings in the other."

"I wasn't possessed," he growled.

"Possession isn't always demonic, Reilly. I think you were being guided by a benevolent being. Maybe even your higher self."

"Higher self," he latched onto that, "Some part of me that knew more than my conscious mind." He seemed to accept that.

"Which would explain why you drew the magical runes Kenaz and Laguz in the bottom quadrants," Jim assumed. "Fire and water. The power of knowledge and the power of imagination."

"They were just decoration," Reilly swore.

Jim gave his friend an assessing look, "There's no need to be spooked by this. You accept telepathy. The logical explanation is that you picked these symbols from the back recesses of my mind. My grandfather Olaf was, after all, a Norwegian immigrant to the States."

I had an aha moment, "Of course, Northey. A variant of Northman or Norseman. Well," I eyed our dinner plates and got up to deal with them. "I can't wait to hear what it sounds like."

11

Jim had swept the area for me. I hadn't been really ready to go barefoot but now I felt obliged.

"Some people believe it helps you absorb electrons from the Earth. I'm not sure about that but there are plenty of studies that show it reduces inflammation in the body, helps with the regulation of the nervous system and improves sleep patterns," Jim explained his interest in encouraging me to give it a go.

"If it's so good why haven't I heard of it?" I wondered. I hadn't ever seen any sick people wandering around in bare feet.

"Because most of the world is asphalt and concrete and not at all pleasant to walk on barefoot. Then there's the fact that most people have lost the degree of awareness to walk around without stubbing their toes, stepping on an ants' nest or worse, stepping in shit."

I winced, "Yeah, that would discourage me too. Okay, I'll give it a try." I ditched the shoes, assured that Jim had checked the ground for anything cringe worthy.

Reilly brought out a camp chair and his tin whistle, setting up position just outside the circle. "You want a chair too, Jim?"

"Thanks, but I'll sit on the ground. It will be easier to play the drum that way."

Clyde wandered over to settle next to Jim. They were becoming firm friends. Possibly because Jim was often the one who fed him, patted him or took him for walks, but who knew. I trusted my intuition that the dog would not interfere with my dance. Just to be sure I sent him a non-verbal communication to that effect, much in the same way as I communicated with Horatio who was currently hunting the day's quota of bugs in the truck's cab.

We could have set up a fire pot in the centre of the circle but for my first attempt at ecstatic dance I didn't want to have to worry about getting burned if I lost myself in trance and got too close to the fire. Instead the guys had positioned a fire pot towards the northern side of the circle, and had set themselves up close to it.

Jim gave one beat on his drum as a sign for me to begin but I hesitated, not really knowing how to start.

Surprisingly it was Reilly who took up the responsibility of guiding me. "Sit for a moment. Feel the ground beneath ya. Imagine ye're the ground."

Yeah, I could do that. And it had the desired effect of both grounding me and making me feel less separate from the landscape.

Jim's single beat of the drum centred my awareness. I felt the beat reverberate through me. I felt its aftermath as the wave of sound passed through me.

"Feel the warm desert wind touching your skin. Breath it in. Deep into your belly. Hold. Now let it out, lettin' go of all your mental activity. That's one breath. Place your palms, face up, on yer thighs. Take a moment to clench them on the in breath. Hold the clench as you hold your breath. Now release your breath and yer palms. Breath in, clench, holdin', lettin' go. Now do it with the beat of the drum. Jim, if ya please. A four beat. Breath in, hold, breath out, hold. One, two, three, four. Jim will match whatever pace ya choose."

Reilly entered my mind, monitoring my state. When he thought I was ready, relaxed but not too light headed, he took me to the next stage. "Stand up and raise yer hands in gratitude to the sky. Lower them and thank the earth. Turn to the left, keep turnin'. Like a slow movin' eddy of wind. Feel into everything around ya. Not too fast or ya'll lose balance. Yeah, like that."

I had no idea how he knew any of this but I trusted him so I listened and I did.

"As you're turnin', imagine you're a bird takin' flight. Raise your arms on the in breath and lower on the out breath. Do that for a bit and see where it takes you."

I was flying. I was a bird. Black with red tail feathers. A black cockatoo. Joyous, liberated, playful. A harbinger of weather change. I was one with the weather. The weather was me. I felt its shifts and turns. I smelled the dust on the wind yet the promise of dew on the night air. Another warm day tomorrow.

The drum beats were slowing. I drifted with the lilting tones of Reilly's tin whistle, immersing myself in the melody but knowing intuitively it was time to return from the no-time-space back to the world of linear time and solid reality. I folded my wings and came to settle back on the rich red soil of the desert and sent my gratitude into the ground.

Reilly brought over a mug of mulled wine, offering it to my lips, letting me sip at my own pace. "Food?"

"No, that's fine, thanks." Unused to drinking too many alcoholic beverages I took the drink slow and savoured it, feeling its warming effects course through my body. I took the moment to review and digest all that I'd felt. Then I looked up and gasped, my eyes and other senses still hyper aware to nature all around me. There was a goanna, pretending to sleep among the rocks but its eyes ever so slightly open, watching Reilly. Two crows flew in on the last rays of the sun, landing not far from Jim, as if foraging for the last of their day's food but casting glances in Jim's directions. "It seems I wasn't the only one to find a spirit animal."

Jim glanced behind him, in the direction of the crows and chuckled.

Reilly frowned as he noticed the large lizard in his vicinity. "A goanna?"

"Australia's version of a dragon," I pointed out. "Now are you going to tell me how you knew how to guide me?"

"I didn't. I just drew upon my martial arts trainin'. Most martial arts were developed from watchin' animals, combinin' breath with movement. Tai chi, in particular, uses a lot of bird-like movements and I just thought it suited ya."

"So Tai chi is shamanic?" I wondered, surprised.

Reilly shrugged, "It may have started out that way."

I thought about this, "Then I've been practising the martial arts that you've been teaching me, all wrong. I need to be the moves, not just do them."

"That's a good point," Reilly agreed, "One I've neglected. We'll change how we practise tomorrow. But for now we need to pack things up and get an early night. Jim?" he asked, meaning the drum.

"It went well. A heavy thing but it does the job."

"We'll see if there's a music shop when we get to Alice Springs. An Irish bodhran would be a lot lighter to cart around."

"As long as you paint it up the same way and I get to keep this one for special occasions."

"Why?" Reilly wondered.

He treasures it because you made it, I mentally pointed out the obvious to Reilly.

"Oh." Reilly smiled at that.

Jim put an arm around me, "And what's this about a black cockatoo? I thought your spirit animal was going to be a spider."

"I guess it's possible to have more than one spirit animal." I'd kind of been expecting a spider too but happy not to have been scrambling across the ground, feeling my way around for prey."

"So you think they have an affinity with weather," Reilly was clearly looking at the strategic advantages of what had chosen me.

"They're traditionally seen as harbingers of weather change. They get pretty excited and playful when it's going to rain and come down from the mountains into the plains country when a cold snap or storm is coming. You won't find any out here in the desert though, they're a bird of the forest."

"What do they look like?" Jim was trying to imagine.

"Mostly like a large parrot. I'll find a picture on the internet for you. They're black with some red among their tail feathers. Except further South, those have yellow tail feathers."

Made sense to Jim, "Kind of goes with the red an black peony scheme you've got going on the tattoo on your back."

I hadn't thought of that, "I hardly think spirit animals would worry about colour co-ordination."

Jim wasn't so sure, "Who's to say?"

"You'd better look up what it means to have a goanna spirit animal while you're at it," Reilly decided.

"Don't you want to intuit what it means?"

"Nah, I'll leave the intuition to you."

I felt like Reilly was avoiding that part of himself but I'd learnt early on that arguing with Reilly logic was like arguing with a rock.

"Hmph," Reilly snorted, not entirely pleased with that thought.

It turned out that goannas symbolised proud, strong, extremely loyal protectors but sometimes they needed to protect themselves from themselves. Protectors who often needed to do inner work to find their true selves. They also possessed a strong earth magic that could bring about balance and harmony.

Reilly didn't say too much about that but clearly he was thinking.

"Think in your dreams, time to sleep if we're going to get up early," Jim reminded him.

We didn't ask what Jim had thought of his crows as it had been an obvious fit with what Reilly had painted on his drum.

I think we all had things going through our heads as we drifted off to sleep, except perhaps Clyde who was already snoring softly at the foot of the bed.

12

My dreams took me to dark places. A prison. Hell, I was the prisoner. My first day and I was surrounded by the thugs who ruled here.

"New flesh," one, with a scar down his cheek, commented appreciatively

"I get first dibs," this from a man who towered above all the others.

The rest of the onlookers nodded their assent, knowing their lives wouldn't be worth it if they went against him.

"No one's taking a bite out of me," I grumbled.

Scarface chuckled evilly, "We're not vampires pretty boy. We just want that cute ass of yours."

"Boy?" Were they blind? I eyed up the odds. Not good. "I can't exactly stop you but if you expect me not to fight back you're sadly mistaken. The first one that tries me will regret it. I promise you that."

They circled like sharks moving in on their prey. They knew they only had to catch hold of me and then they could do what they liked. The first tried and I kicked him in the groin then swung out the way. Damn it, where were the prison guards when you wanted them?

"Now boy," the big man tutted, "You're only going to make it harder for yourself."

I knew my best chance to do damage was to get him on his own, "If you're so tough why do you need your lackeys to do your work? Take me like a man."

This gave the enormous ogre a moment's pause. He nodded to the others who backed away. "Okay then. Have it your way. But you'll regret your insolence."

While he postured and prowled I decided my target and as he came in to grab me I went for his left eye. The sensation was hideous as my nails ripped into his face…"

"Ry, wake up now." came the stern demand. "Get out of there. It's just my memories."

Reilly's memories, of course, I sighed as I woke, nestling into his arms. "Damn, you didn't have it easy did you?"

His hand stroked my forehead lovingly, "No prison is good. That was worse than most."

"You would have made an enemy for the rest of your time there."

"I did but strangely my act of defiance got me not just two weeks in solitary but also a lot of cred amongst the other inmates. I had my own gang of thugs after that."

Jim, who'd woken amidst the mixed mental commotion stared at Reilly, forlornly, "Your father, then that. You must hate what I am." He looked ready to flee at a moment's notice.

Reilly glared at him, "Firstly, ye're in my mind. What do ya see there Jim?" he challenged.

JIm relaxed a bit, "Unconditional acceptance."

"Exactly. And secondly, you're not a sexual predator. Those men were. You're not after taking or controlling another against their will. Heterosexual, homosexual, vanilla, a bit of kink or anything in between, there is no excuse for taking what's not freely given." With that he got up and stalked to the other side of the bed. Jim got up to meet him, watching him intently. Reilly backed him to the wall, sizing him up. Then reaching forward so that his strong muscular arms hemmed Jim in he leaned forward. His lips hovered a hair's breadth from Jim's. "Say please."

"Please", Jim's voice was a hoarse whisper.

Then Reilly took him, crushing his mouth before breaking off to judge if he'd made his point. "I may be more heterosexual than you. My subconscious biases may have been moulded by my past but don't for one minute think that I've anythin' other than the deepest respect and affection for ya. So for fuck's sake, stop expecting me to judge ya."

Jim was still trying to recover from his surprise kiss. "I'll do my best." We all knew he still had issues from his upbringing. No one was expecting miracles, from either of my men.

"I'm going for a walk," Reilly decided. "I need to shake off Ry's dream."

Did someone say walk? Clyde was instantly up and bright eyed, watching Reilly expectantly.

But I felt something. "Wait, Reilly. There's someone out there. Not close but still…"

"Hmm," Reilly pulled a gun from a spare sock near the bed. Where'd that come from? It looked like a handgun out of some futuristic movie.

Reilly acknowledged my thoughts as he pulled his jeans on, " A Luago Alien. 9mm. New on the market. Made in Czechoslovakia."

Reilly was good on facts. "I think whoever it is is too far off to shoot at either you or Clyde but take care out there."

"Stay in my mind. Be my navigation."

I could do that.

"I'll come with ya," Jim offered.

Reilly shook his head. "Not this time. I really could do with a few moments to myself. Guard her!"

Oh, he meant me. Well I could be in two places, as we well knew.

It was only three in the morning but that didn't stop Clyde's enthusiasm for a walk. Reilly patted him on the head. "Let's go huntin', big fella."

I felt the cool night air on Reilly's face. I saw through his eyes the myriad of stars you could only experience this far away from the bright lights of the cities. The milky way, as clear as a road, painted the sky. My black cockatoo spirit guide smelled rain to the South of us and rejoiced but I, for one, was happy it wouldn't muddy our track.

Where to Ry? Reilly asked plainly

You're not going to hunt him down now? Was he?

I haven't decided yet. But the idea of doing just that had already cleared his mind of the bad memories of the past.

I sighed, resignedly, *Nor-norwest. There's a rocky outcrop out there.*

I see it. Can they see us?

I have no sense of being watched. Just a presence. What's he thinkin'?

Come off it Reilly, I'm not that good. That's the skill you're going to perfect isn't it, but, *I sense he's dozing by a small fire.*

I see that now too, he acknowledged. I felt him mentally trying to instruct Clyde to keep quiet but the big dog seemed to know anyway. Maybe the dog had his own extra senses. No doubt.

Just then the stranger looked up, startled, "Well hello bro. Didn't expect anyone else to be out here."

Reilly relaxed and discreetly hid the gun in the small of his back. "What brings you here?

"Car trouble. Started sputtering about five k's up the road. Got it in limp mode this far. Figured I'd ring one of my mates in Warbuton in the morning to come out and take a look or tow me in."

"Want me to take a look?"

The man looked surprised but hopeful, "Sure," he jumped up. "By the way, Elf's the name."

"Reilly," I could feel Reilly thinking that the man, all six feet of wiry muscle, didn't look much like an elf.

Or short for Elphinstone, I suggested.

Who names their kid Elphinstone? he wondered.

Jim's on the way over. He said you might need something called an OBDC reader.

Great. He was already looking under the bonnet of the car with his torch, poking and giving bits a tug to see if anything was loose. The white Ford Territory was in reasonably good condition for an outback car, apart from the lack of plastic accessories that had fallen off long ago and the ceiling material that had somehow unglued itself and was being held up by the sun visors. "Try and start it, Elf. I want to hear what it sounds like." He listened. "Uh huh, switch her off. I've got a hunch but my mate's coming over with some gear. We'll get a computer read out to be sure."

Elf noted the bobbing torch light coming in their direction, "Appreciate it. Didn't mean to wake you guys." He eyed the uber large dog. He'd also noted the gun tacked into the back of Reilly's belt, causing him at least one raised eyebrow and no small amount of uncertainty.

"You didn't. We were awake anyway. Clyde was keen for a walk and, anyway, we want to make an early start before the sun rises. We fancy stopping up the road for breakfast, before the flies come out."

It sounded plausible but, "How'd you guys even know I was here?"

Reilly took the measure of the man and decided on bare bones honesty. "My woman's psychic. She sensed you were out here."

His woman, eh? But I mentally bit my tongue, after all I kind of liked that I was 'his' even if no-one in this world or the next owned me. Though there was no escaping the fact that the three of us belonged together. *What's up with the car?* I asked, curious to know.

Tell ya in a minute. He had a hunch but he wanted to be sure.

"Plug her in", he said to Jim, who'd arrived with a toolbox in hand.

Jim read the codes, "Coils. Um, all of them." he sounded surprised.

Now what causes four coils to all fail at once? Reilly thought to himself. "Elf, did ya just put new coils in this car?"

Elf looked puzzled, "Er, yeah. Oh, don't tell me they're faulty." He groaned.

"Ya got them off the internet?" Reilly asked.

"Only way to get stuff out here." Elf admitted.

"Send them back, they sent ya the wrong ones. Don't suppose you still have the old ones with ya."

Elf brightened. "Yeah, as it happens. I was going to chuck them on the tip the first chance I got. Hell, I thought I was doing the right thing. Fixing the car up before I went to The Alice to see the girlfriend."

Reilly reassured the man, "It was good thinking. This wasn't yer fault. Let's see these old coils of yours."

Within half an hour the car was purring again, not just from the coils but also from a few other tweaks and adjustments Reilly and Jim had given it.

Elf was over the moon but worried, "I don't know how to thank you. Er, I don't have much on me to pay you."

Reilly dismissed his concern. "Wheels and roundabouts."

"Huh?"

"What goes around comes around. We help you today. One day you'll help someone else. It's the way the world should work."

Elf grinned, appreciating that. "Right on Bro. Er, can I offer you at least a cuppa?"

Jim shook his head, answering for all of us, "No we'll head on our way. We're on a bit of mission." He gave Elf a meaningful look.

Elf looked to Reilly again, the gun, the high power torches, the extremely well trained dog, "Uh huh. Never saw you. You were never here."

Jim nodded approvingly, "Good man."

Reilly shook Elf's hand, "Maybe we'll see ya down the road somewhere. Good luck with the girl friend."

As they walked back to our camp Reilly quizzed Jim, "What made you think to hint we were on a secret mission?"

"Just a hunch."

13

There was little sense in going back to bed. "So we're going to do this?" I wondered, excitement and curiosity coursing through my veins. My inner journalist, inquisitive gatherer of information and experiences, was well and truly awake.

Reilly pursed his lips. "Just a mere blip of a test first. 50 kilometres. Anything up ahead on the sensors Jim?"

"Nothing bigger than a rat."

"And your internal sensors, Ry?"

Wow, when had my abilities become part of the test? But I was honoured by the question. "I don't sense any danger."

"Excellent," Reilly initiated a start sequence on the onboard computer, locked in our destination coordinates then engaged the radically alternative drive. Like some miracle we didn't explode into a mushroom cloud of bits. Bonus!

Except … in the next instant I found myself floating in the otherworld, along with Jim, Reilly, Horatio and Clyde. A rainbow of coloured lights rippled past us in waves. "Um, was this meant to happen?"

Jim floated towards me, as if in anti-gravity. "Well this is fun. So this is where you get to when you astral travel."

"Not exactly. I'm usually a lot more grounded, how should I say, stationary than this. I'm not sure what's happening," but I didn't feel panicked about it.

Reilly, however, was frowning. "No, in answer to your question Ry, this wasn't in the briefing."

"Well it's nice seeing you all here." I held out a hand to Horatio, allowing him to grab a lift. Horatio seemed the least perplexed of us. Clyde's eyes, however, were huge with wonder. His four legs, floundering around as he experimented with the space he found himself in. "I guess we'll go back to our bodies when the truck reaches our destination."

Reilly made a mental calculation, "That should be any second now."

"Er, time is irrelevant here Reilly," I reminded him.

But the next minute I was back in my body. The truck was on auto-pilot and once more on solid road, if you called the Gun Barrel Highway a road.

Clyde woofed. Reilly frowned. Jim blinked and then asked if we needed a coffee. I opened the glove box compartment to check on Horatio who seemed none the worse for his trip out of this dimension. He waved a leg at me.

While Jim went off to check the instrument readings and organise breakfast Reilly decided we needed intel on the unintended dimensional shift. "You consult with Lydia. Even Aranya if you need to. I'll give Deman and Tess, the engineer, a call."

Bothering Lydia sounded the preferable of my options. I didn't like bothering Aranya as I figured goddesses didn't like their day interrupted unduly. But Aranya decided otherwise. "You were in an astral wormhole," she explained. "Not something I've seen many do."

"Are there any risks and benefits to doing that?" I figured Reilly would be wanting a risk assessment. "What's an astral wormhole used for?"

The goddess rolled her eyes at me, as much as I sensed her eyes. "Travel of course. Going anywhere in time or space. The rules that govern the physical dimension mean that vast amounts of power are needed to travel even a brief distance within your solar system. However, if you go through what you might consider no-space you can go anywhere in creation. Even time travel, though I would advise against it as that can shift what you call reality to another timeline with different scenarios to the one your world is experiencing now. Which wouldn't bother the universe but it might bother you and those you care about. Normally only highly enlightened or ascended beings can travel the rainbow track. Though sometimes just having the experience under the guidance of an adept is enough to awaken the ability."

Hmm. "There could be a danger then, if unenlightened beings travelled that way. They might use it to travel to places and times where they could meddle with things to their own advantage."

"Yes, but I don't think they would stay unenlightened long. The very experience of being in no-space would begin the process of reconnecting an individual with source."

Worry in the form of Jim and Reilly came to mind, "How would you know if it had affected them?"

"Changes in their behaviour. Strange new abilities. Insights. Though I wouldn't recommend it as a means of soul advancement. Shortcuts often lead to burn out and the types of advancement I'm talking about would shed millennia off an individual's soul growth."

Yikes. "How could the danger of burn-out be avoided?" How could I help those I'd travelled with, even myself?

Aranya seemed to ponder this a moment before answering, "The dog and the spider will be fine but human minds are mired by the filters their beliefs place on them. If a miasma is a noxious atmosphere then you might say that what the human mind has imposed on it from birth and builds upon as it interacts with the collective reality creates such a miasma. Ripping that away can descend the human mind into a deep pit of regret, self doubt, even self-disgust as they reflect on how they have lived their lives in what was effectively a lie."

"So self-acceptance is the bridge."

"Yes, I would say so. Having never been human it's difficult for me to truly relate to the depth of the human delusion. Though the extent of it is obvious from their actions, including their animosity to the natural world. They see it as their enemy, to be conquered, contained and if not that, then destroyed. Minus their miasma I believe humans would begin to see everything in nature as an exchange of energy, keeping a balance. They would be grateful for all the great mother gives them and understand their short lives within the context of that ever shifting flow of energy they call life. Of course the duality of life and death is another kind of illusion but that veers from your question. Keep in mind what you felt when your life as you knew it was ripped away from you, forcing you to find new ways to be. Jim and Reilly will have to come to grips with their new reality, on their own terms. It can't come from you or any outside source but your compassion and understanding will be their support."

And here I'd feared calling on Aranya. I was both awed and reassured by what she told me.

Aranya gave an evil laugh, "You humanise me because that's what you're comfortable with but I will never be anything other than predator, beautiful and deadly." With that she vanished from my consciousness.

I found Jim in our mobile home quarters, dishing up bacon and eggs for Reilly, rice porridge and blueberries for me and some granola and fruit for himself.

I made the tea and coffee, keeping my thoughts to myself until Reilly came to join us. It only took him a second to digest the concern on my face. "Spit it out!"

I let out a sigh and let my tense shoulders go on the outbreath. It wasn't as if I could stop the changes that might come our way because of our trip on the rainbow track. So I told them, pretty much word for word, what Aranya had said.

"Well that explains it," Reilly took a mouthful of bacon and chewed on it, leaving me wondering. Though I could ferret it out of his mind it would be quicker if he told me.

"Auras," Jim explained. "I think both Reilly and I are seeing them now."

Reilly nodded as he continued to shovel food in. Maybe food grounded him.

"Welcome to my world." I'd been seeing auras for a long time now. Though I imagined it might be disconcerting to Jim and Reilly. "You'll learn over time to just let it be in the background unless you focus on it."

Reilly wiped his plate with some bread, "Could be useful." The strategist in him was already looking at how this new trait could be used.

I thoughtfully took my bowl to wash it out in the sink. "That was just a fifty kilometre trip through the rainbow track. We don't know what will happen if we do the 500 kilometre leg of the test."

Jim leaned back in his chair and considered, "You said time and space are irrelevant there so the distance we travel should be equally irrelevant."

I doubted it could be that easy, "In the no-space, yes, but in the physical world a greater period of time will pass. A longer time for there to be an effect on our physical bodies."

Reilly's phone rang and he answered it. "Deman. Thanks for getting back to me. No, it's more complicated than that. Ry needs to bring you up to date. There are, how should I say, unforeseen ramifications for those involved in the test. No, I don't want to explain all this a hundred times over. Give us fifteen minutes to finish breakfast then we'll have an online conference. Can I leave it to you to rustle up the others? Yeah, great. Just send us the link. We'll be here." He hung up, then eyed the blueberries in my bowl.

"You want to try one?" I asked, stunned. He'd never been much of one for fruit before. I offered a berry up to his lips and he bit it, closed his eyes and looked thoughtful.

"I had no idea," he murmured in delight. "Got any more of those stashed away Jim?"

"Hey!" I protested. "Those are my blueberries."

Jim patted my hand understandingly, "I'll buy you more once we get to The Alice."

"They have blueberries in The Alice?" I wondered.

"They have supermarkets, so, therefore…"

"Oh, okay, give him some blueberries then." Not that I was truly going to deny him.

Reilly nibbled my ear, "I'll make it up to you."

"Except not now," I pouted. "Conference call, remember." There went our rest break.

Reilly chuckled, "I'll write you an IOU."

Jim rolled his eyes, "They're just berries."

Reilly shook his head vehemently, "Uh, uh, fruit never tasted like that before."

Jim and I glanced at each other and we knew. It wasn't just auras being visible that was new.

14

We cleared our cups off the mobile camper's pint sized coffee table and set up the laptop so we could all see the screen. Jim, being proficient with the technology, logged us onto the meeting room where everyone was already waiting. A couple of the faces we hadn't seen before.

"Deman," I acknowledged my friend, "thanks for sparing the time."

"It's no real chore Ry, I've a lot invested in this project."

That he'd invested in the technology, I hadn't known. "Um let me just introduce us." I thought it might help the newcomers. "I'm Rylee Jackson, general assistant on this little odyssey and this is Jim Northey, our electrical engineer and finally to my left, Reilly O'Reilly, our boss and mechanical engineer." Which Reilly had been before he'd moved out of marine engineering into the deck officer career path.

"Ry's a bit more than a general assistant," Deman assured the others. "Ex frontline journalist, trainee deck officer and dimensional traveller. Now let me introduce you to those you don't know. Over in the top left of your screen you'll see Seren, who's," he hesitated, "a computational whizz and a seer. Next to her on the screen is Russell, an adept in many things metaphysical."

Delightfully Russell seemed embarrassed by this introduction, shaking his head in denial. But Deman continued on. Of course you know Tess, Dan and Terri. I've asked Lydia along as well."

"Mahala?" I wondered why she wasn't in on this meeting.

Deman frowned, "I assumed we were just having a discussion about the metaphysical ramifications of using this technology."

"Well the dog she loaned us, he joined us on the rainbow track." That got a few surprised looks.

Dan leaned forward into view. "Explain this rainbow track."

Er, "I have a guardian. You might call her a goddess or an angelic protector of all spiders."

No-one seemed too perturbed by that statement. "What did she have to say, Ry?"

So I brought them up to date.

"Even, the spider?" Deman sounded incredulous.

"Hey! Don't underestimate Horatio. He's had my back on more than one occasion. It's not the first time for him to travel in another dimension. More surprising was Clyde."

Clyde acknowledged his name by coming over to sit next to me.

"That's one huge dog," Terri gasped.

"He belongs to Border Force," Reilly explained. "He's on loan to us because of the cargo issue."

Terri grinned, "And being spoiled rotten, I expect"

Clyde woofed his happy agreement to that.

"Seren," Dan addressed the seer, who was notable for the dark glasses she was wearing. Why was she hiding her eyes? I wondered.

"Because she's an android," Reilly decided.

How did he know, I wondered. "You can't see auras through digital technology."

Reilly shrugged his shoulders casually, "When I look at her picture on the screen I feel crackling inside my head."

Dan laughed, "It seems you've been outed Seren."

Seren removed her glasses and stared at us with unearthly eyes of deepest purple, sparkling with electrical energy. "Technically I'm an artificially created sentient being, like Thallon who've you met. More than that I'm not discussing over the internet, even a heavily encrypted channel such as this. I am however a seer, of a kind. I see potential outcomes. It's not possible, even for me, to compute all potential outcomes of any event but what I have seen eventuating from your short journey in what you call the rainbow track doesn't give me any cause for concern."

"Is that a long way of saying we're not doomed?" Just so I was clear.

Seren laughed, "No, you're not doomed. This was meant to happen."

The one called Russell interrupted, "Can we just clarify what we're calling the rainbow track? I'm familiar with teleporting through a medium where no time and space exists but I've never noticed a rainbow of colours."

Terri mused, "It may be a function of the technology. To do with how it uses the electromagnetic currents that surround the Earth and flow out into space."

Lydia butted in, suddenly very excited. "Yes of course. That's it. Ancient shamanic tribes often equated those electromagnetic currents with a cosmic snake."

"A snake?" I couldn't see the connection.

But Jim saw it. "A rainbow serpent?"

"If you equate the serpent with primordial light, the seven rays that generate creation," Lydia mused.

"Hang on!" Russell interrupted again. "Coming back to my earlier point. When I teleport I go through a single point of no-space and no-time. It's like blinking out of existence and then you get to where you're going. I've never noticed a rainbow of light."

"It may all be a matter of perspective." Lydia drew a line on a piece of paper and held it up to the camera for us to see. "Imagine this a line of infinitely small diameter. If you pass through the line at right angles to it you're interacting with an infinitely small point, in effect nothing. But if you're travelling inside the line it may be an entirely different experience."

Seren leaned back in her chair and considered. "What Russell passes through when teleporting is the original singularity. We'll call it a point but as we know there is nothing there except infinite potential, infinite energy, nothing yet defined. From that single origin of the universe light, energy, spirals out fractally. An infinite, holographic fractal. Any one location in the fractal contains the essence of everything such that more infinite spiralling out of energy can proceed from that or any other location. Ry, Jim and Reilly, and of course Clyde and Horatio, were within the energy spiral. As we all are but they were perceiving it from the perspective of a dimension unbound by the physical and the limits of space-time."

We collectively stared at her, no doubt all trying to fathom what she'd just said.

Lydia pursed her lips, "Probably better not to try and fathom that. Something just to be open to and aware of."

"Here, here!" Dan heartily agreed.

"But does that mean it's safe to continue with the test?" Reilly brought us back to the crux of our concerns. "If that short test radically altered us in any way then isn't the damage already done."

Seren smiled enigmatically. "There are times I am not at liberty to influence choice so I won't answer that definitively. Yes, annoying, I know," she answered Reilly's glare. "I will say that I think no other living beings should be subjected to this technology. We don't know how affecting too many beings in this way might alter events on this timeline. I would recommend that after this trip, if you decide on a further human controlled test, future use of the technology should be automated and that its use in transport be limited only to inanimate goods."

Terri, who'd been quiet through all this, nodded her assent. "Sounds like a wise decision to me. Dan?"

"Agreed. I trust this doesn't void your investment Deman?"

"Not at all. The transportation of inanimate goods generally gives us less trouble anyway so I've no problems with limiting its use to that."

"But, we continue with the 500 kilometre test?" I had to ask, strangely keen when I should be worried for our collective safety. The safety of those I loved.

"It's your choice," Seren reminded us.

Deman's brow furrowed with uncharacteristic worry lines, "Is it really necessary?"

Jim cleared his throat. "I've analysed the data from the first test and I've sent it to you but I think you'll agree a further test is needed to validate the data."

Reilly glared at his friend, "The risks aren't worth it, Jim. The tests can be automated later. We proceed to Alice Springs on a slower schedule, that's all."

"But…"

"No Jim. I know travellin' through the rainbow track might make ya into some kind of super Jim but I love ya the way y'are. I accept ya fully as y'are. Ya don't need to satisfy some crazed curiosity."

Jim's jaw dropped, "You said 'love'."

Reilly groaned, he should have known Jim would latch on to that.

It was time to put my cards on the table. "The journalist in me itches with what Reilly calls crazed curiosity, but I'm also loath to risk those I love let alone two animals I have a deep affection for who can't cast a vote on the matter."

"Then it's decided," or at least it was decided as far as Dan was concerned and since it was his project I figured that was the end of the matter.

Tess looked a little disappointed but nodded her assent, "I'll crunch your data Jim. See where we go to from here."

"Could you keep me updated," Jim asked hopefully.

Terri raised an eyebrow and looked at Dan. Clearly there were unspoken thoughts shared but Dan nodded his head. "You may consult with Jim, Tess. But clear any major findings with me first. Okay. Thank you all for your time. Safe travels to our friends."

"Here, here."

Reilly ended the conference call, all of us experiencing a mixture of both relief and disappointment.

"Well if we're not doing the test I suggest we go back to bed for a bit," I waggled my eyebrows. The distraction of sex would do us good and ground us back in the 'real world'.

Reilly growled. "We've got 500 extra kilometres ahead of us. Not to mention we haven't done any martial arts practise for the day."

There was only one way to counter such logic. I got down on my knees and proceeded to unzip Reilly's Jeans.

An hour and a half later we were back on the road, with our 'boss' grumbling about lost time. It was a long haul to Warakurna with only modest rest stops along the way, though it was easy to keep those brief as the flies were up and about for the day, making it unpleasant to try and eat or drink outside. So Jim would fix something for us then bring it to the cab so we could eat on the way.

It was getting dark and we were getting exhausted by the time we got to the outskirts of the town.

"Is it just my imagination or is it bigger than the other communities we've been through?" I wondered.

Jim looked it up on the computer, "A population of about 270, most of whom speak a language called Ngaanyatjarra as their first language. There's a campsite at the roadhouse. Seems like it might be pet friendly. We could ask."

Reilly liked that idea. "Yeah, it would be nice if we didn't have to go any further today. It's still over 780 kilometres to Alice Springs. Our next stop tomorrow might be Yulara, near the rock. That's only 330 kilometres."

Jim was still reading down the webpage about Warakurna. "We're too late for takeaways but we can ring a bell at the campground to get access there. If we're only going as far as Yulara tomorrow we might have time to look at their art gallery in the morning," he looked hopeful.

"Art gallery? Cool," I agreed.

Reilly groaned, "If we must. Any rules or customs we need to know about?"

Jim ran his finger down the information page, "Just the usual, no drinking alcohol. No taking photos of the locals without their permission."

"Oh well" It looked like I would be limited to scenery shots again. Though I could ask.

The friendly manager showed us around the campground which included a large amenities block with coin operated washing machines and hot showers. I was so going to look forward to nearly drowning myself under a stream of hot water.

We parked our rig close to the nearby picnic table. We could eat under the stars tonight. There weren't many other travellers in the campground tonight. There was a Range Rover, caked in dirt, and towing one of those off road trailers with a fold out tent. Its owner looked in our direction and frowned. Obviously we didn't tick the right boxes to be considered travellers of his ilk. A middle-aged couple in a beat up old Toyota ute with a built on canopy and a makeshift annex waved in our direction. We waved back. Invite duly accepted to chat around their firepot later.

Just as Jim was putting Clyde's leash on to take him for a walk the white station wagon from the previous night meandered in. Elf, I assumed. He'd made it. Reilly went over to greet him while I went to find our camp chairs and some nibbles to take over to the friendlies' fire pot. My next priority, that shower.

By the time I came out the local law enforcement had turned up to check us out. You could see their eyes scanning the campground and its inhabitants, assessing the risks. The taller of the two was talking to Reilly.

"You made good time." Apparently Warbuton had briefed them we were coming.

"We got an early start."

Elf must have sensed the cops had concerns and came over to put in a good word for us, "What they mean is they got up in the middle of the night and fixed my car. Otherwise I'd be back in Warbuton, on the phone, explaining to my girlfriend why I wasn't on my way."

The cop took this on board. "No trouble?" he asked Reilly.

"None. Jim'll activate our security system, including movement sensors and cameras, once we go to bed. And we have Clyde." He nodded to the dog who was seated loyally at Jim's side.

It was clear the cops didn't want us in their town or the trouble our presence might bring, "I don't want any shootings, stabbings or any other commotion. If I get woken up by a call out in the middle of the night I'm going to be seriously pissed off. I want no inhabitants of this town or any innocent travellers coming to any harm."

It was on the tip of my tongue to butt in and ask if that meant crims were free game but I didn't think that would go down too well.

The senior of the two cops came to a decision. "I'll let you stay because you helped Elf out but I want you gone as soon as possible."

Now I did butt in, doing my best to look cute and harmless, "We were hoping to check out the gallery in the morning."

The cop sighed heavily, "Two of you can. One stays with your rig. Then go."

"Suits me," Reilly agreed readily. I felt his glee that he didn't have to go to that particular attraction.

We watched the cops leave. Range Rover man was frowning at us even more but Elf patted Reilly on the back. "The cops are worried about your mission, aren't they? Don't worry mate, I'll be another set of eyes for you. I'm a bit of an insomniac you see. Nothing sneaks past my camp without me knowing."

Reilly didn't remind him that he'd nearly snuck up on him. "Appreciated Elf. Are you coming over to meet the couple over there?" Reilly pointed in the direction of the beat up Toyota.

Elf grinned, "Yeah, hell, why not. I'll go get my camp chair."

As he wandered off to his own camp I whispered in Reilly's ear, "I think we should hire him as security. He looks so unassuming no-one would ever suspect him."

"He's one of those innocents the cops were worried about," Reilly reminded me.

But Jim agreed with me. "Since we're not going to be travelling at warp speed he's going to be on the road at the same time as us, heading in the same direction. He might be safer from harm if we word him up a bit. It's not like we're asking him to wrestle any unfriendlies to the ground, just that he uses his eyes and ears and gives us a heads up if he senses anything."

"Hmm," was all Reilly would say but we could tell he was thinking.

I went to get my camp chair, struggling to get it out of storage with my one arm, but a hand reached around me and took it from me. Jim.

"We know you can but there's no need, let me."

I was just trying to pull my weight but was glad of the help.

Jim reached in for a kiss before straightening and smiling. "You're worth more to us than the ability to carry one chair, which you're quite capable of doing but it's easier for me."

Yes, but, "Just don't deskill me. I don't want to wake up one day to find myself weak and dependent."

"You'll never let that happen Ry. You're no-one's dependent. No-one's victim. I think sometimes you're made of some kind of resilient form of spring steel. You bounce back no matter what's thrown at you."

My cheeks reddened with embarrassment. "I'm not trying to prove myself."

"I know, and that's what makes you so special."

Susie and William were warm and welcoming, like many 'grey nomads' I'd so far met. They'd retired long ago from their jobs, the children were all grown up and, while enjoying the occasional grandchildren babysitting duties, they didn't want to spend the rest of their time at home waiting until the day they ended up in an old age home. They wanted to live, meet new and interesting people and see some of the amazingly vast landscapes their country had to offer. So they'd sold their four bedroom house on the outskirts of Sydney for a song. With the proceeds they'd bought a humble shack by the coast, their trusty Toyota and they were happily paying for hopefully many years on the road with the rest of their funds. During the wet season they usually spent time at their shack or visiting their large extended family. The rest of the time they lived on the road.

Reilly turned up with an armload of dry sticks he'd gathered on a walk.

Clyde, gleefully presented us with a large stick of his own, that he'd carried in his mouth. Jim extracted it from him, drool and all, "Why, thanks Clyde." Affectionately he patted the large dog who seemed immensely pleased to have made his contribution.

It was a peaceful wind down from a long day on the road. I felt Jim's mind drifting off as he watched the flames of their fire pot. The peace was broken by the terror that ripped through him, his white knuckle gripped the sides of his chair. I didn't want to spook him further but I did want to reassure him. Gently I murmured in his mind. *Jim, take a deep breath. You're here now. Whatever you saw, it was just a dream.*

That's the problem, it wasn't, just a dream. It was very real.

"Your friend just had a vision in the flames," William observed, startling all of us with his insight.

"William has a sense of these things. He's been watching the campfire flames for a few years now himself," Susie explained. "It's okay. If you want to tell us what you saw. We won't blab."

"I'm not sure," face still deathly pale, he looked to Reilly.

I felt Reilly take the measure of the couple, then he nodded, "What do you know of fire visions, William?"

"I know they can be pretty scary. I've seen my own death in them, enough to know I must treasure what time I have on the planet."

Susie leaned into him, reassuring, "We have time yet William."

"None of us has as much time as we'd like. What did you see, young Jim?"

"I saw that if we continue on to Yulara, Ry will die."

Fuck, I hadn't expected that but should have known whatever it was was pretty scary, given Jim's terror.

In Reilly's world it was simple. "Then we turn around and go home. We're not risking Ry."

Jim agreed, "but what do we tell our bosses, including Border Force?"

"Hey!" I interrupted, "I'm sure I can hitch a ride back while you two continue on."

"No," Reilly stated emphatically. "We don't know that doing that won't bring about a different scenario where you're still at risk. I want you where I can protect you. Both of you," he looked to Jim.

"It may be that I can ask the fire spirits for advice," William offered. "They have a way of not intervening yet giving you what you need to get the most of any situation."

"What I want to know is how I die at Yulara?" curiosity had me in its grips.

Reilly shook his head, "That's not a question because you're not going."

But William was already lost in trance, staring at the flames, "There is a way," he announced in an unnaturally deep voice. "You have the means already to solve the problem so why do you ask?" Then the entity or whatever it was threw William out of the trance. "Do you know what it meant?"

"I might." I thought.

"No! Damn it no Ry. We already agreed." Reilly swore a few choice phases no-one could understand

"We agreed that the potential consequences for you and Jim weren't worth the risk. But for me. Well. What's going to happen to me that hasn't already. I've faced major trauma and upheaval in my life and come through. Psychologically I've got my shit together." Oops, "Not saying…"

Jim disagreed, "no, you're right Ry. I still have a whole barrow load of issues around other people accepting me as I am."

"And what? I'd argue I've got my shit together," Reilly grumbled. "I've faced a load of crap in my life. I've been beaten, framed, incarcerated. I'm not ashamed of what I did to survive. I'm fully aware I'm a grouch at times. And I'm not going to have a dark night of the soul worse than what I've already had."

"A loveable grouch," I nibbled his ear, ignoring the others present.

Reilly warmed. "So it's agreed, I'll go with you."

Ah hm, "Jim cleared his throat, wondering. "While you two bypass Yulara. How do I get there and on to Alice Springs? Don't for one minute think you're leaving me behind for my own safety."

"Easy," Elf declared. "You come with me. If that heap of mechanical shit of mine is ever going to get me to my girlfriend I could use an onboard engineer."

Reilly liked this, "Could you take Clyde with you? He might be extra protection."

I put the stop on that idea, "Clyde's pretty recognizable. If our enemies are on the watch for us Clyde would be a give-away. Elf and Jim need to go under the radar, for Jim's safety, let alone Elf's."

"We're assuming scumbag won't recognise me." Jim pointed out

"He won't by the time I've finished with you," Elf grinned.

"And you'll contact us as soon as we get to The Alice and let us know where you're both at." I knew Jim knew I meant telepathically but Elf and the nomads didn't have to know that.

"Very well," Reilly muttered, still not entirely sure. "I'll go and let the powers that be know what we're up to." He wandered off to our rig so he could either ring or telepathically contact Deman to discuss the whole thing on the quiet.

William and Susie appeared pleased to have helped, even if they didn't know much about our situation. Respectfully they didn't ask. But Susie had one more thing to offer. "Come with me for a moment Ry."

I felt her need to hide what she was about to do, though William rolled his eyes heavenward, so he probably knew.

I climbed, as invited, into the front cab of their Toyota.

Susie reached into the vehicle's glove box but paused. "I'm hesitant to do this as so many frown on Tarot but, well, what's your thoughts on it? I won't read the cards if you don't want me to. I don't believe in pushing."

"I have no thoughts one way or the other on it, Susie, but I was a journalist once so I'm always curious. Show me what you've got."

Like Jim, Susie sought acceptance. Having found it she retrieved her cards and placed the deck in the space between us. "I'm not big on using the cards for fortune telling," she explained. "My relationship with them is more one of seeking different perspectives on a situation. Insights I might not have easily chanced upon. Honestly, they're really a picture book that tells a tale called the Fool's Journey. They were made at a time when few were literate. Later on secret societies took the story and began to hide some of their wisdom in the pictures, wisdom they knew they'd get burned at the stake for if caught. But hey, they're only playing cards."

"So the ordinary deck of cards is related to them."

Susie nodded, "You could say they had a common ancestor. It's possible for some tarot readers to use an ordinary deck of cards but I prefer these. They have more colour, more symbols and the very pictures on them tell their meaning if you know how to look. William looks in the flames. I look into these."

I was intrigued now, "So tell me what you see."

"First you need to get your question clear in your mind. What do you want to know? Be very precise. Get a picture in your head if you can."

I thought for a moment. What did I urgently need to know? Then I felt with my gut and knew at once my priority. "What do I need to know to make sure that Reilly, Jim, me, Clyde, Horatio and Elf, if he's going to be with Jim, all survive our trip to The Alice."

Susie raised an eyebrow, "Horatio? Who's he?"

"The truck's spider. Best not to ask more than that."

Susie made a face but turned to study the pack of cards "I'm going to do a celtic cross spread then. It should give you the most insight." She handed me the cards, "Shuffle them while you keep your question in mind then hand the deck back to me."

I did as instructed and then she laid the cards out, face down. One in the centre, one crossed over it. Four surrounding it and then four off to the right side. Ten cards in all. Then she began to turn them over. "The first card relates to your question. You've drawn the Fool but that doesn't mean you're foolish, only that you are about to start a journey."

"Okay," that much was clear.

"And this card crossing it?"

"The Emperor, note the dog beside him. He's holding a sceptre of power. He represents control, worldly knowledge and fatherliness."

I frowned, "Is Reilly an obstacle?"

Susie nodded, "He might be, if that is who you see as the Emperor. His ways might not be the way to succeed in your aim of keeping everyone safe. Now the third card, above those two, represents a future possibility. The five of swords. It indicates a conflict, hostility or tension."

Probably with scumbag. That seemed obvious. "Go on."

"The Two of Swords. It suggests that you are hoping the problem will just go away but you are at a point where you need to choose your next step carefully. The fifth card is the World. It shows you the past you must let go of to achieve your goals. Essentially all the achievements, honours and triumphs you have identified with over time."

"I haven't had much choice in that. My past ended the day I got blown up and lost my arm."

"Then it might mean more than that. Maybe there's something of your past identity you're still holding on to. Free yourself of what you've come to believe about yourself. It may be limiting you."

"Hmm, freeing myself sounds good."

"The sixth card, Judgement, relates to the root of the situation. It indicates that you or someone you care about is being judged too harshly by others"

"Yeah, well scumbag definitely hates Reilly. That's definitely the root."

Susie gave me a moment to muse then considered the next four cards. "These four advise on your course of action. The seventh card shows where you're currently at yourself, resilience, courage, perseverance and fighting through tough times. The eighth card shows your surroundings and the expectations of those around you. It suggests you might be struggling under the weight of expectations of others. Trying to be all things to all people. It reminds you to shed that load, here shown as a stack of wands, and just be true to yourself."

I pursed my lips. "Okay, perhaps I do try a bit too much to stay on the right side of Reilly and a certain protective spirit," Aranya. "It's not just the people in my life. I've been trying to prove my worth since I lost my arm."

"Well the cure for that is trusting yourself and the abilities you now have. Moving on, the Page of Wands is in the position that represents your current mental state. An excellent card as it shows good fortune arising from your current mental state, drawing on your courage, enthusiasm and talents. Again, trust yourself." Finally we have the tenth card, the outcome."

I held my breath.

"The King of Cups. Kindness, compassion and wisdom will achieve the outcome you seek. Keep a rein on your emotions. Don't be goaded. Stay in your heart space."

"Could the King of Cups be a person, like the Emperor being Reilly?"

"Jim?" Susie guessed.

"Yeah," that's what I thought but I had no idea how Jim would play into our goal of keeping everyone safe if we were hiding him with Elf.

"Well, that's all they're telling me today." Susie picked up the cards and put them away.

"Actually, that has given me a broader perspective on the situation. Thank you so much. I'll keep all that in mind."

Susie was pleased, "My pleasure. But I feel the frowning eyes of your emperor boring into me. Go, but remember the card's advice, you don't always have to try to please everyone."

It was good advice. Now I just needed to work out how I was going to apply it.

15

Reilly was leaning against our rig. "So I'm an obstacle am I?"

Fuck. "Can it Reilly. Are you complaining about me comparing you with the Emperor in the tarot deck? Do you deny that you're protective, strategic and like control. The card even showed Clyde at your feet."

"Hmph. More likely Clyde would be at Jim's feet, not mine. They've formed quite a bond."

"I think Clyde's formed a bond with all of us, and you're changing the topic."

"Me being an obstacle. I wasn't overly fond of the idea."

"It could just be the type of approach you'd naturally use. It's telling us to think outside your normal responses to potential conflict."

"Taking him out, ya mean."

"Which wouldn't earn you any points with Border Force or our police friends in the Seychelles. Don't blot your record because of Frederick James Leary."

Reilly sighed heavily. "Then what do ya suggest? Ya who drew the Fool's card," he got that one in for good measure.

"A Fool who came up elsewhere in the reading as resilient and enthusiastic."

"Starry eyed idealist, more like it," Reilly muttered. "So, I'm still coming with ya," this time there was a query in his voice.

"I can't see a reason why not."

"It leaves the question though, how do we get to Elf and Jim if they get into any trouble."

"I have no idea."

"Hmm, I don't like unknowns."

"Neither does the Emperor," I reminded him. "He would want everything controlled, regulated and protected. That's not always possible and seemingly, in this case, not desirable. We have to trust Jim and Elf to look out for themselves."

"We don't even know what Elf's strengths and weaknesses are," and that worried Reilly.

"You took his measure Reilly. That's something you seem to have gotten good at since our first test run."

"It's not exactly readin' minds or knowin' someone's deepest and darkest secrets, is it now?" He'd grown used to the luxury of knowing where he stood with me and Jim.

I shrugged my shoulders. "It's a start. You're just going to have to trust your intuition with Elf. I know you want more data, more facts but that's all we have."

Reilly sighed heavily again. "Okay. Well I for one have had enough of this day. Let's have supper and go to bed."

That brightened my mood, "As in bed to sleep or bed for…?"

Jim wandered over, "Did someone call?" He asked with a twinkle in his eyes and a smug look on his face.

Reilly shook his head, amazed, "youse two are insatiable."

"And your problem is?" I asked, knowing he had none.

"You like control, Reilly," Jim pointed out what was well known to all of us but it was his lead into his next suggestion. "Fancy learning the fine art of kinbaku?"

Reilly frowned slightly, analysing the images in Jim's head. "Ya mean, tie her up. Isn't that shibari?"

"Technically hojojutsu is the art of tying up prisoners so they can't escape their bonds and as a means of torture, constraining them in humiliating and uncomfortable positions. Shibari is tying someone up, for artistic purposes. A naked erotic display. The beauty of it resides in both the subject and the shapes created with the rope that accentuate and draw the eye to that beauty. Kinbaku is more an interaction between the person doing the tying and the one being tied. It's intimate, intense, precise. The rope master, or rigger, must feel just how much tension to apply so as not to injure their subject yet bridge that fine line between comfort and discomfort. The subject must be at peace with being temporarily constrained in his or her choices and options. It's the interaction of the subject, the rigger and the rope that brings pleasure to the participants. But the reality is that in the world of kink there is often little boundary between all three styles. It's more a fusion that depends on the limits of the particular subject and what brings them pleasure. The question is would you like to explore what gives our subject pleasure? Would you let me mentor you?"

"I'd get to actually tie her up, not just watch?" his look was intense now, glancing over towards me, heat searing his eyes.

"What do you think Ry?" Jim asked me. "You and I've explored a little bit of the pleasures of constraint. This would take it to the next step."

I was wet and hot just thinking about it, "Hell yeah." And it might help to vent some of Reilly's control issues.

"I heard that thought," Reilly growled.

"Do you want me to think a lie?" I asked. "Wouldn't you enjoy being in control of me, however briefly?"

Reilly's eyes gleamed mischief, "When ya say it like that. Yeah. And no I don't want either of ya trying to think lies to placate me. You're right. I enjoy having control, in most things. It frustrates me when I haven't got it." He turned to Jim, "Okay, I'll be yer apprentice. I doubt I'll enjoy taking instruction but if we're doing this I want Ry safe."

"As do I," Jim agreed. "Okay I'll get my ropes."

"You brought some bondage rope on this trip?" I asked in wonder.

Jim waggled his eyebrows, "You just never know."

As we watched Jim go to retrieve his gear I whispered to Reilly, "That man has depths we've yet to fully explore."

Reilly stared after Jim's back, "You don't say."

Fast forward and I was standing in the middle of our mobile home. The door was locked, blinds pulled down and the table folded away. Clyde had, grudgingly, been tied up outside and told to guard. We were on our own.

Jim unpacked his new rope, running it methodically through his hands, looking for snags or catches that might cut or abrade my skin. He passed the rope he'd just checked to Reilly, "You can check too, for practice. Anything that might hurt her skin."

Reilly, as always, took his new task seriously. Stopping to check with Jim if he wasn't sure. "So, how basic are we startin'?"

"Quite basic," Jim acknowledged, "but with those basics you can do quite a bit. We'll start with TK or Takate Kote. It translates into English as a Box Tie. It's one of the most widely used knots in Shibari. But before we start there are three essentials. You need safety scissors to get Ry out of her knots quicker than untying them, in case she's in discomfort, physical or mental." He placed his scissors on the nearby bed, within easy reach. "Find out if she needs a loo stop, as it's a pity to have to stop a session part way through. And finally we have to check Ry's natural range of movement. We don't want to put her into unnatural positions that might cause either great pain or musclo spasm. Ry, are you good to go?"

"Ready and salivating in anticipation."

Jim laughed, "Well then. Do you have a safe word if we take you where you don't want to go?"

"Just the normal, pink for uneasy or uncomfortable and red for cease and desist now."

"Cool." He took me at my word that I was ready. "Remove your clothes," leaving me to follow that instruction he turned to Reilly to explain. "This can be done with the subject partially clothed but for our purposes naked is better."

"Agreed", I felt the weight of Reilly's word boring into me.

Jim placed a palm on me, making an intimate connection. "Give me you right hand Ry," he commanded and I was instantly on alert. We were on.

Jim firmly grasped my wrist and wrapped the rope around twice. Then he placed a finger under the rope to ensure there was space.

"To check that the rope won't cut off her circulation," Reilly assumed.

"Exactly."

With slow and steady purpose he took my arm behind me. "Normally we would then tie both hands together but for Ry," because of my missing arm, "we'll wrap the rope twice around her waist like this. Then tie it off in a knot behind her." He continued on, proceeding to construct what he called a chest harness that accentuated my boobs. I felt embraced by the rope. It was in some ways like being dressed up to show off my best assets. Not that my boobs were big, quite the contrary. But with the rope I felt like they were being shown off to best effect.

Jim continued his instruction. "You can use a harness like this for a partial suspension."

"Interestin'," Reilly mused.

"Now I'll undo it and you try."

"Aw," I complained, though I knew it wasn't allowed.

Jim took me firmly by my hair and turned my face to him, "Are you trying to take control, sub?"

"No sir, sorry sir."

"I don't want to hear anything from you except moans of pleasure or a safe word if you need. Is that understood?"

"Yes sir." Though I was unsure how we'd get to moans of pleasure if he kept untying me.

"Now, where were we?" Jim's nimble fingers had already undone the harness and he was passing the rope to Reilly.

I felt Reilly's hands on me, large, rough and calloused. So different from the smooth and gentle touch of Jim's long and slender fingers. Just like the men themselves. One rough, one smooth. And I was the lucky one who didn't have to make a choice between them. Where Jim's kinbaku had been firm but gentle, almost respectful as well as intimate, Reilly's touch was like that of a pirate's and I was his prisoner. There was a light fear factor in laying myself at his mercy.

Jim chuckled at my thoughts, "I've obviously been going too easy on you girl." He inspected Reilly's work and nodded, pleased. "Excellent. You've got the hang of it. So connect with my mind. See what I want to do."

I, too, saw in Jim's mind. An intricate hip harness. "We'll keep the chest harness but add this." He passed Reilly more rope. "While you see into my mind I want you to feel into hers. Let her pleasure and desires guide you. Yes, like that. Open your heart to hers."

My rope clothing was like an intimate hug. I felt loved.

Reilly stood back and admired his handy work, "Very satisfying. He glanced at the mobile home's roof."

Jim chuckled, "Yeah, I thought of that too. It would be nice to try a little suspension but I think we'd have to reinforce the ceiling. I'm not sure what Dan's transport company might say."

"Hmm, he shares his woman with another. I'll ask. I might be able to find a bit of steel in Alice Springs to do the job."

I coughed to get their attention, risking a reprimand.

Jim raised an eyebrow. A look passed between him and Reilly, whereupon Reilly swooped me up in his arms and carried me to the bed. I wondered who I'd get where today. It was always a mystery to me how they decided. But Reilly had already made up his mind and was propping himself up against the bedhead. "On your knees wench."

Wench indeed! The feminist in me was duly horrified though secretly I liked the pretend roleplay. I knew his mind and knew he was worshipping, not demeaning me. I found a space between his spread legs. He was waiting. So was his penis, eager and erect. I licked the insides of my mouth and slid it down over his rigid flesh.

While Reilly moaned in contentment Jim nestled behind me, "Spread your knees wider girl, yes like that." The next thing I knew he'd put a pillow between my legs then he was on his back, head under me, his tongue finding places I hadn't been prepared for."

Reilly growled, "Concentrate on yer work wench. Or do I need to punish ya?"

Heat flooded my core at the thought, my imagination launching into a wild fantasy about what he might do to punish me. Later! I did my best to ignore Jim's ministrations and shifted my mind to my mouth rather than my cunt. Or at least I tried to. There was a war going on inside me and the guys knew it. They were revelling in my torment. I realised, in that moment, that they were so in my mind they were waiting to ride my orgasm. Well two, sorry three, could play that game. I fought off my orgasm as long as humanly possible but then my mind perceived they were near their own edge. I danced us all, teetering on that cliff as long as I could and then I threw us over. We cried out together. It was only after, in a moment's embarrassment, I wondered if the whole campground had heard us.

"And probably hi-fived us," Jim reassured as he extracted himself then snuggled down beside us. For once, none of us worried about keeping the space between Jim and Reilly. I checked in their minds but I only found contentment.

"Relax Ry," Reilly grumbled, "I trust him."

And that made Jim's smile light up our world.

16

I woke in the early hours in the morning, entirely naked under the sheets. How anyone had removed my ropes without waking me was beyond me.

"Because ya were out like a stone," Reilly announced. "Now, up and at 'em. We're leavin' Jim here to travel with Elf, then we're off."

Jim couldn't possibly be the man standing beside him, in a slouch hat, check shirt, distressed denim jeans, an RM Williams buckled belt and workmen's leather pull on boots. But then I looked at the hands. Dead give away.

Reilly noticed then too, "She's right. Those hands are those of an artist or musician, not a workman. Hold that thought," and he raced out of our mobile home to fetch something.

"Who dressed you I wondered?" I hadn't noticed any outfitters in the area.

"Did a deal with William. He's about my size and since the clothes are second hand they look more the part."

"They sure do. I would have picked you for a jackaroo, um station hand."

"Except for the hands", he mused. "At least I've acquired a little bit of a tan in the last few days on the road."

Reilly was back. With a jar of something that looked nasty. He passed it to Jim who eyed it with no small horror.

"You want me to put what on my hands?"

"Don't look like that. It's just a bit of harmless axle grease. I mixed in a bit of diesel for good measure. Rub that in. Then I've got a bar of workman's soap I borrowed from the men's amenity block. Together that should give the right aroma."

Jim groaned but followed instruction. He glanced at me with vengeance in his eyes, "This is your fault."

"If I hadn't noticed, someone else would have. You need to be believable to stay safe. Now, that accent. It's going to attract attention."

"What about my accent? It's a perfectly good West Coast American accent. Couldn't I have just landed in the country?"

I shook my head, "Not if you've been working on cattle stations for a bit. Try almost dropping the Gs in your 'ings'."

"What, like Reilly does?"

"What tha' hell da ya mean? I don't go droppin' any Gs." Reilly grumbled.

Jim and I both rolled our eyes.

"Actually more nasal than Reilly does. Say that last n as if it was more in your nose. There should be just a hint that you're about to say the 'g' but then you don't."

Jim tried. "I'm just passin' through."

"Yeah, that'll do. Just enough to sound like you've been here long enough to pick up some of the local speech patterns. Now whatever you do, don't call aluminium 'al-LOO-min-um'. It's 'Al-you-MIN-ee-um'. And refuse goes in the rubbish not the trash."

"It does?"

"Aha, did you just hear that upward inflection at the end of your question. Try to add a little bit of that at the end of all your sentences. But keep it subtle. We don't need you sounding like a bogan."

"A what?"

"Uneducated."

"Oh."

"Importantly, if a word ends in an 'r', drop it."

"And do what?"

"Say a very shortened 'a' instead of 'er'."

"So water becomes 'worta'?"

"Right. Now say something."

"Mary had a little lamb…"

"No, no, no. That won't do. That 'little's all wrong. It needs just the slightest touch of an oi instead of the i."

He gave it another go.

"It'll have to do, if anyone asks just say you haven't been out here that long."

"Out here? As in the vast outback?"

"Exactly."

Reilly smirked, having enjoyed the scene all too much. "Well, if you two are finished."

"Hell, get me out of here before she has me sounding like some comic strip Hollywood actor."

"Actually I think she's got you sounding a bit like her."

Jim smiled at that, "Oh, well that's not so bad."

Elf banged on the side of our accommodation. "Ready?"

Jim bruised my lips with a kiss then gave Reilly a manly hug.

"Just don't come to any harm," Reilly growled. "It's no point saving Ry if we lose you. Hmm, that didn't come out right."

Jim, wisely, said nothing to that, just smiled and threw his duffle bag over his shoulder. "I'll be seeing you both in The Alice." With that he left.

Reluctantly we watched as Elf's vehicle took our best friend away, a cloud of dust following in their wake.

"We'd better feed the critters before we go." My thought being, particularly, to check on Horatio.

"Good thinking. I'll feed Clyde and get the engine warmed up."

A woof from outside showed Clyde had heard.

All checks and preparation done, Reilly sat down in the driver's seat while I entered our destination coordinates into the computer interface. While I checked the scanner for low flying aircraft activity or other obstacles Reilly made a quick call to base.

"We good to go?" he asked when he'd finished his call.

"Just about." I reached over and planted a kiss on his mouth that left us both gasping for breath as I pulled away. "Now I'm ready." I put on my seatbelt for good measure. Not that it would be of any use in the other dimensions but for my physical body, it might keep me safe. Losing one arm had made me more safety conscious, even if it hadn't slowed me down any. I didn't need more challenges than I already had.

Reilly hit the go button and launched us all onto the rainbow track.

17

Jim eyed the lolly wrappers and other detritus on the front passenger's floor. The whole interior of the car needed a makeover but it wasn't his car. "So we'll stopover in Yulara."

"Sure thing. Got family there I've been meaning to catch up with."

"Should we ring them or something, you know, warn them we're coming."

"Hell no, they'd think I'd gone all citified on them. They'll be happy to see me. There'll be floor space for us there somewhere."

Which was exactly what Jim was worried about given the state of the car floor. He'd just have to rough it. "Ry says my American accent is a draw card for the curious. She's given me a few pointers. Would you be offended if I tried to mimic some of your way of saying things?"

"Good grief, no, I'd be honoured. Where do we start?"

"How about telling one of the tales of your people. One that outsiders like me are allowed to hear. Just stop occasionally to allow me to repeat."

"Hey, I've got myself my own personal student. Cool! Wait til I tell the others about this."

Distracted by their endeavours the hours and the hundred of kilometres soon passed, with only the briefest of breaks to pour spare fuel in the tank, to stretch the legs, deal with bodily needs and attempt not to swallow any of the flies that amassed around them every time they got out of the car.

"I can see a sign for Yulara up ahead," Jim noted.

In timely fashion the car let out a warning 'bing' to alert them to their diminishing fuel supply.

"Sounds like we could all do with a stop before I head out to my uncle's place. There's a roadhouse up ahead. We'll stop there."

"Is that an emu farm?" Jim gaped. He'd never seen so many emu in one place.

"Bit of a tourist attraction around here," Elf acknowledged. "The kids love seeing them. Just have to keep them from sticking their little fingers through the wire."

"Emus bite?" Jim wondered at that.

"Vicious as. Haven't got an ounce of politeness or table manners in them. But they're amazing creatures. When one turns its head and looks you in the eyes, well you know you've been seen. And while they're looking they're checking you out for any food they might steal off of you."

"I guess they're just small feathered dinosaurs afterall."

Elf laughed nervously, "Yeah, well, I wouldn't want to meet a T-Rex sized one."

"Is there any WiFi at the roadhouse? I'm getting worried as I haven't heard from my friends yet." Not that he'd expected even a phone call on the road as there was only satellite coverage out there. But he had expected to hear their thoughts by now, their trip time being, supposedly, much much shorter.

"Friends, ha! Say it like it is Jim, your woman and your man."

"No you've got it wrong Elf. Yes Ry's my woman but Reilly's Ry's other man. He's my best friend though."

"Whatever you want to call it. I've seen the way he watches both of you. You're his. Maybe you two keep your distance but it don't change what's there between you."

Jim was starting to feel uncomfortable with the direction of the conversation. Time for a change. "Go fill the car, Elf. I'll go in and pay as soon as you've finished."

Elf noticed the change of topic but only smirked, "Okay Jim, I appreciate it. I'll wash the windscreen while you're in there. Get me a Coke?"

"Sure thing."

As soon as he walked through the door of the roadhouse he felt trouble. It wasn't the place as such. The staff seemed friendly enough. He found a couple of cold drinks in the fridge and then took them to the counter. "These and the fuel on the pump out there." He bit his tongue from saying ma'am as Elf had furthered his training in Aussie-speak and had told him it would give him away as American for sure.

The attendant, sun tanned and probably in her forties, smiled, "You with Elf then?"

"Er, yeah." He had no wish to outline too many details as he knew somewhere in the roadhouse someone was listening, such was the itch down his spine.

"Well you're a shy one aren't you? Where're you from, handsome?"

Obviously he was new in town and therefore the potential source of news or newsworthy in himself. "Nowhere in particular. I live on the road. Get work where I can."

"Well you'll get plenty around here if you want. Hard to get skilled hands in these parts."

"Actually, Elf and I have business elsewhere. He's headed to his girlfriend and just giving me a lift."

"Well, if you come back this way and you're after work, call in here and ask for Miranda, that's me. Now, paying by card or cash?"

"Card," he passed it over the reader until it duly binged.

Miranda appeared happy, "Yeah, that's gone through."

Jim couldn't help himself, even if it might give him away as someone more than he looked, "Been having problems?"

"Drops out occasionally. Usually at the most inconvenient times. Like when I have a queue at the counter."

"You on wireless, fixed or satellite internet?"

"Satellite. Have to be out here."

"Has it always played up or only recently?" Jim started diagnosing the possible problems in his head.

"Recently?"

"Was there a storm or maybe someone was up on the roof and bumped something?"

"Well now," Miranda looked at him hopefully, "we did have one hell of a sand storm a few weeks back."

"Hmm," Jim chewed on that. Could a particularly strong gust of wind have moved the antenna or damaged its connection to the roof? Could sand particles have gotten into the connections somehow? "Have you got a ladder? Perhaps I could have a look. If I don't see anything obvious I won't touch anything."

"I'll get Jason to mind the counter. Just a minute." Miranda disappeared before he could think more about the threat he was putting himself in, and maybe Elf and Miranda. That itch in his back was still there. Maybe someone in the eatery.

Elf came in and sidled up to him, "Problem?"

Jim passed him the coke and ripped open his for a drink while they waited for Miranda. "Just going to have a look at Miranda's internet antenna."

"Wow, you're on first name terms with Miranda already. She must like you."

Jim rolled his eyes. "It's not like that. Just helping her out. But that's not the main problem. I've got an itch."

Elf frowned, not knowing what to make of that, "You've got an itch?"

"As in I sense something. Why don't you take your drink over to the eatery area and scout out who's there? Don't engage anyone, just make out as if you're resting at one of the tables while you finish your drink. I'll wait here for Miranda."

"Spy duty, cool."

"Shush, Elf, keep it down."

Elf grinned and went off with his drink, on a mission, just as Miranda returned with her offsider in tow. "Did I just see Elf here?"

Jim nodded. "He's just finishing his drink. He'll catch up with us in a minute."

"Excellent, he can take some of yesterday's leftover muffins to his aunt. She's got one hungry horde of children."

Jim's mind flicked back to his vision of their accommodation for the night. First, camped on the floor, now adding a vision of being trampled in the rush. He pushed it from his mind. "Lead the way."

The last storm had indeed loosened the brackets holding the satellite dish to the roof. Given the state of the roof Jim wasn't sure any quick fix he could do would last long but he could tighten a few screws. He'd brought up his computer tablet with him and used that to check the position of the satellite the dish was pointed to. He made a few adjustments then drilled some extra screws into place. "Coming down."

No answer. That itch was back. He looked over the edge of the roof and saw Elf and Miranda, side by side, kneeling on the ground, their hands behind their heads. The reason being the man with the gun trained on them. There was nothing for it. He couldn't stay on the roof and leave his friends to their fate but he could do one thing. Surreptitiously he turned the volume down on his phone and called emergency. He whispered to them the when, where and how of the situation then hung up. Better still he left his phone on the roof so that Scumbag, as Ry not so affectionately called Fred Leary, wouldn't check to see the last call he made.

Jim grabbed his tool box to make it look like he had everything and then he clambered down. When he reached the ground he carefully and slowly lowered his tool box and then spread his hands wide to show he had no weapons. He couldn't read auras with the same clarity as Ry but he could see enough to know the man was a grenade with a loose pin. He said nothing and waited for the man to make his move, not once letting his eyes off of him.

"Nothing to say?" Leary seemed perplexed by Jim's silence.

"Looks like you've got us at a disadvantage. I thought you might be the one making demands." Jim gave his all, delivering his best over the top Aussie accent. This man wouldn't understand subtle anyway.

Leary frowned, "You can start by telling me where Reilly is?"

"Crickey mate, ya've got me at a disadvantage. Is this Reilly fella a pal of yours? If he's gone missing we might be able to help to find him? Dangerous getting lost hereabouts."

"Don't go playing the idiot with me Jim Northey, electro technical officer for the Merkwood II that runs out of Perth. Has to be you or why would you be on the roof fixing a satellite dish?"

Hell man, it doesn't take brains to put a few screws in the roof to hold things together. I'm just a jackaroo, Mike Sanderson's the name."

"Jacka what? Never mind. Turn around."

"Please don't shoot me, mate, I've a wife and a baby girl who depend on me," Jim played the sob card.

Leary patted him down, checking his pockets, "Where's your phone?"

"In Elf's car. I'd be happy to get it for you. Really, anything you want mate. Just don't hurt us."

"Gah, ya sound like a coward. I hate cowards. What's in that toolbox? Open it?"

Jim opened it and stepped back knowing the game was up. If Leary knew anything about electronics he was sunk.

"And just why the hell do you have a multimeter Mr Sanderson?" Leary asked with no small amount of suspicion.

"For checking fuses and flat batteries. Comes in handy. Geez mate, you going to kill a guy just because he's got a damn multimeter."

Leary snarled, "I said nothing about killing, but a few hostages, yeah that suits me fine. Now why don't you all get up very carefully and we'll walk very casually to your car. We'll check your phone and if there's no one named Reilly on it I'll let you all go, how about that? But if you've been spinning me a yarn I'll shoot your friends here.

Elf paled but Miranda looked angry as all hell. We all started walking to the parking lot but the sudden sound of a police siren changed our circumstances in an instant.

Momentarily distracted, Leary didn't see Miranda's leg sweep. With a precision any martial artist would be proud of, she had him on the ground, his arm in an awkward and painful position that forced him to drop the gun which Elf quickly kicked out of the way.

"Bitch," Leary screeched.

"No one comes into my roadhouse and threatens my customers or my employees." She wrenched his wrist around further, causing him to howl in pain.

The cops strode up, amused. "Didn't need us I see?"

"Yeah, well I'm just glad Jason in the shop must have caught us on the security camera."

Jim glanced around but he was sure there was no security camera pointing in their direction. All credit to Miranda, she'd figured he'd made the call but was keeping him out of it.

One of the cops yanked Leary's other hand around putting both in cuffs. Relieved of her duty Miranda got up and brushed herself down. If she noticed the awe and admiration in Elf's eyes she didn't let on. "Do you need me for paperwork or can I get back to the counter Steve?" she asked the cop.

"Go have a cold one on me. We'll come back later once we have this one in the hold."

"Much appreciated." Then she looked at Jim and winked, "Well what are you standing around for Mike. Get back to work. And Elf, go put that can of yours in the bin."

"Sure thing Mir," Elf beamed.

Miranda groaned, not being entirely fond of having her name shortened.

Jim watched the cops go, just to make sure Leary didn't bolt, then he went back up the ladder to fetch his phone. With that little scene over he went back to worrying about Reilly and Ry. He couldn't touch them with his mind.

When he came back into the roadhouse he found Elf and Miranda sitting in the eatery, drinking. Miranda passed him a small squat brown bottle she called a stubbie, that was encased in a rubber sleeve called a stubbie holder.

Jim accepted the stubbie, studying the label. A beer, but not his usual. Something called Centralian Ale. He took a sip, not bad. Hell anything tasted good after that little debacle. Apologies were in order. "Sorry Elf. If I hadn't offered to help Miranda I wouldn't have alerted Leary to us."

"Mate, if you hadn't helped Miranda when you could I would have been disappointed in you. By the way, I loved your impersonation of the crocodile man."

Jim laughed. "Well, I figured he wouldn't tell one accent from another so I thought I'd just go all out."

"Bloody fool," Miranda swore without malice. "If that bastard didn't have me and Elf on our knees at the time I would have cracked up laughing. It was you who called the police wasn't it?"

Jim nodded. "Had my phone with me on the roof."

"So is someone going to introduce me?" Miranda asked casually.

Jim apologised again, "I'm awfully sorry, Jim Northey. And I am indeed an electro-technical officer onboard the ship Merkwood II, as Scumbag accused."

"Scumbag?" Miranda queried with a smirk.

"It's what my girlfriend calls Frederick James Leary, arms dealer, drug trafficker, human slave trafficker, sometime assassin and whatever else nasty you want to think up. But it's not him we're truly after. We want the links to further up the train."

"Sounds like Scumbag's a really good name for him. Also sounds like you're on a bit of a mission," Miranda noted, putting two and two together. "So where's this girl of yours?"

"I wish I knew," Jim answered, worried. "I've tried phoning her and Reilly but no answer."

"You don't think Scumbag's got others out looking for them," Elf asked, now worried as well.

"Possible but I don't think that's it. I have a feeling it's something to do with the prototype engine they were giving a test drive. They were supposed to do the test after we left this morning, after the rest of the campers had left for the day. It should have only taken a few moments."

Miranda decided it might be best not to ask about missions or prototype engines, sensing she was only being included in the conversation because of their recent shared ordeal. "I could ask Steve to keep an eye out for their vehicle."

"Couldn't hurt but they could be anywhere between Warakurna and Alice Springs." Forlornly Jim took another sip of his beer.

"How could they be further than here if they left after you?" Miranda frowned, curiosity starting to get the better of her.

"I'm not authorised to tell you, sorry Miranda". Jim apologised for the inevitable secrecy.

Miranda leaned back in her chair. "Well, I must say this has been a most interesting day. And you Elf, how'd you get messed up in all this?"

"Jim kindly offered to keep my car going so I can get to Alice Springs to meet up with my girlfriend."

"Hmph," Miranda clearly didn't like that idea. "Well I hope she appreciates the trouble you've gone to to visit her." With that she got up and strode back to her work, clearly not happy.

"I think she's got a soft spot for you Elf," Jim noted.

"What?" Elf choked on his drink.

Jim shook his head and laughed, "You must be blind. Drink up. Let's go and visit your people. The day's getting on." And he wanted to get somewhere he could try a mind to mind hook up.

211

18

Streams of light, all the colours of the rainbow, engulfed us. We were swimming in a river of energy. Were we here physically or just astrally? I was confused. Reilly's eyes shone with a healthy brightness that I'd never seen in the so-called real world.

Horatio was entertaining himself, jumping between the different strands of light.

Clyde stayed put, as if guarding us, which I guessed he was.

"Reilly," I queried, still mesmerised by the light, "Do you get a sense that these different strands go to different places and times?"

Reilly studied the patterns, some more fractal, some organised, some down right chaotic. "They're like a weave."

"Literally the fabric of space time," I posited. Something caught my eye. Embedded in the light were scenes of different people's as well different beings' lives. "Look there, that's you isn't it?"

Reilly peered in the direction I pointed and moved … well less of a movement and more of a shift of focus that brought him into connection with what I had seen. He followed the strand back. "Look, there's m' mother. And there's Fogal, entering the Pig and Whistle where they're fated to meet."

"Is it fate though?"

Reilly frowned, "Are ya thinkin' what I'm thinkin'?"

"Reilly," I gasped. "We can't tamper with what's been?"

"Come on Ry, It's not like I'm tryin' to stop World War Three. Just one little change."

"Your Mum going back to the Isle of Man with Fogal? You growing up with a fisherman for a father? How do we know that's for the best? Maybe in a future life her experience now is important to what she evolves into? Aranya warned us against travelling back in time."

"I'm sorry but I can't believe whatever made this space-time fabric meant for me and my Mum to have it so hard. Or maybe it just doesn't care. It just spurts out all this creative energy and stuff happens at random."

"You think there's no purpose to it all?"

"D' ya?" he challenged.

I sighed. "Let's ask?"

"Do ya think yer protective goddess can hear ya here?"

"I don't know. Someone might."

"How do we call them?"

Intuitively I knew. "We put the question clearly in our minds and then open our hearts."

As if in answer we were suddenly no longer in the light stream but standing on the road outside the Pig and Whistle. Horatio shuffled around in my top pocket, where he'd somehow ended up. He seemed to find a comfortable position and settled. Clyde stood loyally at Reilly's side.

"I wonder if they let dogs inside?"

"Let's find out?" Reilly pushed the door of the tavern open and the rest of us followed. It was a dimly lit interior, filled with smoke which surprised me but then I remembered we'd gone back in time, back before antismoking campaigns and laws.

We spied Fogal at his table. The waitress, Reilly's Mum, was flirting with him.

"What do we do?" I wondered.

"We wait. Even if it takes all night. Fancy a drink?"

"Do they have something other than Guinness?"

"Philistine," Reilly laughed. He waved a different waitress over. I felt his reluctance to call his own, future, mother over. "A pint of your best and a lemon, lime and bitters for the lady."

"Do we even have money for this?" I worried as the waitress walked away with our orders.

Reilly put some of his change on the table. "I felt it in my pockets, back out on the street."

I examined one of the coins. "Check it out, it's even the right year."

19

Elf's mob, as he called them, was large and extended. Most of them seemed to be either living in his Uncle Monaro's large rambling turn of the century homestead or on nearby properties. Nearly all of them had come over to catch up with Elf and to take a look at the stranger who'd come in with him. Children ran races, barefoot, up and down the length of the corridor, yelling and giggling. Some of the younger children had made a cubby house under the dining table, hiding under the oversized tablecloth, playing contentedly with their lego and plastic cars. Elf's Aunt Kirra was busy in the kitchen, rustling up a small feast, with the help of some distant cousins, Yindi and Maali. Somewhere out on the shady wide verandah Elf's cousin Birrani strummed a familiar sounding country music tune on his guitar.

Elf's cousin Jiemba passed Jim a cold beer. "You get used to it."

He'd obviously recognised the overwhelmed look on the guest's face. "Actually, I think I kind of like it. There's a feeling of family and togetherness here. My own upbringing was dry, baren and regimented compared to this."

"Which is why you travelled to the other side of the ocean," Jiemba guessed.

"I do love the freedom of the sea. And being my own boss. I only have the Captain to answer to, though occasionally the other officers pass on orders."

From within his weather worn face Uncle Monaro's alert eyes considered Jim, seeing things that others couldn't. There was a deep kind of knowledge there but Jim couldn't penetrate his thoughts. All he could say was that the man seemed inscrutable.

"You worry for your friends," Monaro said after a moment of all consuming silence.

"They should have reached their destination hours ago. At the very least I should have heard from them. I don't get any answer when I try their phones."

"Or from their minds," Uncle Monaro added, his face still unreadable. "Where they are you have to use something other than your mind. Let your heart become like an open cup, empty and ready to receive. You cannot learn or gain wisdom if you're full." He passed Jim a tray of nibbles, "Eat! It will ground you. Your connection to the earth is weak."

Jim felt judged and found wanting but listened to the old man's advice. "Can you show me how to be this empty cup? How to deepen my connection with the earth?"

"No," he said succinctly. "It's not something that can be shown, only done. You must do. You have it in you. I have seen. Do it now!"

Jim had thought to find a quiet place to try but the old man was determined and seemed to have some faith in him after all. He'd best damn well try.

"Not with effort," the old man instructed. "Just do. Don't be inside your head. Don't turn within yourself. Just open. Find the openness," he urged.

"So, close my eyes?" Jim wondered if the man wasn't some sci fi spiritual master in disguise but then maybe he'd watched those movies a few too many times.

"No, no closing your eyes or you will go into your imagination and that won't work. Just soften your gaze. Don't focus on any one thing in particular but be aware, of everything. Open to that."

Suddenly Jim was aware of more than the room. He heard the chatter of the women in the kitchen, the play of the children, Jiemba sipping his beer as he watched proceedings. A flock of cockatoos flew over the house, he just knew. A small lizard watched the men from the window sill. Overhead the fan turned, stirring the air into pleasing currents of cooling air. He felt the pulse of the earth beneath his feet. It was alive. The land was alive. Everything was alive and everything was energy, vibrating in a cacophony of frequencies that made music, cosmic music. And there they were, Reilly and Ry, Clyde and Horatio, watched over by various guardian spirits. He drew back, knowing they were safe.

"And?" Uncle Monaro, quizzed, knowing Jim had succeeded but wanting to hear the tale.

"They're fine. I just need to be patient. They're busy."

"Well then," Jiemba slapped Jim on the back, "drink up, there's more cold ones in the fridge."

Jim relaxed and thought, *yeah, what the hell.* Tomorrow would be another day.

20

The barman called time but we explained we were waiting for Fogal Quayle, who'd long since disappeared upstairs with the young waitress in tow.

The barman chuckled. "He could be a while."

Fortunately for us he assumed we were crew from Fogal's fishing boat and with a storm raging outside he decided against evicting us. Instead he threw us a couple of blankets. "I've got no spare rooms for you but if you're willing to sleep in those chairs good luck to you. I'll have to turn out the lights though or the cops will come."

"We'll be fine," Reilly asserted. "But could we trouble you for a bowl of water for our dog?"

"Hmm," was all he said. But he went to the kitchens and came back with a plastic bowl and a few scraps. "If he needs to do his business take him out the back, via the fire exit but make sure you prop the door open if you do as once closed it only opens from the inside." He frowned, considering us both, "I'm trusting you two not to raid the bar or the till."

"You'll have no worries with us," I put a good word in for us both, giving my sweetest, most innocent smile but trying not to overdo it.

"Make sure it, or I'll be billing Fogal and he can take it out of your hides." Having said his piece he left us to it.

Reilly and I pushed our chairs together, it was as close as we could get to each other but we made the best of it, leaning into each other. I snuggled as best as I could against his shoulder. "Have you thought yet how you're going to convince Fogal and your Mum? What was your Mum's name anyway?"

"Mum, though possibly it might be Muire. Honestly, it wasn't the done thing to call her anything other than Mum."

"You don't know your mother's name?"

"I don't think I ever heard her husband call her anything other than bitch or other expletives I won't repeat."

"But she must have had friends come around."

"Uh, uh, he didn't allow that. She was his property and he wanted her all to himself, as his personal slave and punching bag."

"Bloody hell!" I was appalled.

"You could say that. And no, I don't know what we're going to say. Go to sleep. I'll keep watch for them."

"Wake me when you want a break," though I knew he wouldn't. Not because he didn't trust me but because he saw it as his job. I wasn't going to argue. I snuggled and slept.

Towards dawn, as the storm ebbed. Fogal surfaced. Tiptoelng down the stairs. No doubt trying to make a strategic exit before the woman he'd just left woke. Reilly rose and blocked his path. "A moment of your time Fogal Quayle."

Fogal immediately positioned himself in a fighting stance. Then he looked square into Reilly's face and gasped. "Aulee? No, you're dead. We buried you. Not two summers back."

"I'm related to you but not in the way you think. Please let me explain." He motioned to a free seat at our table.

Fogal looked nervously back up the stairs but he was curious. Spying me he smiled. "Well now, a pretty lady you do have there."

Reilly introduced us. "Ry's a cadet deck officer on the vessel I serve on."

That Reilly was a seafaring man seemed to gain him a bit of cred with the man. "I serve as Third Officer on a merchant vessel that operates mostly on the Indian Ocean."

"You're a long way from the Indian Ocean and since when did they take women on as crew?"

"The ship's owner's fairly open minded." It was no point telling him that in our time such things, while still rare, were not unheard of. Too much detail.

"Must be. Okay, mystery man. You've avoided telling me your name yet." Fogal didn't miss the evasion. "So tell me, who are you and how do we come to be related?"

Reilly looked helplessly to me, perhaps hoping I'd give him some guidance telepathically.

"Just tell him Reilly, there's about a chance in hell that he's going to believe us anyway so there's nothing to be lost in being honest."

"Some help you are," Reilly swore.

Fogal seemed amused, "Reilly then. A common enough name in these parts. But I know of no cousins named Reilly. The lady's right though. I value honesty."

Reilly sighed. "Then let me tell you a tale and you can decide."

So he did.

When he finished Fogal leaned back in his chair and considered us. "Well I'd say that that was a lie with a lid on it but you both seem earnest. So you're saying I could change the future? How do you know you'd prefer me as your father?"

"Because you are my father," Reilly said simply, as if that answered it.

I intervened. "Reilly's still being cautious in how much he tells you but I will."

Reilly groaned and covered his head in his hand.

"Reilly's met you, at least your oversoul. They got on really well. And even if that wasn't the case, which it is, could you really leave that poor woman upstairs with the choice of a backyard abortion or marrying the bully who will beat and brutalise both her and your son?"

Fogal frowned, uncertain, "I suppose if you're from the future then conversing with beings in the other world isn't much more of a stretch. If you've talked so much with my alter ego then tell me some of it."

So Reilly did. Only I noticed Muire coming down the stairs. While the two men were deep in conversation I surreptitiously waved her over. When she spied Reilly she choked. "Do I know you?"

Suddenly nervous, Reilly extended a hand, "Not as yet." Though something cautioned him to not enlighten her further. He rose from the table. "Ry and I must be going. Consider what I've told you, Fogal, but let it stay between us." His eyes darted to his mother. "I only ask that when the time comes I actually like my name and my career in the merchant navy. My love is the sea, and Ry." He didn't complicate his cryptic message to Fogal any further by admitting there was another love in his life.

Throughout all this Horatio, thankfully stayed still in my shirt pocket, where he'd returned after his night's hunt. I could somehow image Reilly's Mum might have screamed if she'd seen him.

Reilly reached down to pat Clyde who was comfortable at his feet. "Come on Clyde. It's time we went home."

I followed them both out the front door of the bar, overhearing Reilly's mum say, "Strange pair those two."

"Fascinating those," Fogal mused to himself. "Fancy having breakfast with me Muire?"

I felt Muire's blush even if I didn't see it. "Well, I don't mind if I do. Let me go and fix something up for us."

Out on the street Reilly looked at me, inquiring, "Where to now?"

"Now we find our way home."

"How? We're no longer on the rainbow track. We're somewhere in the physical world, stuck in the past."

But I trusted we wouldn't be stuck for long. Whatever had brought us here would see to that. I widened my awareness to take in the whole street. A narrow doorway looked sharper and brighter, almost beckoning. Which I think it was. "This way."

21

With Reilly and Clyde standing patiently behind me I knocked on the door. There was no answer. Not at first. Then there was a bit of distant swearing to be heard and the sound of staggering footsteps coming down a hall. A bolt was pulled and a single eye looked out the peephole.

Swearing still, the woman opened the door. "You picked your time. I was expecting you last night. Do you know what time it is?"

"You were expecting us?" I parroted.

"Well of course. I read the signs in the cards and checked it against the charts. Even the cat's been expecting you."

Said cat, black, spied Clyde and hissed. Clyde went into launch mode but Reilly managed to grab and restrain him.

"Behave, the both of you," the woman ordered and both cat and dog let their hackles down looking to their respective humans for further instruction.

"I think you'd better go in the kitchen for now Sheila," the woman picked up the black cat, now purring in her arms and she took her to another room, closing the door firmly before returning. "Sorry about that. The bigger the dog the more her ego says attack and I think she'd come off second best in a brawl with that one," She nodded to Clyde. "Follow me then, I have everything set up ready to go."

"But we haven't told ya what we need?" Reilly glanced at her, dumbfounded.

The woman looked to me, "He always this slow?"

"Only on some of the metaphysical stuff. On anything else I'd trust him with my life."

The woman smiled at that. "She loves you, big man. Let me introduce myself. Not that it really matters. You can call me Bonny and you'd be two of the same name. At least that's what the spirits said."

"Reilly and Rylee," I explained, before offering my hand.

"Cute," but if she was amused by our names her mind was already elsewhere. She was busy holding my hand then closing her eyes. She opened them again and then examined the lines in my palm. "Now your hand," she commanded Reilly.

Reilly watched Bonny intently as she made a similar study of his hand.

Then she laughed, "Well, well. So there are three of you entwined. Where's the other?"

"Where we came from," I was uncertain of divulging too many details.

"Then he waits and worries, let's get you back before you create any more ripples in the fabric of time."

"It wasn't really our intention to mess with the timeline," Reilly defended us.

"Ah, but the wish was in your heart. Newbies. They have all the luck because they know no better. The spirits aren't angry with you this time but try not to do it again. Okay?"

"Happily," I agreed, knowing the spirits might not help us find a way back if we mucked up the past.

Elf's Uncle Monaro found Jim outside in the dawn light, practising his karate kata. He studied Jim's motions for a moment then decided to intervene, "Don't do it, be it."

Jim raised an eyebrow but decided to be polite and ask. "How?"

Monaro came to his side, "Show me your moves again. Okay, stop there. You're just directing individual body parts with your mind. Making a kind of ritual. Too much mind and not enough power," he patted his belly. "Try like this." He mimicked Jim's stance but widened it slightly and lowered it so the thighs were doing more of the balance work. Then he did the exact same moves."

Jim watched, interested now, "Okay, I can see how that's different now. You've lowered your centre of gravity. The moves are engaging the whole body."

"And flowing, one move into the next, but slowly. You need to give time for the power to build."

"I'm not sure I'd have that sort of time if someone was coming at me," Jim reasoned.

"Try coming at me," the wizened and weathered old man dared. He took up a position in front of Jim.

Jim pulled a punch, not really wanting to hit the old man.

Surprisingly Monaro countered at the same time as spinning elegantly out of harm's way. He rounded on Jim, coming at him with the palm of his right hand and somehow pushing him with ease. As Jim started to fall he grabbed him by his arm and swung him easily back into a standing position. "See your opponent as a dance partner. You don't want him landing one on you so widen your awareness. Feel into the opponent's movements. Know their mind. Try again."

Once again he bested Jim, a much younger and stronger man. "How are you doing this?" Jim asked bemused. "Did you already know martial arts?"

"No I didn't. This isn't martial arts. It's being. I'm one with land and the sky, drawing on their energy, flowing and feeling into that energy. Watching and witnessing until I am simply the witnesser. Knowing there is no division between the observer and what is observed."

"And become like an empty cup?" Jim assumed, remembering their conversation from the night before.

"Exactly."

"So if there's no division between observer and what is observed, does that mean there's no division between me and an enemy?"

"The two energies become entwined but if you were to look to where one energy begins and one ends you would find no actual boundary, only a sea of energy."

"Uncle!" Elf, who'd come out to watch and had bided his time, complained. "You'll blow his mind."

Monaro's eagle eyes studied Jim. "His mind is blowable. If it wasn't I wouldn't be out here."

"Auntie says breakfast's ready," Elf announced.

Jim did have an awful lot now on his mind, not least of which was the whereabouts of his friends. And now this whole entire worldview shift Monaro had thrust on him. Yeah, food sounded good. It might bring him back to planet Earth. "Let's eat and then we'd better head off Elf. See if we can locate the truck."

Monaro patted him on the shoulder as they walked back into the house. "Don't try to understand what we talked about. Let it permeate you. If you're interested in knowing more, come back this way again."

"I'd like that but honestly I don't know whether that will happen. I spend most of my life at sea."

Monaro didn't seem to think that would be an obstacle. "I hear they might seal the road out here. Your next trip will be easier. And there is another way?"

"I'm listening," Jim encouraged him, thirsting for more of what the old man had shared.

"Make yourself like an empty cup before you go to sleep. Make it your intent to meet up with me. If you are open to it, which I think you are, we can meet up in the dream world. At least on the edge of your dreams. Most likely on the edge that exists between early morning dreams and waking."

"You'd take me on as your student even though I am not of your people?" Jim was overwhelmed and honoured.

"In the greater cosmos we are all just unbounded energy. Where is the boundary between your tribe and mine?"

Jim considered that, on the basis of what the old man had shared. "There is no boundary. The only boundaries are the fictions we create with our minds."

Monaro smiled at him. "You'll do."

Jim assumed that meant he'd passed some test.

Several hours later and some four hundred and sixty more kilometres down the road Elf and Jim found the truck. "It looks deserted," Elf commented, worrying for his new friends. "What do we do now?"

Jim took a moment to feel into the awareness Monaro had awakened him to. Straight away he felt the answer. "We wait."

22

The mysterious woman, who refused to give too much information about herself because knowing it could affect the future more than we already had, led us down a staircase into her basement.

If I'd been expecting to see a pentagram on the floor, a ritual altar or other magical paraphernalia I was so wrong. The room was more like a lab, benches lining the walls and on those benches an array of electrical equipment including an oscilloscope, directional antennas, a radio transceiver and all sorts of other gadgets I couldn't identify. Wiring ran all over the walls and it could have been my imagination but I thought those walls were of some kind of metal, lined with metallic mesh. I wished we had Jim with us, he'd know.

"A faraday cage," Reilly mused.

The woman smiled, impressed. "Very good."

"You're a scientist," I assumed.

"And a practitioner of magick. Despite what some think there isn't such a chasm between those two wisdoms. Quantum physics and yet to be officially discovered physics is the bridge."

"Any sufficiently advanced technology is indistinguishable from magic." Reilly nodded in understanding.

"Arthur C. Clarke?" was the name that came to my mind.

"An insightful man," the woman commented. "I have to confess I'm a sci-fi fan." She threw a switch and a pentagram, contained within a circle, that I'd kind've been expecting, lit the floor in iridescent green. "If you'd step into the middle please. Might best keep a hold of that dog and please keep that spider I know's in your pocket contained."

"What are you going to do?" Reilly now asked suspiciously.

The woman sighed. "I can't give you that knowledge. You'll have to discover it for yourself in your own time, if someone hasn't already. What I can tell you is that it involves frequency. Everything in the known universe is a manifestation of frequency. We just need to get your frequency to match the space-time stream you travelled on. Once there it's up to you to find your jump off point and your way home. And, repeating myself, don't do this again. For sure you can travel the space-time bypass to move location but there are ramifications if you travel through time, as you can probably guess."

"So what happens when we fall back into our own location in space-time. Will we remember any of this?"

The woman closed her eyes as if seeking the answer, then looked directly at me. "I believe you will remember. There will be no changes for you, the dog or the spider but for him," she pointed at Reilly, "I can't be sure as I have never attempted what you've done."

"I didn't do it on purpose," Reilly growled.

"But the intent was in your mind. Intent is a big percentage of what makes magick. As you both seem to be progressing rapidly on your soul growth paths I will give you this warning. The more awakened you become to the true nature of reality the more you must be careful of your thoughts. Your ability to create and modify your reality will increase. If it was me I would take a vow to not interfere with reality in ways that interfere with the free will of others. It is a fundamental law of this universe that free will must be preserved. It is for every sentient being to find their own way out of their messes. You can support and guide but don't interfere, as you have with your mother."

"I should have let both of us suffer?" Reilly spat. "Why should I have suffered as a child when I had no say in who my mother married."

The woman sighed, "That, my friend, is a question that many disgruntled or wounded children have asked through millennia. The simplest explanation is that you come into life where the frequencies best match your own. If you don't like those frequencies then change yourself. Change your beliefs, your choices, your world view, your habitual reactions."

Reilly frowned, "So not fate, but my own doing." He clearly didn't like that either.

The woman now smiled at him, "You're not to blame. The circumstances of your life are a nudge to change. A chance to heal your ancestral wounds. You're a mechanic so I will remind you of this fundamental mechanical law - an engine needs a load to push against or work isn't done. In effect nothing changes and your life, indeed the universe itself, becomes stagnant. It's you who chooses either to fall into the ruts of your ancestors and your own prior lifetimes or to heal and move on from where you're at. More and more, as you grow you will realise that you are your own creator. It's like I created your coming here today. You come at a point in time when I wanted some test subjects. My higher mind perceived my need and drew what I needed to me."

It was my turn to groan, "Just what I need to be, a lab rat. But if what you say is true then we created you as our solution to our problem of how to get home."

The woman grinned, and not in a reassuring way. "Exactly, co-creation. Keeps things interesting as you can never be quite sure what the other players of the co-creation game might bring about."

My head was spinning and Horatio was moving agitatedly in my pocket, he was getting hungry. I knew I had a few insects I'd caught in the desert, stashed in the fridge back in the truck. "We need to go."

"Agreed," Reilly had had enough of the woman's philosophy, especially as he wasn't entirely comfortable with it.

Clyde merely woofed.

"Okay, move closer together." The woman instructed. "Yes, like that but hold on to each other."

Reilly put his arm around me and grabbed hold of Clyde's mane which the dog didn't seem to object to. Clyde just looked up at him with absolute trust.

The woman threw a switch, turning the room into a buzz of electromagnetic energy. I felt my hair crackle. "Good luck," she wished us and then we were gone.

We were back in the stream of rainbow coloured light. I felt the anguish in Reilly's mind as the two different timelines, the one we'd come from originally and the one we'd just started back on the island of his birth, collided.

Through our close mental and spiritual links there was no escaping that his struggles were mine. And I didn't want to escape. I reached out and placed a hand over his heart. His pained eyes met mine, "I don't know who I am." That one simple statement encapsulated his confusion.

"Perhaps you are both and neither, simultaneously."

"Not helping."

Reilly had never loved philosophy. I decided to go instead with what was real, well, at the moment etherically real. "Feel my hand. Be in that feeling, here, now. Those other realities stem from you and entwine you but they are not your core. Here is your core." I craned my neck up and pressed my lips to his. A burst of light shot out from our combined etheric bodies. We were the light. That was our reality, in that moment. I watched, with an inner awareness, as the pain eased from his mind.

"I see us in the streams of light. Not just two timelines but a myriad. Each one splittin' off into new paths at the points of key choices in our lives. Not just this universe. Multiple instances of the universe. Multiple universes…"

He was getting lost in it again, "Reilly! Focus on my hand! Come back to me!"

His attention snapped back. "I am here but I suspect if you kiss me again things will be even better," he winked at me.

I found amusement in the moment and kissed him, devouring him. My life, my breath. And when I next opened my eyes we were back in the truck.

Reilly looked around, getting his bearings, "I guess we've landed then."

"Actually, the truck's been here since yesterday," Jim looked up from the game of cards he was playing with Elf. "I've used up my store of interesting stories, about pirates, the Seychelles and life at sea. Elf was just about to start teaching me some of his music."

My mouth dropped, "It's the next day?"

"Afraid so. And I don't know about you two but it's been a while since Elf and I had lunch. Shall I cook us something? Are you two even hungry?"

Clyde, who was sitting at Reilly's feet, woofed a yes to that. Even Horatio squirmed in my pocket. "I'm guessing we're all pretty hungry. I'll get Horatio fed and back into his glove compartment."

"Then we head into The Alice and find us some pizza and a secure campsite," Reilly decided for us. Our Reilly was back. And the mention of pizza had my tastebuds watering.

Elf drew our attention. "Um your phone's buzzing Mr Reilly, um, boss Sir."

Reilly scowled, "Just Reilly." He took the call "Mahala, good to hear from you. What's up? What!" he yelled. "Okay, I'm putting you on speaker phone so the others can hear this." He indicated to Elf to keep his mouth zipped. Elf wasn't officially in on this, yet.

Elf smirked but nodded so Reilly pressed the button, "Go ahead."

"So I was just telling Reilly," Mahala announced. "We'd sent one of our investigators, John Dudley, to interrogate Frederick James Leary but two bizarre things happened. Firstly, by the time John got there Frederick's surname had mysteriously changed to Reilly and all documentation supported this. Even though I and others in this office remember seeing his original data, which has since disappeared into the ether. Not unlike Frederick, who John was in the process of interviewing when he suddenly disappeared right in front of his eyes. A local officer who was assisting at the time is witness to this. No trace of him could be found around Yulara but camera feeds from Alice Springs show him there not long after and there's no way he travelled hundreds of kilometres in that time."

Jim frowned, "But you have the security camera footage from the roadhouse in Yulara. That proves he was there."

Mahala cleared her throat, "He no longer appears on that footage. It's like he's been perfectly photoshopped out and the background of the roadhouse put in its place."

"Damn." Was all Jim could say.

We've changed the timeline, I reminded Reilly.

Reilly groaned, "We have a theory about what's happened but I'm not sure you're goin' to believe us." Then he told her.

"Fuck!" Mahala swore uncharacteristically. "What did you think you were doing? You mess with the timeline, you mess with all our lives."

"Try havin' the memories of two instances of yourself," Reilly grumbled. "And don't tell me that if ya could change a moment in time that would save someone ya loved from a lifetime of torment ya wouldn't take the chance."

Silence. "I lost a sister to a freak accident so I guess I understand but some things are bigger than our personal wants."

"I've already had this lecture," Reilly countered. "And it's not as if I consciously meant to go back in time."

"But the desire was in you and your subconscious took you there. Hell. This technology Merkwood and Sutton have you testing is too dangerous. The technology, if it goes ahead, is going to have to be unmanned. So what now? Do you still have a cargo to deliver or has that disappeared too?"

Jim, who'd snuck out during the heat of the discussion came back in, "It's there, I just checked. Like you figured, if a man could disappear from where we knew he'd been then other things might have changed, but it's okay."

Mahala sighed, on the other end of the phone. "That's something. Okay, the criminal network is still there for us to bust. We proceed as if nothing has changed."

Reilly thought, as he looked at Elf, "One thing has changed. We've taken on some security."

"Is this the guy that was with Jim and the roadhouse owner when Frederick confronted them? Elphinstone Mundy, aka Elf. Skipped school from age 14. Itinerant worker, though currently unemployed. Two slaps for drunk and disorderly, five years back. Presented a tablet for purity testing at a recent music festival. Prone to posting cute cat videos on his social media accounts but we won't hold that against him. Otherwise clean record. No known criminal or terrorist associates."

Elf put his head in his hands but peeked out, guiltily through his fingers.

"I'll vouch for him," Jim put in a good word.

"Elf's okay, Mahala," Reilly added.

"And he's there with you right now, I'm assuming. Damn it Reilly, what does he know of this operation?"

"Just the bare bones, enough to keep watch for us," I put in. "The first night he was just camped near us and offered to keep a lookout in case anyone came close to the vehicle. When Reilly and I went on our little odyssey he gave Jim a lift to Yulara as we believed, at the time, that Frederick wouldn't have associated him with Reilly, at least not as anything more than an employee. Whereas he might have tried to kill me out of spite."

Mahala sighed heavily, "It's hard to say in hindsight that Jim would have been safer with you, especially as he could've added to the timeline tampering you two did. Well, put him on, Elf, I mean."

Reilly nodded at Elf, "Say hello to Inspector Mahala de Plankas from Border Force."

Elf gulped, "Er, hello Inspector."

"If you're working with this lot you'd better call me Mahala. Now, understand this Elf. If you divulge this operation to anyone, other than those Reilly or I authorise, and that includes your rather large family. If you fail in your assigned duties, whatever they may be. If you so much as partake of a whiff of an illicit substance on my watch. While I wouldn't be allowed to ship you to some offshore prison to rot, believe me when I say I would personally make it my responsibility to make your life a misery. Do you understand?"

"Shit! You're one scary woman Mahala."

Reilly glared at him.

"Uh, yeah, I understand."

"You'd better. I'll send Reilly through some paperwork that you will sign."

"You bet."

"Even so, you can take me off speaker phone now Reilly and clear the room."

Jim grabbed hold of Elf by his shirt sleeve, "That means us Elf. You coming Ry?"

"Yeah, Clyde could use a walk." For the dog had an unlimited appreciation of walks. Though if Mahala thought she could keep anything between just her and Reilly she didn't fully understand the extent of our telepathy.

When we came back Reilly was off the phone but when he saw us he threw Jim the keys to the truck. "You drive. I need to check on Mum," and he pulled out his phone again.

I had a moment to wonder if he checked the time zone discrepancy. The choice words I soon heard on the other end of the phone suggested he hadn't.

23

Mahala had found us some private land to camp on. As we didn't want anyone trying to steal the cargo in the middle of the night we were behind a ring lock fence with a security detail patrolling the perimeter at irregular intervals, assuring us a peaceful night. Clyde stayed alert but we kept him inside in case some enterprising crim decided to throw poisoned meat over the fence. If not Clyde then Horatio, with his spidey senses, would wake me and let me know if anything stirred in the dark.

Nothing did.

In the morning Elf came with me to scout out the Persian rug shop's so-called 'closing down' sale.

The shopkeeper took one look at Elf and went on the offensive. "His kind are not welcome in here."

Elf paled and went to retreat but I latched onto his wrist, firmly.

Shit. I calmed my hackles and played dumb. "What men? That must halve your customer base."

"Typical," the man swore but I'll bleep those out. "You from the city?"

He meant Sydney or Melbourne but I continued to play dumb. "Alice Springs?" I asked innocently, egging him on. I was enjoying this. And The Alice was classed as a city, even if I knew he meant somewhere bigger.

"Foolish woman, go back to where you came from and take him with you," he added pointing at Elf.

I smiled, knowing I held an ace. "So I guess that means you don't want your delivery of rugs that we've brought here for you all the way from Western Australia. No problem. We'll write them up as damaged goods and send you the bill for the cartage."

Shock hit the man like an oncoming bus. "The rugs? You didn't say that was why you were here."

"You didn't give us a chance. You were too busy being a racist git."

Mr Salesman went red in the face but swallowed his pride. "I'm sorry, I thought he was one of the locals."

"And that excuses it?"

"You'd understand if you lived here. Youth crime is rampant."

Youth crime was a problem in a lot of the bigger towns in the outback but that was no reason for Elf to have to put up with this man's hostility. "So all Persians are carpet salesmen?"

"Irianians," he wrinkled his nose, "and no, of course not."

"So would you say that all Italians are members of the mafia?" I continued the theme I was on.

"Don't be stupid. There are plenty of hard working designers, cafe owners, cooks and concrete labourers amongst them."

"And Russians? Do they all run debt collection agencies?"

He frowned, "I can think of a few astronauts, scientists, musicians and ballet dancers, so no. What's your point?"

"My point is you're not allowing for the fact that there are plenty of people that don't fit your very narrow stereotypes. And as for youth crime, it's a niche you'll find in any society where there's a wide gap between the rich and the poor. Where there's generational poverty, lack of job opportunities, lack of self esteem, lack of any hope for a better future or indeed any way out. That doesn't excuse their behaviour. That's a choice and it's a bad one. But I'm mindful of the fact that there was a suburb close to where I grew up, only there the inhabitants were all descendants of anglo-saxon-celts. Let me see," I counted off on my fingers: "arson, drugs, domestic violence, brawls, stealing and burning cars, rocks hurled at public transport. Doesn't sound that different to me. Should I then be racist against my own kind?" It was time to get off my soapbox. "Now, do you want these carpets or not?"

He'd taken my rant because he knew I could walk away. "You should have rung so I knew to expect you."

"There was no need. We knew your opening hours," and we really hadn't wanted to give him warning. Better getting a feel for the place if he hadn't tidied up for our arrival. "We weren't going to bring the truck into the town until we knew we could park it close to your premises. Or perhaps you have an alleyway out the back?"

The salesman seemed relieved at the change of topic and recovered his politeness, although it came off as slimy, "Forgive me, I forgot to introduce myself. Sal Brusq, owner of this emporium."

Reluctantly I shook his hand. "Trainee Deck Officer Jackson, representing the Merkwood Line and this is Mr Mundy who's in our employ." My look dared him to say anything further about it but he didn't. He even shook Elf's hand. "If I could look at your loading bay then, Mr Brusq."

"Certainly, this way ma'am."

"I prefer Officer Jackson or just Jackson." It was rude and unAustralian of me not to offer my first name but I wasn't feeling friendly.

On our way back to camp Elf cornered me, "You know, you didn't have to say all that. I'm used to that reaction."

"It's a reaction that doesn't give you a chance does it?'

"No, it doesn't."

"The thing is, Elf, I saw a lot back when I was a journalist. I've reported from some of the more unsavoury spots on the planet. There's a lot of bad out there Elf. Organised crime gangs that thrive off of protection rackets, kidnapping, scamming little old ladies, kiddie porn, drug pushing, the slave trade and I won't go on because it gets me in a mood.

Now I'm not saying there isn't crime in the most affluent areas of the planet but you have to admit it thrives in places where there's either corrupt regimes, entrenched poverty, or, for whatever reason, a lack of hope. And the horrible reality is that there are always some good people in those places, stuck with no way out. Racism is one of the things that blocks their way. When I was a journalist I tried to highlight the injustices and inequalities I saw."

Elf smiled, "I think you're one of the good people Ry. Jim too. Even Reilly, though he seems grumpy and bossy at times."

"It's just Reilly's outer layer of clothing. His soul's good." But I steered the conversation away from defending Reilly's foibles, back to something I'd been mulling over. "Talking of ways out Elf. If you or anyone you think enough of to recommend would be interested in a life at sea there might be opportunities. It's hard work and long hours but the pay's good and so's the shore leave." I didn't try and oversell it by telling him some of that shore leave was in exotic places, the likes of which he'd probably never imagined visiting. "I emphasise the 'might' because ultimately it comes down to the Captain and Wilcher's no pushover, but think about it."

"Hmm. There's the girlfriend you see."

I shrugged, I could see how that would be an issue. "Oh well. You would have been a nice addition to the crew. We'll all miss you when this is over. We'd better get back. Mahala's flying in and her colleague John Dudley will be here shortly too. We have a briefing as soon as they get here."

"The local cops?"

"Yeah, them too."

As the truck was limited in space we met in a private conference room Mahala had rented for the occasion. It was conveniently located on the outskirts of town close to where we were camped. We waited while it was checked for listening devices. We didn't expect any but since it was in a public place we had to be sure.

Reilly and Elf helped to bring in the electronic screen while Jim dealt with all the connections to equipment and getting a secure internet channel. Once that was all hooked up Deman Merkwood and Daniel Sutton came on screen. I greeted them both.

"So the engine had some unexpected side effects?" Dan wanted to know all about it so I went back over what had happened, though I knew Reilly had already been in touch.

"We can't be sure of the long term effects on any living organisms." I was acutely aware that Clyde and Horatio had been test subjects as well as us. No-one had expected consequences so the risks to them hadn't entered our minds when we'd decided to engage the drive. I looked up as John Dudley entered, along with some of the local constabulary, "Um, we have company guys," I warned Dan and Deman. We ended our discussion of all things metaphysical there.

Mahala was dressed in plain clothes, like a tourist, in a pale blue tank top, denim shorts and thongs. Though I notice the brown leather thongs were of a quality you could go bushwalking in. She took centre stage and asked everyone to take a seat.

"As you have been briefed I won't go over too much of the background except to Introduce Jim Northey, Ry-lee Jackson and Reilly Quayle who first alerted us to the nature of the cargo they were carrying."

Nods and acknowledgements ensued but John Dudley frowned, "I thought his name was Reilly O'Reilly."

"He goes by both," Mahala winced, not wanting to go into the unbelievable complexities of how that had happened. She forged on. "Jim comes to us with considerable field experience with our allies in the US. Reilly is in charge of his ship's security. Ry-lee is a trainee Deck Officer now working for the Merkwood shipping line.

A few eyes zeroed in on my obvious disability, the lack of most of my left arm. It took all my inner steel not to wilt under those stares.

"Can you use a firearm Ms Jackson?" John queried.

"I couldn't hit the side of a barn," I answered honestly.

"I've trained her myself in mixed martial arts," Reilly came to my defense. "She's more than capable of lookin' after herself but that won't be necessary as she'll be safely out of sight in the trucks' accommodation. Jim and I will be in communication with her at all times." What Reilly didn't say was that communication would be telepathic and that I would be busy, walking in the etheric realm where I could give them intel they might not otherwise access. Guarding my being while I was out to it would be the protective stones Reilly had been given in the Seychelles and Horatio. But none of the authorities needed to know about the illegal wildlife we harboured onboard.

A few brows knitted so I added to Reilly's explanation of my involvement. "Jim has installed a number of discretely positioned sensors and cameras around our cargo. I'll be in a position to monitor that."

Captain Michaelson, one of the local cops, was clearly not happy at what he saw as an unnecessary amount of civilian involvement. "One of our guys could drive your truck and another could watch those sensors."

"That truck is a testbed for highly sensitive innovative technology. No-one but Jim, Ry and Reilly are going in it," Dan declared, via the link.

"You're putting Mr Merkwood's employees in harm's way, unnecessarily," the cop countered.

"They stay with the truck or the cargo gets unloaded onto a different rig. Your pick." Dan was having no-one else near his truck.

Mahala swore, "We don't have time to reload the carpets. Jackson and Mundy have already made contact with the owner. He's expecting delivery after lunch."

Deman piped up. "Have you sailed through Somalian waters Captain Michaelson? My crew have. They've fought off pirates who tried to steal one of my vessels and its cargo. The pirates intended to sell the female crew into slavery and would have no doubt posted hefty ransom demands for the rest of the crew. The people you see before you retook the ship and rescued their Captain before cooperating fully with the authorities from the Seychelles to put the ringleaders away. They've forged, on behalf of my company, an alliance with the Seychelles coast guard to help them counter piracy, illegal fishing and smuggling in their waters." Michaelson seemed to look at us afresh. "That's quite some track record. Though we can't be responsible for your safety."

"Border Force will issue them with body armour," Mahala put in. "Jim and Reilly will be issued with sidearms." She opened a nondescript equipment case she'd brought with her and took out two hand guns."

"Sig Sauer P320 X-Carry Pro," Reilly approved.

"They're brown," I noted. Their colour was the only thing that meant anything to me.

Mahala sniggered, accurately surmising that that was the sum total of my knowledge of guns. "Actually, their marketers call the colour Flat Dark Earth."

"Muddy brown then," I countered, playing the game between us.

Mahala conceded, "Brown then. 9mm, 17 rounds, a safety here," she pointed out the mechanism

"That's one up on the usual Glock," Jim mused.

Reilly kept his mouth shut. He wasn't about to admit he had an unregistered Luago in the truck.

"More than that," Mahala continued. "They come with improved sight capability. Take care of them. They're coming out of my budget."

"One problem," Reilly was ever mindful of the cops in the room. "Neither of us have an Australian firearms licence."

"That won't be a problem will it, Michaelson?" Mahala stared the police captain down. She wasn't asking a question.

"Civilians, unlicensed civilians," Michaelson muttered, rolling his eyes. "Not as long as they hand them back to you at the end of the operation. Mind telling me how we stay in contact with said civilians?"

"All of them will be issued with discrete earpieces and lapel mics so they can hear what's going on and keep out of the way when the time comes."

"And Mr Munday," Inspector Dudley wondered, "What will he be doing?"

"He'll be Clyde's handler," Reilly proposed. "He and the dog will stay out of the way unless needed."

"Actually, I can handle Clyde. I have something else in mind for Mr Mundy," Mahala told them. "If you're agreeable Elf, I wondered if you might meet with the local people and see what they know about Mr Brusq's operations. They may have seen or heard something."

Elf's eyes lit with glee, "Like a spy?"

Mahala winced, "We prefer the term 'intelligence officer'. You up for the task?"

Elf had a think then replied, "I'm a Wiradjuri man. They're Arrente. I have some kinship ties but 'll need to go through their elders."

Mahala seemed relieved to have someone else work out those protocols. "I'll leave the details of how you go about it to you Elf. Would you be able to take a recorder or body cam with you?"

Elf shook his head. "Not without talking to them first."

"They could just come forward and talk to us," Michaelson growled. "We're not exactly the enemy here."

Elf bristled. "And who exactly is the enemy then, Captain?"

"Boys," Mahala intervened. "Play nice on my watch." The threat of very real consequences was there in her tone of voice.

John raised an eyebrow at Elf's involvement but wasn't about to challenge his boss in public. "Okay, moving on. We'll need the local swat squad stationed on top of these buildings. Can we discreetly gain access without alerting the locals?

"We'll be using the cover story that they're survey mapping and need the tops of those buildings to establish trig points," Mahala explained.

Michaelson frowned, he seemed good at doing that, "And people will buy that?"

Mahala smiled, "It's all in the props. They'll be dressed as a survey crew and they'll be carrying tripods on their shoulders. They'll look the part even if the rest of what they're carrying will be military issue and that will be hidden in large, innocuous looking, equipment bags. Keeping with the survey theme we'll establish road detour signs, here and here. That will help to keep civilians out of the area."

"What about the people in the other buildings?"

"We'll trigger a fire evacuation alarm for those, just before we're ready to go in hot. Michaelson, I'll need a couple of uniforms to get those people down the street a safe distance. Use whatever excuse you deem fit."

Michaelson nodded his understanding."A hypothetical kitchen fire in one of the buildings then, We don't need to specify which one. I'll liaise with the fire department. Anything else?"

"It would be helpful if we had a chopper in the air, at a discrete distance. If anyone escapes the cordon we'll try and track them from the sky."

"That can be arranged, But if they try to do a runner with the drugs and they successfully evade us?" Michaelson wondered.

"I've placed tracking devices inside a couple of the bags of drugs," Jim piped up.

John's eyes gleamed at that news, "Excellent."

"Are we a go?" Mahala asked, her eyes scanning the assembled to see if there were unvoiced concerns.

Michaelson nodded. "We'll be ready."

John agreed. "I'll have a forensics team on standby. We need to gather as much evidence as possible and nail this."

"Take care of my crew, Reilly," Deman demanded.

"And don't get my truck shot up," Dan glared.

Michaelson laughed, still not happy with all the civilian involvement. "That will be the least of our concerns."

24

After Mahala had stood over Elf while he signed a short-term employment contract and a non-disclosure agreement we left the authorities to organise their end of things. Elf gave us a mock salute then filtered off, one minute there, the next a vague part of the landscape. I could just make him out, walking up to a group of individuals who were sheltering under the shade of a tree in the nearby park. He sat down on the ground with them, brushing an odd fly from his face.

"You think he'll be alright?" I worried.

"He can handle himself," Jim firmly believed.

"Hmph," Reilly had other things on his mind. "Let's get you and Horatio settled. I'd be a lot happier if I had ya wrapped in something bulletproof. If there's shootin', a stray bullet might pass through the truck."

For once I knew something he didn't. "Actually, the walls of our mobile home are armour plated. They should stop most things, other than perhaps a ballistic missile."

"How d'ya know that?"

"Deman told me."

"I wasn't told," Reilly complained.

Jim groaned. "Boss," he said with emphasis, for that was the mode Reilly was definitely in at the moment. "You have a telepathic link to our brains. We're all getting so used to that that we don't often feel we have to say everything in our heads. Or do you want a full briefing on every conversation we have?" He stared his best friend down.

"Bollocks, I'm responsible for the safety of both of youse," Reilly grumbled.

"As is Deman," I put in. "Not having armour plating would have been an issue you needed to know about. That there wasn't a problem wasn't high on the priority list, was it?" Was that statement a kind of double or triple negative? The ex journalist in me wondered.

Reilly, sighed. "Yer right. Both of youse," he conceded.

"You're on edge," Jim noted. "It's understandable."

"Yer making excuses for me."

He was but Jim thought it better not to say that, instead shaking his head, "Just stating facts." Although Reilly could easily read his real intent from his head. Jim just wanted to settle us all down. "It's only a suggestion, but perhaps you could go and do a light karate workout while I settle Ry and Horatio. It will clear your mind," and take some of the tension out of him, Jim thought.

Fortunately, Reilly saw the sense in that.

I undressed and lay down on the bed. The extreme dry heat in the middle of the day could be oppressive and I didn't fancy astral travelling while my body lay in a pool of sweat. I wasn't even sure if I could achieve a trance state if I was that uncomfortable. When we got underway we wouldn't be running the air conditioner as it might alert undesirables to the fact that someone was inside.

Horatio sat on the bedside table, preening himself.

Jim stood beside the bed, the protective stones in his hands. His eyes raked my body. "Maybe we should relax you first," he placed the stones on the table, next to the spider then knelt on the bed, beside me.

I could read where his mind was going, "We have time?" I arched a brow, questioningly.

"Asks the time traveller. We'll make our own time. Although," he eyed Horatio, "I'd feel more comfortable without an audience."

I chuckled to myself. "Horatio's no prude," I'd watched his own dangerous mating with a female Tarantula in the Seychelles. We'd managed to extract him in time before the female, Delilah, had killed him as the females of the species were inclined to do after, and sometimes before or during sex. But I opened the bedside table drawer and Horatio, sensing my mind, kindly climbed inside. Out of sight, out of mind. "Better?"

"Definitely."

"And Reilly?" we didn't want him getting any more grouchy than he already was. Missing out on sex might just put him over the edge.

"I just checked in with him. He's got into his zone with the kata and enjoying it. I got a mental thumbs up."

"Well then…" My pulse sped up a notch.

"Well then," he moved around to the foot of the bed and took a firm hold of my ankles. Spreading my legs wide he made a place for himself then bent down with intent. I felt his breath on my crotch as he parted the lips of my vagina. His tongue forged an entrance, sending my spine into an arch as I moaned out my pleasure. "Please."

"Please what?"

Game on, "Please master."

"Better, now stay still. I don't want you bucking me off the bed." And with that said his tongue danced around my clitoris, tormenting me with almost unbearable pleasure. But I did manage, somehow to bear it, my mind drifting into a pleasure-scape of sensations, warmth and connection.

His tongue dived in again, keeping me on the edge of the unexpected. Connected with my mind he could read when the volcano inside me started to build. Relentlessly he thrust his hot tongue into me. *Let it come, Ry,* he commanded. Surf the wave of it. Let me surf it with you.

You're asking the impossible, I moaned. *Let it go or hold it back? Which is it?*

Imagine you're releasing the orgasm through a very small hole. He thrust two fingers, deftly, in beside his tongue, alternating the thrusts of his tongue and his fingers. It spilled me over the edge, the dam cracked but met that restraining valve Jim had asked me to imagine. I felt him with me as I cried out, as we rode the wave together. The world pulsed and then I was drifting, vaguely aware that Jim was still there, placing the stones around me and voicing words of intent, that they would keep me safe in my travel.

I drifted out of my body. Horatio was there with me, in his much bigger and scarier etheric form, "Let's go."

We journeyed over the town, finding the shop, then we waited.

Reilly parked the truck in the loading bay as arranged, in the shady alleyway behind the shop. Jim went to tell Brusq we were here while Reilly started to unlock the cargo container. All going well they would just unload the carpets into Brusq's storeroom then high tail it out of there before the raid.

"No problems this end," Reilly whispered into the discrete button mic on his top pocket.

"We've got the building covered," Mahala conveyed. "Let us know when you're clear."

"Any info from Elf?"

"Not as yet."

Reilly saw Jim returning, with Brusq in tow. "We're about to start unloading. I'll get back to you."

"Understood."

It was heavy work in the worst heat of the day. Sweat dripped off both Jim and Reilly. Fortunately Brusq was a dab hand with his forklift, which reduced a lot of the work.

Who was minding the shop? It soon became apparent that Brusq had closed the shop for the duration of the unloading.

I saw Mahala walking Clyde on the other side of the street. She'd meant to come in to browse like some passing tourist, but that wasn't happening.

I noted the SWAT team in their carefully camouflaged positions, visible to me through their etheric signatures.

The snipers had their weapons trained on the entrance and exits of the building. Not that we were expecting anyone on either side to be shot but it was a nice backup.

A helicopter buzzed the dry riverbed downtown, a news channel logo on its side but I expected it wasn't a news chopper.

Then I saw him. I quickly reminded myself that his surname was no longer Leary. Fredrick James O'Reilly, was wandering casually down the street, like he too was a tourist. *FJ approaching*, I sent a quick mental picture to Reilly and Jim, to back up my claim.

Reilly whispered into his mic, low enough that Brusq wouldn't hear, "We have company."

"I see him," Mahala confirmed. "Moving to intercept."

But Fred had a sixth sense, the likes of which only came from surviving on gang ridden backstreets. In one easy turn he swung around and shot Mahala in the chest, right over the heart. She faltered and fell from the impact but I could see her aura, she was alive and well. Meanwhile Clyde had launched into full attack mode, our mild mannered dog ready to tear out the man's throat.

My heart stuttered as I saw Fred take aim and then at the last minute change his mind as he ran for the door of the shop. He quickly opened it with his own key. Damn. *He's in*, I warned my lovers. *Mahala is down but okay. Clyde's trying to tear the door down.*

Get him to back off if you can. We don't need FJ shooting him through the door, Reilly instructed

I called to Clyde, mentally, and he looked up. He shivered when he sensed the spider with me. Our brave Clyde really didn't like tarantulas. I managed to coax him away then ordered him to guard Mahala, who was trying to struggle to her feet. She was already on her communicator assuring them she was okay and requesting them to maintain their positions. There was no need to escalate the situation, yet. We still didn't know who, if anyone, FJ was working with. The whole point of this operation was to find the connections to the global organisation behind the criminal activity.

Reilly felt behind his jacket for the gun he'd stashed in his belt, motioning Jim to move back, out of sight. Jim readied his gun as well. To hell with the red tape mess that would ensue if he used it. He wasn't about to leave Reilly unprotected.

Fred walked in and nodded at Brusq. "They've finally arrived then."

"Just unloading the last."

Reilly kept his head angled down and positioned himself between the already off loaded carpets and the forklift but Fred's sixth sense must have kicked in again. "Well looky here. I know you don't I? Long time ago," he scratched his head, thinking. "Ah yes, I remember now. The Manx fisherman's son. What was it? Something Quayle."

There was no point lying. "Reilly Quayle." Reilly had to remind himself that that was who he was now. He kept himself angled so that Fred didn't see the gun behind his back but Brusq glanced back and saw it.

"He's armed," Brusq noted with alarm.

"Get it off him," Fred commanded.

"What?" Clearly Sal wasn't used to taking orders. "I'm the owner of this shop, not your lackey."

"If you want to live to get your middleman's cut of the merchandise you'd better think again." Fred waved his gun between his two targets.

"Anybody harms or attempts to disarm Reilly I'm shooting them," Jim ordered from his cover position.

Reilly smirked. "Seems we're evenly matched. What now?"

It was Fred's turn to smile. "I just came in to check on the merchandise. My lackeys, as Brusq here would call them, are on their way.

"No they ain't," Mahala whispered into Jim and Reilly's ear pieces. "They were identified and arrested a short time ago. Elf came through with the necessary info. We're about to storm the building, on my signal. Distract them if you can but stay safe. Moving in ten, nine, eight …"

But if Reilly and Jim had any ideas on a distraction Horatio beat them to it. Brushing the back of Fred's neck. Fred swore and swung around, gun at the ready but then screamed out his lungs as he caught sight of Horatio's etheric form. Apparently he had enough Irish fey blood in him to see such things.

Well done Horatio, I praised the spider as Reilly launched himself and took Fred down in a tangled Judo roll.

Sal moved to intervene only to find Jim's gun thrust against his back.

"Do you really want to find out what 9mm will do to your spine?" Jim asked.

"Go!" Mahala was ordering. Her team burst through the door of the shop and in through the back. A group of them went to extract Fred from Reilly.

Fred spat at Reilly, "Bastard, I knew you were no good."

With the man safely handcuffed and restrained by two hefty SWAT members Reilly faced up to him. "I'm no-one's bastard. Not anymore. Actually I kind of feel sorry for you. It was you that ended up growing up under the thumb of oldman O'Reilly."

"Leave my father out of this. Mark my words Reilly Quayle. I'll remember this."

Reilly smirked, "Please do. As I doubt it'll matter where you're going. Have a good life in the clink, Frederick James O'Reilly."

Still pale from being shot at, Mahala moved to intervene. "That's enough Reilly. We'll take him now. We'll debrief in two hours once we have this lot charged. I'll need you to bring your truck to the station later so we can go over that container with a fine tooth comb." She moved to wave in the forensic team. "Stuff's inside the carpet rolls, gather it up and we'll see what we've got."

Captain Michaelson was waiting in the rear. He held his hands out for the guns Jim and Reilly were still carrying, "I'll take those." Then he gave a grudging nod of acknowledgement, "Well done."

25

There wasn't enough space in the observation room at the police station so Michaelson, grudgingly, allowed Jim to set up a secure feed so we could watch the interview from the truck. I think the Captain knew enough of Jim's background to know that he could quite easily hack into the station so rather than having to arrest him and getting Mahala offside after such a successful bust he made an exception for us. The only proviso was that his computer technician, Constable Jenny Singh sat in with us, ready to pull the plug on our feed if Michaelson gave the order.

Michaelson waited until Inspector John Dudley was seated then scraped a chair across the floor for himself. They both stared at Frederick who was currently studiously looking at the ceiling, whistling an Irish tune to himself and pretending they weren't there.

John started things off. "Frederick James O'Reilly, you are charged with entering this country illegally on a falsified visa, attempting, this day, to receive a shipment of drugs delivered to Mr Sal Brusq's store. Before entering the premises you shot at a passerby, a clear shot to her heart area. Upon entering Brusq's premises, by key, since the store was locked at the time, you proceeded to draw a firearm on one of the people unloading the carpets. That's illegal immigration, attempted murder, procurement of illicit substances, threat with a deadly weapon. I must caution you that you are required by the laws of this country to state your true name, date of birth and current residence. You have the right to refuse to answer other questions. You have a right to contact a lawyer. But I should warn you that any lack of cooperation on your part will only go against you. Do you understand the charges against you?

Frederick growled "They're bullshit charges. I'm saying nothing until I talk to my lawyer."

John leaned back in his chair, "I must inform you that we have checked your financial situation, which appears to be rather healthy. You are therefore not entitled to a court appointed lawyer. If you have funds to pay a solicitor of your choice I can provide you with a list of locally available lawyers."

"Then do it."

John motioned to the guard at the door, "Take him back to the holding room. We'll resume this interview as soon as the lawyer arrives. Dudley and Michaelson exiting interview room A."

"Well that was a bit of a non-event," I mumbled to no-one in particular.

"Standard procedure," Constable Singh explained.

Jim got up from his seat at the table. "This is going to take a while. Anyone for coffee? Jenny, that includes you too."

"Ooh, that's very kind of you. Yes please."

"How do you have it?" Jim asked. He knew what the rest of us had.

Jenny smiled guiltily. "I know it's cliche but, hell, I like it uber strong, black, thanks."

Reilly moved to the freezer, "Just so happens we still have a few frozen danishes. Um apricot, cherry, strawberry and a cinnamon and almond scroll."

My mouth was already watering, "Whack 'em in the microwave Reilly. I'll hand whisk some cream."

Jenny looked like her mouth was watering as much as mine. "Wow, I didn't expect all this."

So we enjoyed afternoon tea while we waited for instalment two.

It was nearly four o'clock by the time the lawyer arrived. At least the day outside was starting to cool off for the afternoon. I was just outside stretching my legs, and Clyde's, when Jim poked his nose out the door. "We're back on."

The lawyer looked annoyed at having had to rearrange his agenda for the afternoon. His white shirt was crisply pressed. His simple steel grey tie matched the colour of his trousers.

Michaelson extended a hand, "Simon, thanks for coming at such short notice."

Simon Bealy, of Bealy & Sons, sighed. "Makes a change from the usual mix of acrimonious divorces, child custody suits and drunk and disorderly charges."

"You've had plenty of time to talk to your client?"

"I have. The client wishes to know if there is a deal on the table?"

Captain Michaelson laughed, heartily, turning to Frederick. "You've got some gall. Even on the attempted murder and illegally being in the country we've got enough to put you away for ten, maybe fifteen years. Our local circuit judge doesn't take kindly to authorities being shot at."

"How the hell was I to know she was from Border Force. I thought she was just a tourist."

"Mr O'Reilly!" Bealy swore, "Desist from speaking until I tell you otherwise." Bealy pushed a document across the table to the two seated officers, "My client wishes to submit this statement."

Dudley and Michaelson read it. Dudley's eyebrows arched. Michaelson just laughed. "So according to this you didn't realise your travel agent hadn't arranged the appropriate documents for your travel. Are you going to tell me you've never travelled and don't know what a visa is?"

The lawyer nodded curtly for Frederick to speak. "Do not elaborate, just answer their question."

"Yeah, okay, I know what a damn travel visa is. But on the day I travelled I left the paperwork at home. Belfast is part of the United kingdom and Australia's just a left over bit of its empire, I shouldn't need a fucking visa."

John studied him, "It depends how long you're intending to stay and the purpose of your visit."

"I'm just a tourist. Only here for the week. Wanted to see Ayers Rock."

"We'll check with the local tourist companies and see if there are any bookings that would support your claim of wanting to visit Uluru but that still leaves the matter of your passport. Is there a reason your passport lists you as Frederick James Leary? Leary does not appear to be your current surname. Did you somehow mysteriously change your name while in transit to this country."

Frederick looked momentarily confused. "It's always been O'Reilly," though he looked like he wasn't sure, "I don't know how that happened. Someone must have stolen my identity and substituted a false passport to land me in trouble with the authorities."

Captain Michaelson banged angrily on the table making everyone start. "Bullshit, bullshit, bullshit. Tourists don't go shooting at people walking down the street."

"I've got a phobia of large dogs. That dog she had with her looked like it was about to charge me. I meant to hit the dog, not her."

"She had the dog on a leash. It was nowhere near you at the time. Where'd you get the gun? Who sold it to you? Where's your Australian gun licence?" Michaelson hammered the suspect with questions.

Bealy intervened. "Captain. My poor client cannot be expected to answer more than one question at a time. Mr O'Reilly can you outline the circumstances of how you came into possession of that firearm."

"It's not mine," Frederick tried to claim. "I'd just found it on the street, behind some bushes. I didn't know it was loaded."

Clearly Frederick's fudging was wearing on Michaelson. "So in fear of a large dog you pointed a gun you didn't know was loaded, pulled the trigger and inadvertently shot the officer who had full control of the dog at the time."

"That's what I'm saying."

"Yet officers we had on the roofs of nearby buildings state that you clearly aimed the gun at the woman."

Frederick shrugged his shoulders, "They need their eyes checked."

John made a show of putting a restraining hand on Michaelson who looked like he was about to launch across the desk. "Be that as it may. We still have the matter of what happened inside Sal Brusq's carpet emporium. Why were you in possession of a key to his shop?"

Frederick's eyes flicked from side to side, clearly thinking up some lie, "Sal and I are friends from way back. He knew I was in the country and invited me to have a private look at the carpets that had just come in. He was most proud of their quality."

"So you're claiming that you didn't know that drugs were hidden inside the shipment of carpets."

"Had no idea."

Mahala came quietly into the interview room.

John looked up and smiled as Mahala passed him a plain folder, which actually contained nothing. "Inspector Mahala de Plancas entering the interview room."

"Sal's been most forthcoming," Mahala didn't exactly say what about as she wasn't in a position to lie within an interview room.

Frederick tried to rise from the table. "That's bullshit, he wouldn't dare."

Michaelson laughed. "You expect Brusq and your local contacts, who by the way, we've rounded up as well. You expect them to take the flak while you walk away on lesser charges? You've got mush for brains."

John cautioned the Captain, all part of the act, "There's no need for name calling Captain. "I'm sure Frederick here understands that we know he's only a minor, bit player, in this whole operation."

Frederick went beetroot in the face but John continued. "It's the really important people who pull your strings Fred, can I call you Fred? It's those with power over you that we're after."

Fred's anger exploded, "I'm nobody's bloody puppet."

Bealy tried to calm him but Fred angrily shrugged his hand from his shoulder. "Who the hell do you all think you are? Do you know who I am? How important I am?"

John steepled his hands, calmly assessing the man. "Actually, Fred, we know quite a bit about you. Under your various pseudonyms you own a palatial home in Bermuda, a small stately home in the Scottish highlands, a chain of carpet stores in a number of counties, including Brusq's. At this very moment authorities in those countries are swooping on your operations and gathering further evidence for our case. Oh, and by the way. Your funds in the Cayman Islands have been frozen."

Frederick sputtered, "You can't do that? That money's off the grid."

John smiled, benignly, "Oh, you'd be surprised what we can do, with a word in the right ear. Make it easier on yourself. Who are your bosses?"

"I don't know anything about any bosses." Frederick swore, " I was just picking up a shipment of carpets. I had no idea there were drugs inside."

Mahala leaned against the wall, still hurting from the earlier slug to her bullet proof vest but too tough to admit it. "That's not what we heard, Frederick. Our sources say you've been working with this crime syndicate for a while now. And let's not forget about the charge of using a firearm to shoot at a Border Force officer, me.

Frederick eyed her up and down, "Should have gone for a headshot."

It was Bealy's turn to swear. "A moment with my client, please."

"You've got five," Michaelson allowed, brusquely. " I could do with something to wash the nasty taste out of my mouth. You ask me, Frederick, you're of no use to us. Prepare yourself for a long stay in prison."

John sidled up to the Captain as they exited the room, still fully in earshot of Frederick "Let's not give up on Frederick yet, Captain. There must be something he knows, something that would help us take down this crime syndicate and in the process take a decade or two off his sentence." He shut the interview room door and smiled. "That should give him something to think about."

"Simon won't want this to drag on. He's got a backlog of cases on his plate. There's only so many lies he'll tolerate from his client. He'll lean on him."

John laughed at that, "Is he working for his client or you guys?"

Michaelson grinned. "Oh, I think you could definitely say Simon is working in his own best interests. He knows we've got enough on his client that the case won't drag on in the courts. He'll want a quick turnaround on this one."

"That mix up with his passport though. It's odd. I could have sworn when we first started investigating this his surname was Leary, not O'Reilly."

Michaelson frowned. "Yeah, just quietly, you're not the only one but all the paperwork I can now find says he's always been O'Reilly."

"Someone could have accessed his files and changed it." John couldn't discount the idea but it would take a high level hacker to get into their files.

"For what purpose? It doesn't change who he is and my IT technician, Constable Singh, couldn't find any evidence of tampering. I had her look."

"Well then, just thought it was me going crackers, glad I'm not."

I leaned back against Reilly and sighed. "This is taking a while." I was pleasantly hemmed in by my two favourite men though.

Jenny, at the other end of the cramped table, didn't seem bothered. "It's not like in the movies. Crims aren't in any hurry to confess. Though I suspect they'll entice this one to do so. Won't take long now. You'll see."

Five minutes later Frederick's lawyer, Simon, called the interviewers back in. "My client may be prepared to change his statement but he wants to know his options."

"Options," Michaelson laughed. "We've got the evidence stacked against you. You're not coming out for a long time."

Back in good cop mode John took a softer approach, "Now Captain. You know he's just small fry. We want to know who he's working for."

Frederick bristled, "Enough with the small fry. You want something, you have to give me something for it."

John leaned back in his chair and looked at Michaelson, "I suppose we could drop the illegal immigration charges. It's possibly just a mix up."

The Captain rolled his eyes, "Some mixup. The man didn't even notice the surname on his own passport."

Frederick folded his arms, "Not enough. There's not much jail time in that one. You're going to have to be a little bit more flexible than that."

"There is one possibility," John whipped out his phone, "Inspector de Plankas. Could you spare a moment in the interview room? "

They waited a moment, staring at each other, each trying to guess the other's thoughts. It was like a poker game.

Mahala knocked on the interview door and the guard let her in.

John got up to greet her, "Inspector, thanks for joining us. How you feeling?"

Mahala raised an eyebrow, "What's this about Inspector Dudley?" she asked, trying for suspicious and hostile though they both knew what they were about. "Don't tell me you want me to drop my charges against him."

John made a show of wincing, "Eh, not exactly. I thought the suspect might be more cooperative if we lessened the charge to accidental discharge of an illegal firearm."

"That's bullshit. The man fired at me with intent to kill. He's just messing with us. We don't need him. We can gather the evidence ourselves. It's what we're good at."

Frederick paled a little, seeing his chances of a lesser charge going out the window. "Give me a pen," he demanded of Simon. He took the lawyer's designer pen and scribbled a note on the paper the lawyer grudgingly handed to him. He pushed the paper across the table to where John grabbed it.

"Plokamia," John read the single word out.

Mahala snorted, "Yes we know who you work for. I'll need more than that before I consider dropping the attempted murder charge."

Fredrick looked at her, trying to gauge what he could get away with. "What do you want?"

"We already told you what we want, slimeball," Michaelson roared at him.

"Steady Captain, let's hear him out."

"No." Mahala surprised them all, "I don't just want the bosses names. I want a complete flowchart with the whole hierarchy. Who you report to. Who they report to and so on. Names of the branches of the organisation. What businesses they operate under. I don't just want the body of the beast, I want the tentacles as well."

"Then drop all the charges," Frederick demanded.

"Not going to happen," Mahala glared back at him. "You're going down for drug trafficking at the very least."

"But," John intervened, "we could turn a blind eye to your funds in the Cayman Islands." Truthfully they had no way of touching those funds anyway but Frederick didn't need to know that. "Of course," he carefully added. "If we find you've lied or omitted anything then all deals are off. Those funds could disappear in a keystroke." Could being the operative word but technically John wasn't lying. "So what's it to be? Thirty years before parole and no money stashed away or…?

Frederick grumbled, none too happy. "I'll want protection inside the jail, a cell with a window and access to plenty of good Irish fiction."

John's eyes widened, surprised by the last part of his request, "Agreed."

"Then you'd better get me more paper. In fact, get me some butcher's paper. This is going to be a big flow chart."

"How about an electronic whiteboard," Mahala offered, pleased at how things had turned out. "Just a minute." She went out to arrange it.

Inside our makeshift observation suite Jenny offered a high-five.

Reilly high-fived her back. "I think this deserves a drink. I don't suppose there's a pub in town that serves Guinness?"

"You're inviting me?" Jenny looked surprised.

"You bet. Better ask Mahala and John too. And I suppose Michaelson."

"Anyone see Elf?" I wondered.

"He took Clyde for a walk," Jim replied.

I took out my phone, "Hey Elf. We're going to a pub to celebrate. Yeah that's right. Uh, where? Not sure. Hang on a minute." I handed the phone over to Jenny for directions. "Do they allow dogs," I wondered.

"This place will," Jenny took the phone, "Hey, Elf, got a pen?"

Epilogue

The next morning I stepped out of the truck to stretch my legs. Jim was making breakfast and Reilly was giving the rig the once over, tyre pressure, fuel and oil levels. I was already missing Clyde who'd gone with Mahala. He was a work dog after all so we couldn't keep him and I doubted he would have been suited to a life at sea. Before he'd departed we'd smothered him in cuddles and pats which he'd lapped up with glee. Though I did have one thing at the back of my mind. How had multidimensional travel on the rainbow track affected him?

I looked over at Elf's camp. Since he'd bought himself a small two man tent, out of what Mahala had paid him for his work, he'd moved to sleeping in that instead of his car at night. His tent was there but his car wasn't. Where was he? We'd be going soon and I for one dearly wanted to say goodbye before we left. I knew the guys felt the same.

I went back inside, "Jim, seen Elf?"

"Why you asking me Ry, reach out with your mind?" Jim was always encouraging me to use my 'super powers' as he called them, to hone and refine them.

I did as he suggested and let my mind go wide and empty. If I'd tried to use my thinking mind it would have been like looking for a needle in a vast haystack but by going into what I was starting to call my inner 'eagle vision' I quickly found Elf's location. It had merely been a matter of being clear and definite about my intent to find Elf. "He's with his girlfriend but it hasn't gone well. I get a sense that she had another bloke in her bed when Elf turned up."

"Bloke?" Jim queried. "That's an Aussie term for guy?"

"It is."

"Well, if Elf's headed back here I'd better set another place for breakfast."

He was doing a French breakfast today. Strong black, perfectly brewed coffee, a choice of freshly squeezed orange juice or mango juice. Fresh crusty bread rolls from a nearby bakery, including gluten-free for me. Locally made jam and butter from grass-fed cows adorned the table in tiny dishes. The butter was neatly curled. Somewhere he must have snuck out and found a device to do that. And of course there were pastries. Today's pastries had chocolate centres.

Jim saw me admiring them, "Pain au Chocolat aka chocolate bread. And since I know you don't much go on chocolate there's a peach centred one for you."

"Hell, Jim, you've really spoiled us on this trip. You're not aiming to take over Cook's job are you?" The ship's cook had a long unpronounceable Zulu name so we all called him Cook. Occasionally, when I was feeling brave, I'd call him Becky, a very shortened version of his name. But he was a big man and at times intimidating. He was also my friend and fellow escapee from a former life, Adela's partner.

"Nah, I'm happy with who I am, Ry. I wouldn't want to have to cook for a shipload of hungry crew, three times a day for the rest of my working life. I'd probably end up as grumpy as Cook. But I do enjoy dabbling."

"Next time we're in the Seychelles I'll look forward to you dabbling again," amongst other things. We had use of a remote beachside shack in the Seychelles, where I had dual citizenship. It was our land base, though I still called Australia home. My Mum was here. Or at least in another state on the other side of the country. Which reminded me I should ring her. Being on central time now there wasn't as much of a time difference between here and there. "Mum," I called her. "We're about to head back to WA. Sorry but we're going to be pushed for time." I hoped she'd understand I couldn't fly over for a quick visit.

"Not to worry luv, we'll catch up next time."

Guilt afflicted me but there was nothing I could do about it. "Things just got a bit more complicated than we expected." Honestly, I hadn't told her about the whole deal working with Border Force.

"I know you, you're feeling you should have come. Don't. You've got those two luscious guys now."

"Mum!"

She laughed. "Want to know what I found out about our heritage?"

Guilt was replaced by curiosity, "What."

"Well I paid the genetic company I originally had my DNA tested with to delve deeper. Though going further back costs."

Hell. "Not too much I hope."

"Luv, this is my hobby," I felt her enthusiasm through the phone.

I couldn't quibble with that. "Tell me."

"I'd rather wait until we get confirmation from your data. We'll get a better picture of what you've inherited from me then. Did those testing kits I had sent to you turn up yet?"

Oh hell, I'd completely forgotten. "Picking them up from the post office this morning." Reilly wouldn't be pleased with the delay but it would give us a better chance of seeing Elf before we left. Elf had to come back to his camp some time. "I guess this means you're not going to even give me a hint."

"Well."

By the time I returned from the post office, and a very quick tourist look at the shopping district, Elf was having a belated breakfast and commiserating with Jim and Reilly. I wasn't sure whether to interrupt. They might have been having a mens' heart to heart. But Elf waved me over, "It's okay Ry, I'm not mad at all women. I'm just confused. I thought she wanted me as much as I wanted her. I must have read her wrong."

I sensed Jim wasn't sure whether now was the time to mention it but he did anyway. "There's at least one other woman out there that wants you Elf, Miranda."

"Miranda? From the roadhouse? Nah. You've got that all wrong."

Jim shook his head, "I don't think so. I saw the way she was looking at you when you weren't watching."

"Well hell. Miranda's hot but she's a bit scary too."

Reilly, listening to this, shook his head, "Where's your balls man? I haven't met the woman but if she wants you I'm sure ya'll work it out. Mr undercover spy."

Elf beamed, it was just the confidence boost he needed, "Yeah, hell, I did that didn't I?"

Jim looked at him earnestly, "Elf, you have a quiet strength and courage. If she likes you it's because you're who you are. Just make sure you start the relationship as equals. If she tries to boss you either call her on it or ignore it but don't give in to it or you'll lose the chance for a true partnership."

It was Reilly's turn to look angst ridden. "Damn it," he looked at me and Jim. "Is that how it is with me?"

Reilly looked like he needed a hug, so I gave him one. "We do follow your lead when there's an obvious need."

Jim felt for his friend. "We accept you as you are Reilly. It's in your nature to be boss. We know that. If we railed against it it would only annoy you and hurt our relationship so, yes, most of the time we just take it in our stride." It was a better phrasing than saying we ignored it. Full marks to Jim.

But Reilly knew we were being tactful. "I don't want ya tippin' toein' around me. I want this complete partnership yer describing to Elf. I want ya to call me out when I get over the top."

I looked thoughtfully at Jim. We both knew the challenge if we went down that path. Neither of us wanted to get our heads bitten off if we went up against him on anything. But if Reilly was wanting to make the effort then we both wanted to support him."

Jim answered for the both of us, "We'll only do that if you accept that we're not after changing you. There's a strength in who you are, just as there is strength in each of us in our own way. No-one expects you to negotiate the next UN peace agreement but If there's a crisis you're the one we're all going to turn to for leadership. So we're not going to pull you up all the time on your innate need to direct and keep us on our toes. Only when you go overboard. When you're treating one of us in a less than equal way or not willing to listen to any dissent. But we need, I think, some safe word or phrase, like 'permission to speak'."

Reilly swore, "I don't want ya askin' permission to challenge me, unless it's in the bedroom," he seemed to cheer at that afterthought. "Okay, safe word, something we wouldn't use in a sexual context either." He paced as he thought.

"How about a word that reminds us all why we're doing this," I mused, "something like 'partner'? It's relatively formal so it's not something we'd naturally call each other. If any one of the three of us is doing something that ignores the partnership we're building with each other then we'll say that one word to remind the other," preferably not in a derisive tone. I'd have to catch myself if I got exasperated.

Elf had watched this whole exchange with avid interest. "So I need to start with Miranda as I mean to continue. Make sure she understands I won't be subordinate to her. Ooh, I like this."

I needed to give a word of warning, "Just remember, a partnership requires all parties to do the work. It's not about changing each other to make it work. Though that may naturally happen to both of you over time. You'll need to start out accepting each other as you are now, both of you, or don't bother. And talk. Men are about action. They want to solve or remove problems. Women are about talk. They want to understand why something is a problem or what caused it. That's cliche and to some extent a bit black and white but a big thing for my kind is the need to be seen and heard. It's probably the result of several thousands of years playing second fiddle to men but there it is."

Jim knew where I was coming from, that I'd had a hard time getting my father's attention as a child. "Wise words Ry, though it's not just women. We all have a need to be noticed, in a good way."

Reilly was getting bored, "Enough of this lonely hearts club stuff. Did the post office have what ya were waitin' for?"

"It did," I put the four, not three as I had been expecting, test kits on our camp table. "Mum sent a spare and I think we should go ahead and use it." I handed one to Elf.

His eyebrows shot up, "Me?"

"It's all paid for," I assured Elf, in case he was worried. I wasn't about to read his mind without an invite. "You don't have to if you don't want to?"

"And this will tell me what?" he asked suspiciously.

I shrugged my shoulders, "You might find people, DNA matches, who can tell you more about your own ancestral links. Much like I've been looking for mine. You might even end up helping other people who've been looking for theirs. It's just a bit of fun, Elf, curiosity."

Elf was curious. "What do I need to do?"

Rather than explain I showed, by doing my test and then doing the documentation while the others took their own samples. "I'll just need to drop this back to the post office. The samples need to be returned as quickly as possible."

Reilly groaned, "More delays. Well if we're going back up town I'm comin' with ya. I've got some things I need up the street."

I couldn't read from his mind what he was up to, he was being cagey.

Elf distracted me. "Once this gets processed how will I find out the results?"

"Well you're going to stay in touch, aren't you?" Reilly demanded, then caught himself, "It would be really nice if ya stayed in touch Elf."

We finally got underway, late morning. Horatio was comfortably in his glove box. Jim was busying himself going over online maps, looking ahead for possible campsites. I was studying the weather maps to make sure we didn't hit any flash floods or freak sand storms on the return trip, though I'd be checking in with my black cockatoo spirit animal. Reilly, of course, was driving. It was strange how quickly we had each slotted into this way of life but I guess it didn't really matter whether we were steering a truck or a ship for home. The scenery was different though.

On our return trip we found time to stop and see Stef Maxwell's private history collection, since Essie had recommended it. By we I mean me. As the boys opted to do maintenance on the truck while I perused the displays. Unfortunately Stef had nothing that shed any more light on my recent ancestors.

A few more days and a few more pleasant overnight camps, chatting with travellers, we found ourselves back at the Homes Estate enjoying an evening meal of tapas, dips and other simple yet elegantly presented finger food. We lounged around the wide verandah, eating, drinking and enjoying the company. It was a welcome celebration after a long and dusty trip. Tomorrow we'd be back at the boat.

Essie was curious to hear about everything I'd found out about my ancestors so we filtered off to her treasure trove room of history, antiques and curios. "Tell me."

So I did, as much as I was at liberty to tell. I described meeting Ed, my vision of my dreamtime ancestor at the rocky outcrop and my astral meeting with the women of my line.

"But no luck connecting the drover and his wife to your family tree," Essie quizzed.

"Mum's tried but the evidence isn't there. We're pinning our hopes on further DNA analysis. Mum paid the DNA company to look further back. There's some tantalising hints but nothing conclusive. Even though I only have half my mother's DNA we've decided to see what mine might tell. But to be perfectly honest, unless we get some useful matches with people with similar DNA we might just have to satisfy ourselves with what we've found. It's certainly more than we knew before and at the very least I feel I've made a deeper connection with those who've gone before me."

"Will you be able to call on them for help, in the astral I mean?" Essie asked. "Even though you don't know who they are specifically."

"I believe so. A very wise woman I know," Lydia, "says that intent is everything. If I reach out to them with an open heart and the right intent there's a good chance they will respond."

"You'll let me know if you find out more," she pleaded. "And, well, you know, just keep in touch."

I gave her a hug, "You know I will."

The next day I met Bosun, before we officially arrived at the ship. I handed over Horatio who was safely stashed inside an insulated cooler bag. Not that it was that cool inside the bag but it wasn't too hot either. Reilly had made a couple of makeshift breather holes in the side, just for good measure.

Our Bosun, a turbaned Sikh in an orange boiler suit, beamed as he took charge of his errant pet. "I've got a shift, assisting on the bridge, tonight. I'll do the change over then."

"I'd keep the plastic spider, just in case." I didn't want to worry Bosun by voicing my suspicion that Horatio had somewhere along the way learnt to teleport. Our shared trip on the rainbow track was yet to reveal all its effects on us. I wondered about Clyde too. I fully approved Dan's decision to go with automation. Far safer. "I'd better go. Captain Wilcher will be expecting our imminent arrival."

"See you on board. And Ry, thanks for looking out for him."

"Actually it was all of us and, well, our pleasure." I bid him a temporary farewell and high tailed it back to the truck where the boys were waiting. Reilly was already looking at his watch meaningfully.

We'd just handed back the truck and were getting ready to board when I noticed a couple of women waiting for us at the bottom of the Merkwood II's gang plank. One was wearing a hoodie and sunglasses, obscuring her face but the other I recognised. "Mum, what are you doing here?"

But before she could answer Jim was beside me. "Mum, is that you?"

The other woman threw back her hood and laughed, "I thought I'd surprise you."

"I'm surprised," he hugged her then gave her a kiss on the cheek. "But how?"

"Lots of help from a lot of your friends actually. Your Reilly had words with a certain Lieutenant Sophie Camille in the Seychelles who then spoke to authorities in her country and here. I'm here on a Seychelles passport and Sally Jackson is sponsoring me so I can work towards getting my residency and eventual citizenship here."

Jim worried. "Dad will try to find you. He's both obsessive and possessive."

"I know. But with your friends' help we think we've laid a trail that will lead him well away from me. That trail should lead him on a wild goose chase through the backblocks of Europe."

"And we've changed her name too," my Mum put in.

"I named myself after my favourite goddess, Freya."

"And your surname," Jim wondered.

Freya actually giggled. "All part of the plot. You see my surname is now Jackson. Sally and I got married in the Seychelles. It seemed the easiest thing all round. We can divorce in a couple of years if we need but in the meantime I'll be living in Sally's garage, at the back of her house, where Ry used to stay. I hope you don't mind Ry. We didn't think you'd be needing it so much."

I was scratching my head on how they'd married when Freya was technically still married to the bastard she had as a husband but what the hell. I laughed, still in awe at what they'd done. "It's all yours. I'm very pleased to meet you, Freya Jackson." *You hatched this plan*? I asked Reilly on the quiet.

Not at all. After that dream you had, about when Jim left home, I just let a few people know of a problem. I left them to come up with a solution. I'm learning to trust and delegate, he grinned.

Jim was still in shock. "You flew all this way to see us off?" He asked his Mum.

"I would've come to see you in a heartbeat, long ago if I could've." Freya looked guilty about that. "We flew in from the Seychelles this morning. We thought we'd stop over and have a catch up with you before we catch our connecting flight home. That's if we're not in the way," she looked meaningfully at me and then at the big man Jim called more than friend.

Reilly stepped forward, graciously, to shake her hand. "Welcome to the family Freya. Come on board. I'm sure Cook and Adelia can whistle up some refreshments for us. Somethin' better than the airline food ya'd have 'ad on the way here." He waved over Seaman Merryman, "I'd appreciate it if ya'd take these two ladies to the canteen and explain that they're our guests for a couple of hours. We'll be along shortly. We just need to stash our things."

The seaman's eyes widened a little at this ranking officer's polite demeanour but nodded quickly. "Yes sir. I'll see if any of the crew are available to assist you with your things as well."

"That would be great. And if it's not too much further trouble could ya get a word in Wilcher's ear that his debriefin' will be delayed for a couple of hours."

"Yes sir," Merryman hurried away before the Third Officer's mood changed.

We made it to Jim's cabin before he burst into tears and cried on Reilly's shoulder. Reilly looked at me helplessly but held the man, rubbing his hand on his back for comfort. "Um."

Jim pulled away, momentarily embarrassed. "I will be forever grateful. And you," he turned to me, "for what your Mum did for mine."

I held my hand up. "Hey, I had nothing to do with this."

"You had the dream that started the ball rolling."

"Well there is that," why not take praise when it was offered?

"I don't know whether this is the right time," Reilly looked awkward, "It'll probably be an anticlimax but…" he passed me a tiny box and Jim a bigger one, from the pile of things the crew had brought up.

Fascinated and eager, I carefully untied the bow on the box, lifted the lid and gasped, "Is that…?"

"Fire opal. It's what I thought suited ya and I checked in with Sophie on its properties. She said it was a perfect stone for such a creative soul so I hunted one up at the local jewellers in Alice Springs, while ya were posting the DNA kits. I thought the pendant would be better than a ring as it wouldn't get in the way of yer work. Plus it would give me the excuse to do this for ya." He took the pendant from the box, and then placed it around my neck, securing the clasp. "Perfect," he muttered. He noted Jim hadn't yet undone his box. "Are ya goin' to undo that thing or what?" he asked exasperated.

"I was just treasuring the moment. Okay," he lifted the lid and pulled out the brand new Irish Bodhran drum. It was plain, with no designs on it.

"I'll paint it up for ya first chance I get," Reilly promised. "Ya wanted the same designs as on the other drum?"

"I do. I don't know what to say. We didn't get you anything."

"You gave yourselves to me, that's enough." He shifted his feet uncomfortably. "We'd best go up to the canteen and see what those two adventurous ladies are up to. Comin'?"

"Just one moment," I had a hunch I should check my incoming email. And there it was. The test results from the DNA company. "Wow, you'll never guess who's my second cousin twice removed."

Jim and Reilly both grinned, having already picked it from my mind, "Elf."